VOICES
OF ASH

VOICES OF ASH

Jill Zeller

Book View Café

Voices of Ash is a work of fiction. Names, characters, places, and incidents either are the products of the author's imagination or are used fictitiously. Any resemblance to actual persons, living or dead, events, or locales is entirely coincidental.

Voices of Ash

A Book View Cafe Book

Published by The Book View Cafe Publishing Cooperative
P.O. Box 1624
Cedar Crest, NM 87008
www.bookviewcafe.com

ISBN 978-1-61138-500-7

First Edition August 2015

Cover design Jill Zeller

Sometimes a thousand twangling instruments
Will hum about mine ears; and sometimes voices
That, if I then had wak'd after long sleep,
Will make me sleep again.

– William Shakespeare
The Tempest

Part I

SUSAN

One

HANK HEARD VOICES as long as he could remember. Not the voices that crazy people hear, but the continual, incessant noise of his life. The only time he didn't hear singing and monologs and radio ad scripts and endless jokes was when he was lying next to Susan. He could lie next to her in complete silence, look at the arcing line of her shoulder and hip turned toward the window, hair the color of burnt cinnamon repeating the line of her body in parallel waves, and his ears would ring with blessed silence.

Over her shoulder Hank could see limbs of a winter-bare tree, slanted roofline of the house next door, irregular rectangle of gray sky through Susan's bedroom. The only sounds were birds, the occasional hiss of a car passing on the wet Venice street, the snap and creak of the old house, Susan's breathing, and his own heart, pumping speedily in his chest as he thought about having to leave her.

Maybe he could stay here another hour. Maybe Joseph the brother would be late coming home from his shrink session at the VA. Three years ago the war ended. World War II, wars named like a serial. Episode 1, the Great War. Episode 2, an

Even Greater War. Joseph would get over his shell-shock and get his own place and be out of Susan's hair.

Maybe Susan would tell Hank he could move in.

Snagging a strand of Susan's hair in his fingers, Hank put it to his nose, inhaled straw and sweat and roses, imagined mornings waking up beside her, making coffee and toast and bringing it back; outside the sun would always be bright. They would dine together, butter running down their chins, laughing. He could get her to laugh. He was the only one, she said, who made him laugh. But even when Susan laughed, it wasn't a great belly laugh or a high giggle, it was a sort of *huff huff*; a smile grazed her cheek and he could see her teeth, a little crooked, that she always tried to hide. But this morning of his imagining, she was holding her stomach laughing. He would have a place in the den to write the novel he was going to write and she would go off to work at the factory, but not before they made love again.

He grew hard thinking about it. He always wanted more than she would give; Susan allowed him to come here on weekdays, when she got home, while Joseph was gone, but there wasn't time for lovemaking more than once. He wanted to be here every day. He didn't have a job; Mom and Dad didn't yet press him to decide about college.

There was no way, he thought pleasantly, leaning back against the headboard, that he would follow Carl and Connie into the entertainment business. This was all he wanted.

Today, as rain started up and brought its own sounds of pattering and slapping, Hank lingered, knowing he would stay until the last second in this blessed silence, day-dreaming about a life that, if things were different, if Susan were different, they could have.

When footsteps sounded on the front porch and the screen

door shrieked, Hank's heart shivered with cold in his chest. Joseph was home early. Only this time, instead of the heavy stomp of Joseph's feet through the vestibule, there came a sharp knock on the door.

Sitting up, Susan clutched the sheets to her, eyes wide. Looking at her, Hank's skin crinkled with goosebumps. Scrambling to her feet, she snatched her robe from the closet door and whirled into it; seized a towel and wrapped it around her head. Hank had to admire her skill at improvisation. What better way to explain being in a bathrobe in the middle of the day than to be showering off the dust and smell of the Pottery?

Hank knew better than to follow but as she disappeared through the door he started to get dressed, pulling on slacks and shirt, running a comb through his unruly black hair, tying his shoes, listening to the voices.

A man's, low, rumbling and slow.

"What happened?" Susan's voice sounded anxious.

A reply came that Hank couldn't quite make out as he walked to the door and listened; imagined Susan, tall and slender in her chenille robe, edges clutched close in her hand, the officer or official or Sargent or whomever he was knowing she was naked under that robe, looking her up and down and wondering if he should make a pass.

Her voice again. "Is he all right?"

Moving to the front window Hank saw a view of the Bermuda grass lawn, palm tree, and a corner of the front porch. The blind was down, of course, to hide their love-making activities from passersby, but if Hank angled his eye a certain way, he could make out a Los Angeles County police car parked on the street.

Joseph was in trouble again.

It happened regularly and Susan dealt with each occurrence in a calm, orderly fashion. But this time, her voice wasn't resigned or angry or frustrated, but genuinely worried. An expert at voices, at timbre and inflection and the different ways a certain story could be told, Hank knew that Joseph had been hurt—not in jail or the crazy house.

The policeman went away, heavy tread sounding on the steps. Hank watched him saunter down the walk and around to the driver's side of the cruiser, hesitate and look back at the house. Hank knew the policeman wasn't looking back to check the grounds or look for clues. He was looking back because he had just been speaking to a beautiful woman in a bathrobe, and he was wishing he didn't have to leave.

The bedroom door squeaked behind Hank. Susan came into the room, jaw set, eyes narrow with purpose. Without a word to Hank she swung out of her robe and let it fall to the floor. Hank was instantly hard, watching the flesh of her hips and butt jiggle as she yanked open her dresser drawer and pulled out her panties. He knew her like this, focused and intent whenever dealing with the issues of her brother Joseph. Hank wanted to ask her what had happened, but he knew better.

More than that, he wanted to touch her, run his hands across her bottom and up her curves and under her arms and onto her breasts. Before he knew what he was doing he had crossed the room, stood behind her and slid one hand under the elastic of her panties. She slapped it away.

"I have to go to the hospital," she said, her voice like rasping insects. Hank loved everything about Susan, piercing, judging glare, firm, no-nonsense lips, little ears, bitten nails and rainbow of colored glazes staining her cuticles. Her crooked teeth. But her voice was hard to take.

Buckling her bra, she yanked a wrinkled yellow sweater from another drawer. Shrugging it over her head, she unloosed her hair from the neck and stopped. Hank waited, breathing in her complex aromas, trying to find himself in there.

She gazed at him in the mirror. "Joseph jumped off the streetcar while it was moving. Yelling something about an old man under the tracks. He broke both his ankles."

"Wow," was all Hank could think to say. He didn't want her to leave to rescue her crazy brother. He wanted her here, with him. Hank wanted her to commit Joseph to Camarillo Nut House forever and let Hank move in with her. Marry her even.

As if she saw all this on his face, Susan's look soured. "Hank, you are such a child. You have to go—wait, do you want a ride? I can drop you off."

Swallowing, Hank shook his head. He didn't want to act like a child. He wanted to act like the adult he was. He was the mature one, anyway, the steady one, the one, his mother said, who didn't need as much attention.

"I have my bike."

"Oh right. Your racing bike."

Hank didn't bother to correct her. The French racing bicycle was in the garage at home, oiled and cleaned and tuned, built for cross country racing. Around town he used the Raleigh, a 3 speed touring bike.

What would a mature guy do, an older guy like the policeman, burly and confident, who had looked Susan up and down?

"Do you want me to go with you? To the hospital, I mean?"

Susan was pulling on a pair of loose slacks. Zipping them

up the side, she gave him a quizzical look.

"No, I'll be OK. I've been doing this a long time now on my own." She looked at him a second. "You're such a boy."

She could be condescending. The subject of the difference between their ages only came up for Susan, never for Hank. Susan had never told Hank how old she was, but he took a peek at her driver's license and knew she was 32.

Thirteen years older than Hank. So what? Hank loved her. He had never met anyone like her before.

Looping a rubber band around her hair, Susan rummaged in her drawer. Watching her, Hank knew she didn't know or care what affect she had on people, her voice, her manners or if she hurt anyone. She pinned a red beret on her head, yanked a plaid wool jacket from her closet and left the room.

He followed her down the hall to the kitchen where she shifted things around in her pocketbook, looking for car keys. She acted as if he wasn't there; she didn't seem nervous or worried in her actions, just efficient, organized. As if she had done this a million times before.

Like Mom, Hank thought, squelched this idea the same second. He didn't want to think about what that meant. Susan didn't always treat him like a child. Not in bed, she didn't. There, she let him take the lead, and even if she did, at first, show him things, now he was an expert at the geography of her body.

She went down the back steps. Her car, a battered black Packard, sat like a swollen beetle before the old wooden garage. Hank's bike leaned against the back porch. Picking it up, he hefted it on his shoulder and followed.

There was never a kiss good-by, an embrace, a tender exchange of endearments. Sometimes he earned a half smile, a look of affection, but most of the time their parting was brusque, business-like. The car door clanged in an authoritative way. She started the engine. The rain had stopped, and the sun, having reached a place in the western sky where it found a rent in the clouds, turned everything to graphite.

As Susan backed the car out, she glanced at Hank and lifted her chin, a recognition, a sign, he thought, that he was still part of her life. He knew he would be back again day after tomorrow, even if she turned him away, even if she wasn't here.

Two

HANK DODGED the late day traffic on Wilshire and Venice or by zigzagging his way northeast through Santa Monica and West Los Angeles. Lights burned in windows as he passed, urged on by the gray rainy day. Traffic was heavy on Sunset Boulevard. The road was wet and his trousers soaked by the time he coasted into his parents' driveway an hour after leaving Susan's Venice bungalow. To his relief, the twins' car wasn't there, but Dad's car was—a little unusual this time of day. Mom would be with the twins and they might not be home for hours. Hank hoped he would find the place empty except for Joaquin.

Still breathless from the long climb up from Wilshire, Hank picked up his bike and carried it down the narrow walk to the back yard. Acacia leaves drifted in the swimming pool and littered the patio, slimy and dead. Beyond through a row of date palms lights of downtown LA glimmered just beyond the tile roof of the house on the slope below them.

Hank spent some time in the garage wiping the water off the bike. Running his hand over the cold metal smoothness of the Peugeot, he thought of Susan again, his groin heavy, wishing she were here right now; they could do it in the garage, on the floor, his parents and brother and sister in the house unknowing.

Letting himself in the back door, he found Joaquin filling the place with steam and odors of chilies and garlic. A pear-shaped dark man, bald head the top of the pear, body flaring out ripely, Joaquin wore a lab coat-like cooking jacket wrapped around his belly. He had a family somewhere; multiple relatives he supported cooking for the Cleveland family, sending money to Mexico and running a lucrative trade in whatever he could buy or barter, an activity carefully ignored by Hank's parents.

Did no one but Hank understand that Joaquin was a fag? If they did, they pretended not to. Mom always asked after Joaquin's wife in Mexico.

Seeing Hank come through the back door, Joaquin raised one eyebrow at him and laid a spatula-laden hand on one hip. They gazed at each other this way every time Hank came home from being with Susan. Each knew the other's secret without having to be told, and each kept their council carefully, for the day might come when information of this kind—Joaquin's nights off spent down in Hollywood and Hank's trysts with a woman more than ten years older—would be worth using to advantage one day.

"Hola, *chicicito*, you are wetter than a goldfish." Joaquin stabbed the spatula at a pile of steaming chorizo. "How was the afternoon in heaven?"

"Heavenly," Hank replied. "Is Dad home?" He snagged an olive off a tray.

"Bad news. You better go see him." Joaquin turned back to his stove where water boiled and tortillas bubbled in oil. "And Bess *la reina* is home already."

"What happened?" Opening the icebox, Hank found a

half-drunk Coke. He didn't really like Coke, but because this was probably Connie's and she forgot about it, he would happily drink it.

"You go see him." Joaquin slapped a tortilla on a plate, where a stack of them was underway.

Exiting the kitchen, glad for something to distract him from thoughts of Susan, Hank followed the sound of his father's voice.

Speaking on the telephone, Kenneth Cleveland's landmark voice was recognizable, and one of the many voices always in Hank's head. Like following crumbs left by Gretel, or a tangled strand from a run-a-way woolen ball, Hank could always follow his father's voice to find him.

Dad stood with his back to Hank, facing the fireplace, holding the receiver to his ear, telephone dangling from his hand. Booming in the big room, bouncing through arched entries and across the tile floor and up the stucco walls, Ken Cleveland's announcer's voice was its own personality, one that everyone turned to see, for which everything stopped.

Able to stop listening to it entirely, paying attention like one does at a movie when the sound is turned off, Hank heard nothing, enjoyed just trying to figure out what was going on.

Sitting on the leather davenport, Hank crossed his legs and sipped his Coke. Dad had seen him come in and shook his head as he spoke to the person on the other end of the line.

Ken Cleveland was not an attractive man. He seemed to go in constant bewilderment, as if his handsome family had been dropped into his life by aliens. His eyes were too narrow and his thin blue lips too weak, his skin flaccid, black hair lank. But his voice was of a Greek god, or an Archangel announcing the end of the world. Everyone who heard him watched him transform banal Midwestern farm-country looks into Adonis or Apollo.

Now his velvet tones were subdued, his gift for gab flown. He sounded genuinely distressed about something. It was then that Hank noticed the shards of a figurine lying on the coffee table, a figurine he had always thought a crass bit of California kitsch, a ceramic, painted courtly French fop, the matched pair to an equally vapid Marie Antoinette look-alike, a pair that was, according to Dad, very expensive and rare.

Obviously it had fallen from its perch on the mantle, probably knocked down by the cleaning lady who was now, inevitably, out of a job.

Finishing the call, settling the gold and white hand piece of the phone onto the gold and white stand, after promising to get on the next train to Oklahoma City, Dad slouched onto the leather couch.

"Grandpa Joel is dead. Drove his car into a ditch. They said he died at the wheel. They didn't know where he was going, though." Dad pushed up his black-rimmed glasses and rubbed his nose, shaking his head as if he still couldn't believe his father was dead.

Hank could think of nothing to say. He barely knew his grandfather, short of a meeting ten years ago when Grandfather's voice came booming across the barnyard at him, frightening the newborn calves, shocking the hell out of Hank and scaring the calves even more. Nine-years-old then, Hank had never been on a farm before.

He did remember that the tasteless figurines lining the mantel belonged in the Cleveland family, and that the marquis and marquess were the latest additions, French, painted in the 19th century.

14

Dad looked at Hank. His eyes were watery, but he didn't appear to be crying; he looked more allergic than anything else. "I guess I have to go out there, even though I've got re-cordings scheduled all week. My sister insists she needs help with deciding what to do with the old place."

Grandmother Annette had died before Hank was born and Aunt Hope lived a few miles away from her dad with her physician husband. As he spoke Dad's lips went side-ways like they did when he had to discipline the children or do anything he didn't like to do.

Dad didn't expect Hank to say anything. All the family talked to Hank, sang to him, recited lines to him, practiced speeches on him and he didn't have to say a thing, just pre-tend that he was listening. The only person he really listened to, wanted to hear about, was Susan.

Dad rattled on about Oklahoma City and how he and his friends would do this and that in the Twenties—they didn't have to worry about money because of the oil, blah blah and it faded, and Hank treated himself to thinking about Susan.

But the sight of the broken marquis twisted his attention away from her. Something about the marquis and marquess, urgent like an important task he was supposed to do but had forgotten about. What was it? Why did he feel as if he had just cut off his own hand?

It had to do with an old photograph. He could see it in his memory, held by a hand not his own, the hand of a girl he once knew and strangely, now, he missed that hand.

He hadn't thought about that girl for years. Staring at the colored shards on the table, the notion of her appeared, shot through his skin like a hypodermic needle. Then gone, flown away. He almost moved his hand to capture it back, but it was not to be.

The twins were home.

The slam of the front door, and the silent house filled with Constance's bird chatter and Carlisle's scatter-shot banter, preceded by the smell of damp shoes and sweat and floral perfume.

"Connie, Carl, get in here." Dad's voice flooded the room, sweeping toward Hank. Hank thought of Susan, the way she flatly told him her brother had been injured. This conversation would be far more entertaining.

With deliberate slowness, Hank set down his barely-touched Coke, rose, and sauntered toward the vestibule arch, where Connie and Carl were having a whispered argument.

When Hank appeared they stopped. Leaning against the archway, folding his arms, Hank said, "Your presence is requested."

Connie gave him an unhappy smile. Her hair, brightened to a platinum sheen for the current picture, went awry as she pulled off her hat. Fatigue deepened the lines of her heart-shaped face, and she looked even thinner than usual, her dancer's calves almost masculine for their lack of feminine fat. Carl glanced down at his jacket, wiped some unseen dander from it, and uncurled one of the silk scarves he had lately taken to wearing. His jaw muscles worked tensely, and he rolled his eyes at his brother.

"We come as commanded, Henry," Carl said, taking Connie by the arm as if to escort her. She flung her arm free.

"Fuck off, Carl."

"Oh my, we are in a pissy mood tonight." Carl leaned close to her ear and lowered his voice. "Or is it a pussy mood?"

Connie slammed open her purse and rummaged out a cigarette. "Carl, go dip your head in acid. Hank, you got a light?"

Hank had recently given up cigarettes, but he kept the lighter Susan had lent him when they first met. He snipped it alight under the cigarette in Connie's shaking hand.

Connie inhaled, eyes crinkling, and gave him a wink. She smelled faintly of gasoline and cigars. "You always were my favorite brother."

"Gotta have someone do the dirty work," Carl said as he brushed past them, especially giving a shove to his little brother. Hank rocked back on one foot, but he said nothing, just waited for Connie to breathe deeply before entering the den of their parent.

Following her, Hank stretched onto a chair near French doors leading out to the patio, far away from Dad who was slouched deep in the sofa.

Connie snuggled beside Dad, and Carl now occupied the place Hank had earlier.

"Where's Mom?"

The three on the couch all looked at Hank. Carl said, "Isn't she home yet?"

"She said she had a meeting at the studio. That she'd meet us back here." This from Connie, who shrugged. "She told us to take the car, that she'd either get a ride or a cab."

Dad stared into his whiskey. Carl and Connie glanced at each other.

Unusual, surely. Mom kept Connie and Carl on a tight leash, supervising their every step, dance step or party step. Making sure they got to bed early to maintain the ruse for their adoring fans that the Cleveland Twins were clean all-American kids.

A thumb of unsettledness pressed under Hank's ribs. "Joaquin said she was home already."

This statement had its promised effect, as Hank knew it

would. Connie sprang from the couch as if levitated by a cable. "Then it's time for her to join the fun and listen to the Big Announcement, whatever it is."

The circus was on. All Hank had to do was be the audience as he so often was for his older brother and sister. Catching Connie's arm, Carl leaped over the coffee table and they began to dance. Connie's sapphire blue dress swirled around Carl's legs.

And the patter. *Ah you look lovely tonight, Countess. Oh prince, you make me swoon.* If Dad weren't here, the dialog would be a lot dirtier.

Dad sank into the couch as if he were deflating balloon in the Macy's Thanksgiving Day Parade. Hank watched him shrivel, fade to gray. Except when he stood at a microphone reading a script, Dad was a dull bird hidden in the shadows behind the cocky brightness of his family.

"Alright, guys. That's enough." Hank got to his feet, grabbed Connie's arm; his hand closed tightly, and Connie gave him an angry look. "Dad has something to tell you morons."

Connie wrenched her arm away. "High priest Hank, we are here to obey." Turning to Dad, Connie bent over to rub one of her knees.

"What is it, Dad. What is the Big Announcement."

When Dad told the twins his father had died, the massive Kenneth Cleveland baritone was oddly broken. Even Carl noticed; his eyebrows came down in suspicious doubt.

Appropriate murmurings of "That's too bad," and "Poor old guy" went around the room at the news of Grandfather Joel's demise. Hank could see that Connie and Carl had even less concern for the loss of another grandparent than himself. As he considered this, another memory shot past, this having to do with his grandfather.

It was that same visit to the farm at Oklahoma City when Hank was nine. The old man, who walked with a pronounced limp, whose hands were the gnarled roots of arthritis, had motioned Hank to follow him to his bedroom. The room held a big four-poster with a dip in one side where grandfather slept, an oak dresser and wardrobe that looked as if they were never opened, and a chair with overalls and flannel shirts piled and pressed by the housekeeper. Grandfather sat on the bed, Hank near the foot, fingering one of the posts, holding on to it like he would the mast of a ship in a heavy sea.

"Your dad says you are a fast runner. I want to show you something."

He had taken out a creased and used-up paper book, removed some photographs tucked inside and showed them to Hank. These were pictures of men racing on bicycles. Hank especially liked one of a man coming straight on, bowed on the handlebars, his feet in black shoes and the calves of his legs wider than grandfather's thighs.

"I told your dad he should get you a bicycle. I used to have one, and I raced it a little, but I was never as good as these guys, going through France before the war." He shuffled the photos, and Hank looked at them, not sure what this conversation was supposed to be about.

"If I still had that cycle I'd give it to you." Grandfather's eyes were blue like Dad's and they scanned Hank's face. "You're going to need something, kid, with a family like the one you got."

When Hank thought about it now, turning sideways in

his chair, gazing through the French doors to a distant splash of neon, he realized his grandfather had done him a great favor that day and Hank had never thanked him.

Three

HANK SAW MOM FIRST. Bess Cleveland stood in the dining hall archway, in an immaculate Navy suit, white corsage, white heels. She leaned against the doorpost, a cigarette in one hand, her other hand caressing her elbow. One minute Hank was remembering the moldy smell of Grandpa Joel's 100 year-old farmhouse, something he had long forgotten. The next he was staring at his mother, and she was staring back at him.

Silent. Standing. Not pacing and talking. As if pacing and talking could not be separated.

She's a ghost. Not really there. Only there for me because for the first time ever she has come into a room without saying anything.

A quirky thing about the Cleveland living room was that the sofa was set with its back to the dining room. An artifice, Hank always thought, so that whomever was seated on the sofa could appreciate the entrance of whomever came through the hallway archway.

"It was so strange," Dad was saying as Bess Cleveland stood silently behind him, "But I as I walked in here the phone rang, and the same time the marquis fell off the mantle and smashed to smithereens."

Dad and Carl each leaned forward to pick up a shard where they lay on the coffee table, Dad a blue-glazed arm and Carl the head.

"That thing was worth a lot of money. Now the set is ruined." Mom inhaled deeply of her cigarette, lifted her chin to Hank and made her entrance.

The three on the couch turned as one to watch her as she crossed the room, stood before them, stared down at the pieces. Turning, she stubbed out her cigarette on the mantle ashtray as if she were squashing a fly.

Hank had always been curious about Mom's concern for the ugly things. She never had paid any attention to them other than to comment on their worth.

"The cleaning lady obviously didn't put it back properly," Carl said, looking through the hollow neck into the fractured head, as if he expected to find a brain inside. "Can it be re-paired?"

Mom snorted and lit another cigarette. Hank noticed her fingers flicking as she smoked. She looked as nervous as a tightrope walker strolling above Times Square.

Dad worked the buttons on his shirt. "I have to go there. Hope says she needs me there."

"Oh great. Why can't she deal with it?" Mom paced across the front of the mantle and back. "She's a grown woman and her husband is a doctor, isn't he? Aren't doctors supposed to be smart?"

Dad shrugged. He said nothing. Mom opened her mouth to speak, but shut it again.

"Oh Daddy, don't go." Kicking off her shoes, Connie curled up next to him. "I promised that you would come to the set and read for the crew, like the Ten Commandments, or something."

He gave Connie a hug and a smile. "I don't have to go to-morrow. I can leave on the weekend." They discussed trains and times and who would drive whom to the station, while Hank swung his feet where they dangled over the arm of the chair.

As if some faucet of his brain was leaking, another memory dripped down.

Hank was in his bedroom with a girl. The door was open, Joaquin in the house, everything above board in terms of propriety. The girl, a friend from high school, more than a friend, had dug out a box of old photographs and gazed a long time at one of Hank's Grandpa Joel and Grandma Annette.

She tapped the photograph with one well-manicured finger, her hair, the color of night woven with the Northern Lights, falling down to hide her face. Hank remembered admiring the swell of her breasts under her sweater, the curve of her butt under her plaid shirt as she lay on his bed, feet in the air. She had grown silent, staring at the photo for so long that he crawled across the floor from his desk chair to tease her about being rude.

"No," she said, her voice only slightly accented with Spanish. "This," she tapped it again, "is important. A message from the past."

Hank sat next to her on the bed. His arm brushed hers but she didn't seem to notice. He looked at the photo, recognized old Grandpa Joel and Grandma Annette, a woman in a flowery hat.

A fist turned under Hank's heart, causing him to sit up, grab a sharp breath, remembering the girl and the photo.

"This," she had said, eyes wide with pleasure and confidence, "Look at what is behind them, on the mantle. The little man and woman. The man is thinking, I hope I don't outlive her, and the woman is thinking, I hope I outlive him. But it wasn't to be."

He wanted to search for more memories, but a door clanged shut somewhere in his mind.

"Hank, I'm talking to you. I wish you would pay attention."

Bess Cleveland's voice flowed from the girl's as Hank tried to remember what happened after she told him the truth of the photo.

He looked at Mom, who was standing in front of him. "I want you to drive your dad to the train. If you don't get your act together, Henry, I'll make you go with him."

Mom's pupils dilated as she pulled on her cigarette. She fumbled the words *if you don't,* an unusual and glaring mistake in one so careful but she was either nervous about something to do with the twins' contracts or she was drunk and it was probably both. But Hank wasn't doing anything wrong. He never did anything wrong. Or if he did, his parents never knew about it because they never paid attention.

And then his mother jerked her gaze toward the hallway, a sign that she wanted to talk to him alone without making a fuss in front of the others.

"Time to take off my shoes," she said rather too gaily, but no one seemed to be listening. Carl's feet were on the coffee table as he stretched out reading the paper, Connie tapped her fingers along the back of the couch and hummed a song Hank had never heard before, reciting phrases and jerking her body around as if she were dancing in place. Dad had a script in front of him and his mouth moved as he murmured the words.

So much for Grandpa Joel. More words were spent on the broken figurine.

Mom led Hank upstairs. A cold pit yawned inside him, eating up and swallowing the intriguing hint of pleasure in remembering his afternoon with_*The Girl*.

Mom led him to his small, serviceable and private bedroom in the back of the house, overlooking palms and city. He didn't spend much time in it any more, except to sleep and dress, and he kept it neat. Clothes folded and put away, closet door shut, bicycle magazines and books in an orderly row in the book case. His desk held a pad of paper, pencils lined up, a battered typewriter he hadn't touched in two years.

Sitting on his desk chair, Mom kicked off her shoes and hunched over as if the stiff rod of cool correctness in her back had broken. Hank hopped onto his bed, fingering Susan's lighter in his pocket.

Leaning back on his elbows Hank waited for the inevitable speech, delivered in proper lawyerly fashion, about how he had to be more supportive of the twins at this difficult time. Having heard the speech many times in different modes throughout his life, he could have recited it by heart.

Instead silence ticked away between them, while Hank waited and watched his mother make squares and rectangles of the pencils on his desk. After a few moments of this, Mom turned toward him, undid the buttons of her jacket, and stretched out her legs.

"I want you to talk to your sister. She is going through something and I can't get it out of her. It's always excuses and don't worry and leave me alone." Mom's voice quivered, from fatigue maybe? She never showed anyone how the life she had chosen was eating away at her.

"It's not easy being a mother and a business manager at the same time. Although I suppose running a home is like running a business. Just that most women don't have the training I have had."

This was certainly true, Hank was thinking. Mom fell silent again, turned back to the desk, formed the pencils into a row and ran her fingers over them, rolling them back and forth.

Hank's warning-system turned up a notch. When Mom started fiddling with things, her buttons, her earrings, her nylons, she was getting ready to reveal something bad.

"There's something else." Mom didn't look at Hank. She watched her pencil game instead, lids blinking mascara-brushed lashes over her blue eyes, a strand of golden hair free from the hairspray to hang dreamily along her chin line.

"I haven't told anyone this and I don't want you to either, especially not your father, not until I say so."

As Hank sat up, his gut tightened. Mom shifted in her chair, and looked at him, stabbed him with a look he had never seen before. Fear? no—*terror*?

But the look was gone a second later, an imagining of Hank's mind and heart. And the moment was thoroughly gone when they heard Connie shouting, running up the steps, along the hall into her room and slamming the door.

Hank watched as his mother collected herself, rearranged her face into her courtroom mask; professional, cool. Getting up, she picked up her shoes, approached, touched Hank's shoulder. "Later. I have to deal with this. You understand."

It was never a question but an assumption that Hank understood Constance and Carlisle Cleveland were driving the Cleveland family, a precision engine of finer quality than that of a Rolls or Porsche. And that Mom had given up her rarified career as a trial lawyer to manage the twins' lives as they climbed the starry ladder of entertainment success.

Hank watched his mother leave, heard her knock on Connie's door, go in, listened to sounds of sobs and cursing. He decided that whatever emotion he had seen on his mother's face had never been there. It was easier that way. It was the way Mom would have wanted it. But it stuck there, like a sliver, and he couldn't quite pull it out.

Stretching back on his bed, Hank waited, wondering if Susan were still at the hospital. Below he could hear the clanking of china as Joaquin set the table for dinner.

A movement at his open door caught his eye and Carl leaned there, chin lowered, scanning Hank's room.

"Must be that time of month."

Hank nodded. Connie's rages did seem to occur routinely every twenty-eight days.

"This room looks like a monk's cell." Carl stuck his hands in his pockets. "Everything so neat it gives me the creeps."

Shrugging, Hank waited for Carl to get bored and go away.

Pulling out the scarf he had worn earlier, silk paisley, Carl wound it around his hand. "She's been even crazier lately, though. I don't know what's the matter with her."

Monk's cell. Everyone comes to *Padre* Hank with their problems. Hank never had to do or say anything except drive people around and carry their baggage. Nobody wanted him to talk. They did all the talking and he just waited.

Used to Hank's silences, Carl continued. "I don't get it. She seems healthy, you know—her dancing is unbelievable. The studio is noticing. Maybe it's the pressure." A frown pulled down those beautiful lips. "I think she's thinking about splitting up the act."

Sitting up, Hank couldn't tell if Carl were talking about Mom or Connie. If this were true the Cleveland family was about to undergo another upheaval. Maybe that was what Mom was going to tell him.

Seeing Hank's quizzical look, Carl sneered. "Yeah, I hope she does. It's making me think I am having rag rages, working with two women all the time. I'd like to dance with a man." He twirled, executed a neat tap dance, and bowed. Then let his wrist drift down limply.

This was funny. Carl was no more a fag than Dad was a matinee idol. A snort escaped Hank's lips, and seeing that he'd gotten a reaction from him, Carl bowed, and his continual haughty smirk had returned. "Thank you Father Hank. Three Hail Mary's for my confession?"

"Twenty-four, and self-flagellation."

Carl's right eyebrow worked up and down. Hank had seen Carl practicing in front of a mirror for hours to get his eyebrows to do that.

He said, "I love it."

Dinner was quiet. The men ringed the big table, the women were late. Hank was halfway through his plate when Mom appeared, Connie trailing her. Her face sweet, relaxed, Connie had taken a shower and wore a soft sweater and skirt; her white hair flowed to her shoulders. Mom had not changed out of her suit, but she had put on slippers.

Mom looked mismatched, as if pieces of herself had been separated and put back together not quite right, like the shattered marquis would look like if someone glued him. Hank saw something broken there, but he didn't know what it was. More than just a business decision, harsh though it was, to break up the Clevelands. But how deep the fracture went, he couldn't tell.

Four

JOSEPH'S INJURY CHANGED THE COURSE of Hank's life in a wonderful way, at least for the following week. Arriving at Susan's bungalow in the afternoon, two days after the accident, convinced that she wouldn't be there, that she would have gone straight from the factory to the hospital, Hank was astonished when Susan opened the back door for him and pressed herself into him.

More than ready for her, instead of waiting until she gave a sign, Hank pushed her back, propelling her through the kitchen and down the hall to her bedroom. Without a word they wrestled to a climax—Hank understood that an urgent energy traveled through Susan, muscles quivering to the point of giving off a burning heat, like making love to the sun. Not for the first time did Hank think this wasn't Susan at all, but the Susan in the hairnet and the colored nails was a shell for something wild and hazardous.

After, she sat up and leaned against the head board, pushed her hair from her eyes, watched him as he lay beside her. Her breasts lay heavily on her chest, nipples pale pink. Hank watched her watching him. There was a glow about her, a contentment and joyousness he had never seen before in her moist chocolate eyes.

Getting up on one elbow, Hank waited for her to speak. They didn't speak much after lovemaking, usually. Sometimes she would talk about her work, the new glazes she was trying, how bored she was with the current line of figurines. Hank didn't know which line she was working on, only that they had something to do with Disney.

Hank thought of the broken marquis, thought he could ask her about it, who might have made it and when, when she folded her hands like a little girl about to recite.

"You haven't asked me why I am home today."

Hank couldn't help feeling wary. Her mood was new to him; he had never known her to say hopeful things or glorify the weather. Their three-month-long affair had been addictive and grief-laden without words of justification.

He agreed to play along, ran his finger along her forearm, pale red hairs tickling.

"Ok. Why are you home today?"

Raising her arms, she ran her fingers along the headboard, tracing the rosettes and ivy carved into it.

"They let me have a week off. I can work at home—so I can spend more time with Joseph."

This mention of Joseph turned slowly in Hank's stomach. He waited, wondering what it would mean for him.

Susan looked at him, his eyes, his mouth, his hair. She rumpled his head, a thing that she had never done before. "I'll miss the money he made at the cemetery—I doubt they'll hire him back after six weeks. But at least I don't have to drag myself back and forth to work or the hospital, silly. I can set up a studio in the garage—you can help me."

Sitting up, Susan seized a rope of hair, tossed it over her shoulder. Now she studied her fingers, spread them wide, wiggled them in a spidery wave.

"You can come every day, if you like."

Numbness followed by a bit of shock roamed Hank's stomach. "Wow," was all he could think to say. It would not sink in, these moments he would have with Susan—he could come over anytime he liked. He could, if she let him, and she had to let him, spend the night.

The rest of the afternoon and into the evening Hank helped Susan clean out the garage, hauling tires and oil cans and brooms and a child's bicycle out into the yard to put in a pile. A merciless and tireless overseer, Susan assigned Hank a series of tasks; wash the walls and floor, repair a broken window and the lock on the side door, oil the garage door hinges. She wanted to paint, but didn't have any.

Finished, they rested in the back yard, Susan in a rusting chair and Hank on a rickety wooden stool. Night closed in bringing faint cold and stars, everything faint, as if all the heavenly bodies felt tentative about the laws of physics.

Hank wanted to have her right here and now, on the damp Bermuda grass, stars observing and neighbors hearing and not quite believing. But he stayed on his stool while she brooded. He thought he knew what was coming.

And when it did, he didn't mind as much as he thought he would.

She must, of course, go to the hospital. Joseph was in a lot of pain, and she had to make certain the nurses brought his hypo every three hours, as prescribed by the doctor. Not for the first time did Hank wonder what she did for money, how she paid the utilities and food and hospital bills on her salary. He knew about Joseph's gruesome job digging graves in the Santa Monica Cemetery but that couldn't bring in much.

"Come back tomorrow, early. I'll make you breakfast, and

then take you out to the factory to get my tools."

He nodded, a little stung. "I could wait here for you until you got back. Have dinner together or something?"

Getting up, Susan stood before him. Dirt smudged her nose and she smelled vaguely of gasoline.

"Dear Hank. Don't push it." Leaning in she kissed him; her hair brushed his neck and he wanted to pull her down on top of him, roll off the stool together.

But something stopped him; Susan stopped him without saying a word because she had set the rules when it came to Joseph. Straightening, she walked into the house. He was dismissed.

On his bike ride home Hank nearly got creamed by a Red Car trolley on Sepulveda, cracked his elbow on the curb, falling and rolling onto the sidewalk to land at the feet of two girls strolling arm and arm along the boulevard. Maybe it was the same Red Car Joseph leapt from, sent by Susan's brother to get Hank out of the way. The girls looked at him and giggled as he lay there cradling his elbow and cursing.

One of them reached down to help him up. They both looked at him shyly, quizzically, out-of-town girls wondering if he were a movie star.

"You OK, mister? You OK?"

Ignoring their whispers and laughter, Hank lifted his bicycle from the gutter and checked it over. It was still useable; the Raleigh was a workhorse, as unbreakable as a mule.

"You want to buy us a soda?"

Forward girls, fast girls. Hank had to smile, shook his head. What if he did go with them, follow an impulse for once, sneak them into Eddie's, where he knew Eddie would serve them cokes spiked with rum? For once he would stop being reliable Mr. Hank, the Cleveland family dog's body.

No one was home. Rehearsals went late. Dad recording, Mom could be anywhere, with the twins, with Dad, at the library where she spent vast amounts of time doing who knew what.

Joaquin served him stoically, saying nothing about Hank's being gone all day. Joaquin said often enough that Hank should get a job. If he wasn't going to go to college he should get a job and help support his family.

Hank had a job, but Joaquin wouldn't understand. Hank's job was to be the glue that held the family together.

The next morning Hank left early on his bike. It was another bright breezy day, cool in the early hours, promising to be sunglasses-and-short-sleeved shirt warm. His elbow ached mercilessly, swelled and bruised in the night. He iced it and dug around in Connie's room for the strong stuff the studio gave her but could only find aspirin.

Coasting into Susan's driveway, he almost lost his balance. Maybe it was his hinky elbow, or maybe it was the vision spooling through his mind; that her car would be gone, she would be at the factory, having left him behind, and all the spinning glee of yesterday was his day dream.

But her car was there. Leaning the bike next to the back porch, he walked right into the kitchen, not waiting to knock as before.

Susan was cooking, wearing her chenille robe. Seeing him, she wiped her forehead with the back of her hand, smiled, kissed him, and motioned him to sit, all in one movement far more graceful than Connie's dancing.

Hank sat before toast and eggs and coffee, but it was as if he was at a banquet of stuffed squab and mint jelly, paper-thin slices of baguette and *pâté*. He had arrived hungry for breakfast, but now he was hungry for her.

When he touched her buttocks Susan was fiddling with the toaster; she allowed him to run his hands up her flank and onto her breasts, free, to his joyful lust, of any brassiere. He held them, heavy, growing hard. Feeling him, she twisted and thrust her hips into him.

She pushed herself onto the counter. He buried his nose and mouth in her, inhaling the soft musk amid curly red hairs and staying hard as she came over and over, biting her hand to keep from screaming. Then she pushed him back, jumped down, forced him into a chair, straddled him, and he struggled not to come, but it took only a minute as he watched her breasts move up and down and she watched him, smiling, waiting for the inevitable.

After, he was famished, and swiped up the cold eggs with the cold toast while Susan sipped coffee. As soon as he was done they left for the factory. Susan took Sepulveda south past the airport, through sandy expanses where derricks drank up rich pools of oil, dipping their dinosaur heads to the ground.

Hank ran his hand along the fabric of the car. His silence with Susan was another companion, sitting between them. He wanted to ask the question but he didn't know how. He wondered how Joseph was doing, and why Susan's mood was in the sky above the clouds. She drove quickly, a heavy copper bracelet on her wrist sliding up and down as she turned the wheel.

Manhattan Beach shouldered itself between El Segundo and Hermosa Beach. Once a shabby little beach town, Man-hattan Beach was filling with post-war families, and Metlox Potteries dominated several city blocks near the railroad. Susan parked on the street in front of a long, low stucco building sitting in the shadows of massive wooden sheds. A salty breeze came off the sea, and gulls swirled overhead. Hank obediently followed her along the sidewalk to an entrance set back from the street, his role about to change from lover to beast of burden.

Inside was a long hallway flanked by offices cluttered with drafting boards, shelf upon shelf of pottery in various experimental shapes and colors, drawings and drafts and pots of glazes. One of these was Susan's.

This studio, drafting table and shelves and bits of clay and glaze like the others, was the smallest, situated in the part of the building with no view of the street, no window at all, in fact. But as soon as Hank was in there, following Susan, a strange feeling came over him, one he couldn't quite describe, having never felt it before, an underlying watchfulness as if he had walked onto a stage in a crowded theater.

Ringing the shelves were dozens of figurines, and taped to the edges of the shelves and the walls were drawings of the same; animals and people in various poses and dress. The room smelled of solvents and mud.

He found himself standing, unable to move. The clutter unnerved him, being of a tidy nature himself. But it was more than that. Something moved here, *alive, observant*.

Susan got him busy, though, ordering him to place pencils, brushes, little bottles of color, boxes of crushed colors, oils, mixtures of talc, blocks of clay in the cartons. Heavy paper tablets. Molds of various shapes and unrecognizable figures. Then he was to take apart and fold her drafting table.

As he worked, someone came into the room. Looking up, he saw two men in white shirts, no ties, one with a pencil behind his ear. The nearer one was older, silver hair ringing a bald spot, the other younger and handsome, brown hair slicked back, head on the broad neck of an athlete.

"Susan, our dear Susan returned to the fold," said the older one. His voice jarred Hank, cross and hoarse. Crouched on the floor, he looked up. The older one scanned him with small, brown eyes above rimless reading glasses.

Susan, holding a large portfolio, turned to look at him. "You, Frank, are just in time to help us carry this stuff to my car."

Silver-haired Frank lifted his hands. "Oh no. I can't be torn away from my creative flow. New line, you know, dinner dishes, vines and all that. Practical stuff, not little Indian statues and fish vases."

Tilting her head, Susan smirked at him in an almost flirty way, a look that Hank had seen before and he wasn't sure he liked.

"Maybe Sam will be my assistant."

The younger man pushed past the older one and saluted. Another returned veteran, this one, seemingly, unmarred by the war.

"Give me an order, ma'am."

Susan thrust the portfolio at him. The older man remained in the doorway. "Who is your other assistant, Miss Chagall? Introductions?"

Rolling her eyes, Susan indicated Hank where he crouched on the floor, screw-driver in hand.

"Hank, my trusty friend, meet Frank and Sam, designer and apprentice."

The two men nodded at him, and Hank returned the nod. He didn't like the way the older man was looking at him, or the way the younger one was looking at Susan. In fact, the tiny windowless room, crowded with four people and the odors of glazes and aftershave and paints, brought a sicken-ing rush to his stomach; his elbow throbbed from using the

36

screwdriver and he inhaled and sat on the floor, pretending to wait or even be sociable, when all he wanted was to rush out and breathe in the heavy mists of the sea.

Susan, however, was in a hurry. Ignoring Frank in the doorway, as he leaned and watched, she directed Sam about which boxes to carry out to her car. The rush of activity distracted Hank long enough for him to get to his feet, remove the table from its stand, shift it all together in a bundle.

"How is the brother, dear Susan," Frank asked as she stretched to capture bottles of caked color from a top shelf. Hank moved to help her.

"Coming along, thank you." Susan turned to roll up sheets of drawings.

"You see him every day, I hear. Sherman gave you the week off, and permission to work at home."

Susan glanced at him, and Hank saw a mask of worry come over her face. "I do see him every day. It comforts him to see me. This way, I can see him during visiting hours and work at night, not get behind on my designs."

Frank nodded, taking his pencil from his ear and tapping his chin. "Oh, yes. Very good."

Relieved to be out of the office, Hank had to force Frank to stand aside as he carried the drafting table to the car, leaving Frank to hover over Susan alone. His elbow stabbed with pain, but he made it to the car without dropping anything, meeting Sam on the way back for more. Sam's eyes crinkled in the bright misty light.

"I've seen you somewhere before. You work in Hollywood?"

You work in Hollywood was a way of asking if someone where an actor. Hank shook his head, picked up a drafting table leg.

"No, sorry. But I know you. I help out in the studio for extra money, working in the prop shop." Sam folded his arms; his smile was friendly enough.

Hank didn't want to say anything about his family. He used to show up at the studio to hang out and watch the twins' rehearsals, but since Susan he hadn't bothered.

"People always tell me I remind them of someone. I got that kind of face, I guess."

Nodding, Sam saluted again, turned away. Hank knew Sam didn't believe him; any time now he would place Hank waiting in the wings of the stage, but Hank didn't care. Busying himself stuffing the table into the trunk, he delayed going back inside the factory building and the stifling studio. He would never see this Sam guy again.

Susan's mood was changed as she drove back through the sunny morning. A frown pulled at the corners of her mouth, and she kept yanking at her hair. Hank leaned back, massaged his elbow, watched towns slide past and a big plane arrow overhead as they returned to Venice, pots of glazes and glassy-eyed figurines in the back seat like nervous passengers.

Five

IF ANYONE, DAD OR MOM OR THE TWINS even noticed that he was gone all day, every day, they said nothing to him about it. They had flown out of his life, and if occasionally he remembered Mom wanting to tell him something important, or Grandfather Joel's death, it was because he was for a moment bored with Susan.

But these moments were fleeting. This past week he was only reminded he had a family when he rode his bike through Hollywood and a flashy billboard message about the new musical, introducing the remarkable Cleveland twins, caught his eye. Susan was his world now, and a world of new smells and colors he had barely imagined.

Susan's garage-cum-studio transformed itself. He was astonished by her ability to bring something of her imagination skillfully to the page and into three dimensions.

And there was the sex, of course, less often now, but longer at each coupling, sweeter and infused with touching and tasting. Hank lost weight, even though he was always hungry and consumed portions of the good food Joaquin provided, and more than portions, because more often than not this week, he ate alone, or maybe with Dad for company, and that wasn't much company. Dad would stare forlornly at a script and whisper the words, gesturing. He didn't even notice when Hank left the table.

Joaquin gave Hank a quizzical look every time Hank crossed the kitchen to get on his bike to see Susan.

"Training for a big race, *chico,* with all this going back and forth?"

"Tijuana, *camarada.* Can't get enough of that town."

Joaquin's nostrils flared. "*Basurero.*" He squinted down at his paper through a pair of rimless glasses. "You talk to your mama yet?"

How did Joaquin know these things? Restarting that conversation with his mother hung heavily from Hank's ribs; he knew he should ask her about it, but the look of her lately unsettled him, and in fact, he knew he was avoiding her. Helping Susan build her home studio was an addictive distraction.

Hank leaned against the kitchen doorway, feeling the lint in his trouser pockets, while Joaquin ran his hands across the paper, a Mexican tabloid his wife sent him from Mexico City.

He said, "Your father doesn't want to go to Oklahoma. Bad memories, I think."

There it was again, the polished certainty of a man who had lived with the Clevelands since before Hank was born.

"I'll take him to the train on the back of my bike. Think he'll like that?"

In truth Hank didn't want to go at all. He didn't want to miss a moment with Susan, watching her draw or paint or crumple a rejected design and toss it into a pile near the garage door.

And she needed his help more than ever now. She was building a kiln.

Hank had never built anything in his life, and he

wondered if Susan understood how it was to be done. She had a set of plans and emphasized how specific it all had to be, which made Hank feel even more inadequate. She purchased the materials, bricks and mortar, a cast iron door, paid a skeptical plumber to lay a gas line to a place near the back fence with Joseph's last paycheck from the cemetery.

Together they suffered through building the walls, getting the mortar mix all wrong, watching the bricks slide and crack. Hank wondered why Susan didn't call one of her colleagues from the Potteries to ask for advice, but she refused. Every late morning and afternoon she left for the hospital, stayed the entire time for visiting hours while Hank fussed and considered the kiln and slowly built the thing. It was not quite done by the next Saturday, when he was to drive Dad to the train station.

He considered not showing up to take Dad. Dad could call a taxi. The family had money, but Dad hated spending money on taxis; he liked to ride around in cars or drive himself, and Hank had to admit it was cool to drive the Cadillac. But the kiln was almost done. Susan wasn't home, still at the hospital, as Hank smoothed the layer of slick clay on the interior, set the cast iron rack inside, tightened the vents and tested the fuel over and over.

The day was warm—it hadn't rained in the past week, and as Hank bicycled home he pulled off his shirt and tied it around his waist. His shoulders and back were already bronzed from the sun while he worked on the kiln.

In spite of the task before him, Hank was in a very good mood. Dad, however, was not in a good mood as Hank swept into the driveway, hopped off his bike, ran into the house for a drink of water. Waiting near the front door, his matching luggage beside him, he pointed at his watch. He carried a heavy gray overcoat, a strange juxtaposition to the heat of the balmy Southern California winter day.

"If I miss this train because of you, I'll send you back to the gypsies who brought you here."

Hank shrugged, gave what he hoped was a look of contrition. No, he would never hear the end of it. Both Mom and Dad would devote more words to it than was necessary.

Dad eyed him over his reading glasses, as if, Hank thought, he was seeing his youngest son for the first time. Hank wondered if his new-found life showed somehow, new glaze painted on his skin as if he were a line of figurines of half-naked men, well-muscled and athletic.

But Dad turned away a moment later, as if knowing that to ask the question would get him either a frustrating nothing or more information than he really wanted. Smiling, Hank pulled on his shirt and picked up the two suitcases, neither of them really very heavy, and followed Dad out to the car, already parked in the driveway by Joaquin, who in addition to cooking, also washed the cars.

The drive through downtown LA to Union Station usually took around 40 minutes. Hank was a careful driver—the twins always complained he was too sedate behind the wheel, like an old woman. Dad didn't seem too agitated, because he preferred that Hank take Sunset the entire way, avoiding the congestion of Wilshire. Hank turned on the radio and found a noisy swing band, the sort of music Dad detested.

The first thing Dad did was roll down his window, push in the lighter, and take a cigar out of his pocket. Mom didn't allow Dad to smoke cigars in the house.

"You've been busy. You got a job or something?"

Hank considered his answer carefully. "Yes, I have a job.

I'm helping a friend do some remodeling."

Giving him a sideways glance, Dad nodded and sucked on his panatela and made no reply, as if that were all that needed to be said. Relief settled deep into Hank's stomach.

"I want you to keep an eye on your mother." Dad's head was turned away, but his voice, the booming, velvet tones, were clear and precise. "I think she's showing signs of strain. Just—keep an eye on her."

Keep an eye on Mom. Talk to Connie. And Hank still didn't know or want to know what Mom tried to tell him the other night. He should hang out a shingle as the Cleveland's personal psychiatrist. Or spiritual counselor.

Dad took Hank's silence as assent, and the rest of the way to the station he flipped through his perpetual script, rehearsing vowels and consonants and inflections. Hank stared through the windows and manned the great car like the captain of a ship through a busy harbor, and wished he were on his way out to sea.

Six

HANK HAD NO CHOICE but to accomplish his assigned family tasks this same weekend.

The Cleveland family attended an innocuous Methodist church in Hollywood. All went, as a group; Bess Cleveland's assumption that a Sunday at church together was never to be missed was never questioned. The facade was laughable to Hank, and the twins . Dad played his role perfectly, and Mom inevitably relished the autograph-seeking that went on after a service delivered by a young reverend whose looks made him more suitable for Hollywood heartthrob than spiritual advisor.

Tomorrow morning, after the church scene, was usually a time when Hank oiled and tuned the Peugeot and cycled to the shore for a sixty-or-more mile round trip. He'd sacrifice his ride to corner his mother and sister and listen to their voices and give them all the attention they craved and that would be that.

But he easily squirmed out of his obligations when Susan asked him to spend Saturday night with her.

The kiln was finished, the night unseasonably warm. When he cycled back to her house after leaving Dad at the

Station, they celebrated with a bottle of wine and the firing of a pig-head cookie jar. Dinner was hamburgers on Susan's rusty grill. Hank brought out the radio and plugged it in and they danced to Harry James and Duke Ellington. Susan, to Hank's astonishment, had gotten rid of her phonograph, something about Joseph breaking all her records.

And then they made love, wrestling on the bed, sheets and blankets sliding to the floor, skin to skin, smells of candle wax and cinnamon. Hours after, Hank lay looking at the special geography of Susan's body as she slept with her back to him, moonlight through the parted curtains providing the back drop to the landscape.

He was thinking of the broken marquis and the crowd of figurines in Susan's studio. He thought of Grandfather Joel, his son on the way to Oklahoma City, sitting in the lounge car with a cocktail and chatting up pretty girls.

Getting up, he pulled on a robe that Susan lent him, an old flannel plaid thing of Joseph's, smelling of cedar-lined closets and cigarettes. He walked through the silent house into the yard, across the icy grass to the studio. The kiln was still warm, the piglet jar still inside. Cool-down or something was called for, Susan said. Hank thought of the piglet alone in the kiln, a lonely pet tied outside.

He wondered at his sad mood. He should feel content and pleased with himself, getting his wish like this, a night with Susan. But grief tugged at him. Maybe it was because the grandfather he barely knew had died. Maybe it was because it was January. Maybe because he somehow he knew this was the first and last time he could stay with her.

A pair of hands slipped around him and into the pockets of the robe. Susan's hair tickled his neck. He turned and kissed her.

She knelt, opened the kiln door, extracted the piglet jar, carried it carefully into the studio and set it on a bench. A little heater on an extension cord—not a safe feature of the studio, but good enough until a wire could be run from the house—kept the place comfortable for the ceramics.

"When my grandfather died, a figurine fell off the mantle." Hank didn't realize he'd said this aloud until he saw Susan looking at him thoughtfully.

"You didn't tell me your grandfather died."

Shrugging, Hank stuck his hands into his armpits. His feet were cold.

"I didn't even know him. But my dad said the figurine fell off the mantle, and then the phone rang. It was Aunt Hope, telling him their father was dead."

He described the figurine to her, and its companion the marquess. Her eyebrows traveled upward as she listened.

"Meissen figures. Could be the Kaendler period. Your mother is right, worth about $1000. Each. More for the set." Susan scanned her shelves, prototypes of animals and people in various poses, extras in a movie hoping to be noticed.

She was silent a long while, then, "She died long before, the little marquess. And waited to push him over the edge, waited all those years, because he loved her more than life, and she despised him."

A cold hand swept over Hank, and he looked at Susan, wondering what in her mind had made her say that. He knew nothing about her past, just that she and Joseph had grown up in this house, inherited it, lived in it after the war. She was a WAC or WAVE in the war, worked for somebody. She would not say her parents were dead and she would not say if they were alive. She would not say anything about that. Nor if she had been married before, or even had children. She didn't want him to ask and he had never asked, and the idea of her telling him all this frightened him anyway. He might fall out of love with her if he knew too much about her.

And it was so like what the Girl had said, the girl who sat on his bed and looked at the photograph of his grandparents.

Susan knew about Hank's brother and sister, his cycling mania, where he was born. But she didn't seem interested in more, and even when he told her these things, her gaze wandered and she seemed to go somewhere else in her head.

But she had relayed to him knowledge of a story about his grandparents that he knew had to be true. Maybe she knew this because she had worked with small clay models of people and animals all her life. She had gone to some fancy design school, he knew, having seen a certificate and diploma in her bedroom. But there was no evidence of early artwork. Her house was vacant of the things she had made over the years.

But there was more, that made him sway and turn, so she wouldn't see his disequilibrium. The broken memory of the Girl saying the same thing. The only memory of the Girl he could summon, and the effort to remember more hammered in his head, deafening him.

Susan was saying, "This is greenware, what we call clay figures or dishes that have not been glazed."

She was looking at the pig head. Hank thought of the broken head of the marquis, how Carl had been peering inside it. Only the top of this pig's head was sitting on the bench beside it. The pig now an empty bowl ready to receive, and then give up, whatever was put in there.

"I'll think about what colors to use tomorrow." Yawning, she turned and walked out of the garage, her hips moving from side to side in her chenille robe.

When Hank woke up Sunday morning he turned to find Susan gone. It was late, sun well over the horizon casting a long shadow of the front palm onto Susan's lawn and the next one and the next. Disappointed with himself, Hank had hoped to be the first to arise, but his sojourn in the middle of the night, and it taking him quite a while to get back to sleep, had caused him to doze far longer than he planned.

And by now of course, his absence from home would be noticed. He didn't want to think about that.

The kitchen was silent and cold. Coffee on the stove was lukewarm. It was as if Susan had been up for hours. For a jittering moment, Hank worried that she had already left for the hospital.

He found her in the studio. She had begun to paint the piglet head, cans of mixed glazes surrounding her, including several of a powdery substance; the talc from Death Valley she was always talking about,.

Ignoring him as he entered, she painted dull shades, which she said would give the little pig's jowls a healthy blush in the fire. Hank propped himself on a stool and watched.

After a long silence, broken only by the creaking of her chair as she worked and the chattering of sparrows in the grass outside, she finally spoke.

"Joseph is coming home three days early."

Hank sagged as if he had been punched in the stomach. "When?"

Glancing at him between two strands of hair loose from the scarf she had wrapped around her head, her look warned him.

"Tuesday."

Sighing, Hank got up, began picking random things off the shelves: a heavy brush, a jar labeled "slip", a page of stencils.

His chest squeezed him, making his face hot and his eyes dry. Why couldn't she just leave Joseph there, make the VA hospital take care of him until he was normal again, then get him an apartment and a job and a wife?

"Now don't pout." Susan's voice was firm, short, different from the wonderment of her pronouncement about the figurines last night. "There's more. I have to get a nurse. I can't take care of him by myself when I go back to work. She'll be a nursing student, a live-in. The doctor is finding one for me."

Now Hank stared at her, unbelieving. The coldness in her voice. But also the acceptance. Of course she would take Joseph home again. Of course she would rearrange her life around Joseph. Hank's mind whirled with hurt.

Susan glanced at him again, then at her silly pig. She gently chewed the end of her brush. A fingerprint of pink dotted her chin. Hank waited for the pronouncement about him: that he couldn't come over any more, they were breaking up. Susan didn't have time for him. And besides, how could he come for his afternoon trysts with a nurse and Joseph in the house?

"We will have to find another place to meet." Susan's words dug into his heart, turned it around. "Actually, I might have a little more freedom with the nurse here."

"I'll look into some places," he said before he could stop himself. Maybe Susan had some place already in mind.

A smirk pulled at the corner of her mouth, as if to say it was funny that a nineteen-year old boy would know of places where lovers could meet.

He shrugged. "My family knows a lot of people. People with cottages they don't use. Something could be worked out."

Giving this statement a short nod of approval, Susan went

back to her painting. Relief poured through Hank, just as if he had been doused with warm water. No more nights over, like this, but he thought maybe that was a good thing. Familiarity breeds contempt, wasn't that the old sobriquet?

To hide his joy, he turned and picked up a paper bag the size of peanuts bought at a carnival. Inside was gray powder; more talc, he assumed. He stuck his finger in it.

"Don't touch that," Susan said sharply. She squinted at him, the morning sun coming in through the garage window, making her face glow like a lightbulb behind a clear mask.

"The oils from your fingers," she added, in a tone more kindly. "It can affect the quality of the glaze."

She let him stay with her until it was time to go to the hospital to visit Joseph. She even asked him to come with her to pick Joseph up on Tuesday, if the nurse wasn't available. Hank rode home on tires of silk, the wind licking his face and tasting of Susan's hair.

He got home about midday, his head spinning with how to ask Carl or Connie if they knew who had an apartment or house they weren't using. After seeing to the Raleigh and lovingly apologizing to the Peugeot for missing their ride this morning, he entered the house to find his mother sitting stiffly in the living room, reading a paper, and looking at him over the edge as if she were a lioness in wait.

Now would come the unpleasantness, but Hank thought he could take it because he was made of light and air and Susan's lips on his cheek.

Going to his chair by the French doors, opened to fill the room with air scented with eucalyptus, Hank sat in what he hoped would be an obedient pose to accept his punishment for being out all night and missing church.

Mom was in her bathrobe. Maybe she had come home for

a swim on this weirdly warm January day. But something wasn't quite right. Her hair hung in ragged shanks, and she wore no make-up at all. The last time Hank had seen her look this way, she was home from the hospital after having her appendix out.

"I don't care that you didn't come home last night, but it would have been nice if you'd shown up for church." she said crisply, crumpling the newspaper into her lap. Cigarette butts overflowed the ash tray and the tumbler beside it was half-filled with whiskey and chunks of half-melted ice.

"And thank you for taking your father to the train. But I do care that you ignored my wishes to indulge your own selfish little whims."

There were odd little catches in her voice, as if she had been speaking in court all day. She didn't argue cases any more, and she didn't do half the speechifying she used to, but her voice was ragged and unsure. Her mouth and lips jerked to one side and she touched her throat, swallowing.

Hank tried to remember what Mom's wishes were this time, besides taking up his role in the pew as the Cleveland's youngest son. He did take Dad to the station and he did remember Dad asking him to 'keep an eye on Mom'. But he didn't dare ask her what she was so pissed about that he didn't do. Instead, he tried to look chagrinned.

"Sorry, mom."

"Sorry won't do it this time, soldier," Mom said, trying to fold up the paper. She folded it and creased it and thrust it at him.

Little scandals had often come to light for the Clevelands. It was the risk the dancing-singing-orating clan ran in the their rush to infamy. Rising, Hank took the paper from his mother's hand and read the title of the article folded for his viewing.

Love nest! Cedric Sigfried's got one in the bush.

The routine hyperbole of the sensation rags filled in the data. The producer's rumored casting couch claimed another victim, this one thirty years younger than he. She got the part but hints of stalking have arisen now that she had been 'cast' away for another 'casting' catch.

Hank gazed at his mother, unbelieving. She thought this stalking starlet was Connie? That was why she was so nervous lately? And then it came to him. He had muffed his assignment to uncover the reason Connie was upset.

"This?" Hank handed the paper back to her. "Mom, c'mon."

To his surprise Mom threw the paper onto the couch beside her. She had been steadily reading through the tabloids, Variety, the Times, looking for angles and news. Always thinking how to apply any little happening to boost the twins' act.

"Then I want you to find out." Snatching the pack of cigarettes from the coffee table, she pushed newspapers aside, looking for her lighter.

In a moment of daring, Hank pulled out Susan's lighter, snapped it open and held it out to Mom. Glancing at him in a startled way, she accepted the light, blew smoke into the air.

"I thought you quit smoking."

"I did. I keep it around as a reminder."

One of Mom's eyebrows went up. Then she went back to her papers; snagging an unstarted crossword puzzle.

"She's in her room."

Hank waited, unsure now, but determined. He remembered Dad's voice, softly worried.

Mom filled in three words with her gold ball point. She

looked up at him from under her eyebrows, both eyebrows up now, her best intimidate-the-witness look.

"The other night," Hank said, the confidence he always felt as he left Susan's beginning to slide away, sucked away. "You were going to tell me something?"

"Yes, well, it can wait." Mom scribbled in another word, looking down now, at her puzzle. "Just go talk to your sister, please."

Hank knew his chance was gone, but he lingered, walked over to the mantle. Nothing filled the space once occupied by the little marquis. The smooth stone was free of dust, the walls rising whitely and curving into the high ceiling. He looked at the marquess, hands resting on her bustles, white wig glinting with a pearl-like glaze.

"You know, you are right. She's Messian, from Dresden, worth about $1000." Hank thought of the photograph of his grandmother, the same flat, unlovely face as his father. Did you despise your husband, just like Susan said? And the Girl said that, too.

"How do you know?" His mother's voice was pointed, sharp.

"A friend. Someone who knows about this kind of stuff." Hank touched the pale blue skirt, rippled with faint colors like motor oil in water.

"Don't touch that."

The same tone as Susan, a mother's tone. Someone accustomed to giving orders.

"Just, don't. We don't want to lose her, too."

"Don't you think that was strange? It jumping off the mantle and then the call comes?"

Mom snorted, sighed abruptly. "Hank, quit bothering me. Go talk to Connie."

The Girl's finger tapped the photo, touched the marquess's dress in the same place Hank just had. This close and pale, a beautiful finger, tracing a line down the photograph, across the bedspread, and onto Hank's hand.

"Mom, do you remember a girl, with dark hair, pretty, who I knew in high school? She used to come over here, a lot, I think. It's so weird, but I can't remember her name."

No answer came. Turning, Hank looked at Mom, and he saw, before her eyes flicked back to her paper, that she had been staring at him, and had she, for a moment, looked afraid?

"You were always bringing girls home. No wonder you can't remember all their names. I certainly couldn't." The funny catch was back in her voice, as if her jaw froze a split second before every other word.

The marquess gazed back at him from under black blots signifying lashes. She was prettier than the dour woman in the photograph, the one that the Girl said was hoping she would outlive the old man, but bitterly never got her wish.

Seven

CONNIE WAS IN HER ROOM, door ajar, and turned from her place on the bed to watch Hank enter after he politely knocked. He always knocked before bursting into either of the twins' room as he used to before he was ten.

Connie wore dungarees, a big plaid shirt that once, and still perhaps did, belonged to Dad. She had tied up her hair in a bandana, the way Susan did, the way women who used to work the war factories did. If there were no extra rehearsals, unlike Carl who disappeared down to Hollywood to loiter with other young actors in restaurants and bars, Connie kept her Sundays private and alone, a day of contemplation and relaxation that had nothing to do with God.

"What do you think of this dress—for me, that is?" She thrust a magazine across the bed, and he sat down on the bed to see. The room was stifling hot, sun burning invasively through her closed French doors to her balcony which faced south west. Connie was always cold. In the drawing, a lanky, curvy woman looked over her shoulder in a soufflé of a dress, poufy sleeves and full, busy skirt.

"It's hideous," Hank said.

Connie seized the magazine, flipped to the next page. "Just

what I thought." She rattled through the pages, the same way Mom rattled through her papers.

"Where were you last night?"

"Out."

"No!" Connie gave the word a sarcastic inflection. Closing her magazine, she sidled closer to him. Uneasiness stiffened him, but he pledged not to move away, just look her full in the eye.

"You are too cute," she said, poking his chest. "You have a girlfriend. Admit it. I can see it on you." Bringing her face so close to his that he could see tiny hairs on her upper lip, she whispered, "You're fucking her."

Hank gazed back at her, hoping his face was fully blank, hoping the warmth he felt spreading up his neck was not visible as blotches of uneasy color.

"Mom wants me to talk to you."

Rolling her eyes, Connie shifted backward, lay down, slung an arm under her head. "About what, for god's sake?"

"She's worried about you, I guess. And you're more wound up than a hop head trying to dry up."

That made her grin. "OK, you can tell her this. Someone has been talking to me about my career—someone very high up and powerful. He says I should ditch the duo dancing act and branch out on my own."

Maybe she had slept with Cedric Sigfried. But that didn't alarm Hank. What did alarm him was what Carl would do when he found out. He already caught the scent of change in the air.

"Why haven't you told Mom yet? She's your business manager."

"I'm going to." Connie turned onto her stomach, stuck her bare feet, toes painted tomato red, into the air. Hank couldn't help noticing the smooth line of her butt under the dungarees. "When the time is right."

Shifting in the bed, Hank crossed his ankles like a yogi, turned his back to her. "Is that why you hit the roof the other night?"

There was a silence. When Hank looked over his shoulder to see what she was doing, he saw her studiously cleaning her nails.

"Yeah, sure, whatever you like."

"I thought I was your favorite brother."

She rolled again, touched his knee. "You are, Hank, you are. Carl is such an asshole sometimes. You have no idea." Her face took on a stony look and Hank wondered if it was for his benefit, because somehow it didn't look real, just as her voice hadn't sounded true or convincing of anything.

"You're wrong about that. I have an idea," Hank said, leaning back on his elbows. But was Carl really more cruel than any other older brother? Connie had her moments as well.

There was another question he wanted to ask, but he couldn't bring himself to do it. He thought he knew why she blew up the other evening. He thought he knew that her moods and disquiet had nothing to do with menstruation or the chance to do a solo act. The thing was, Mom expected an answer. What was he going to tell her?

"You do have an idea, don't you, poor little brother." She leaned on one elbow, watched him, her lips smirking, her eyes—what were they saying? What had they always said? What challenge was she laying down before him?

She said, "This girl you are seeing, she took your cherry, didn't she?" A frown cycled through her face, then caught up in a smile. "You're such a pretty boy. You don't know how lucky you are a girl seduced you before one of the multitude of Hollywood queers got to you first. Carl and I hear them whispering about you, whenever you tag along with Mom to the studio."

"Don't think they didn't try." Hank started to slide off the bed, but Connie playfully tugged at his shirt. Pulling free, Hank turned to look at her. She lay with her head on her el-bow, reaching up to him like a pinup girl, the top several buttons of her shirt undone.

"So, if you don't want to tell me what's really the matter," he said, making a point to keep his gaze pinned to her face. "I guess I'll have to make something up."

Her eyebrows drew down in a scowl. Picking up the magazine, she rolled it and put it to her mouth.

"Why does there have to be something else wrong?" she asked through the tube, her voice low and hollow, ghostly.

Shaking his head, Hank turned and walked away. The magazine hit him square between the shoulder blades and fluttered like a shaggy bird to the floor.

Eight

WAITING IN THE CAR under the Veteran's Hospital *porte cochére*, Hank turned off the wiper blades. The inside of Susan's car was like a submarine, alone in the depths full of sea creatures. Rain fell steadily all day, and night claimed territory early under the steel gray clouds, darker than the hulls of military ships moored at Long Beach.

A few hours ago they had made love. Susan was fiercer with him, pushing him down, getting on top, digging nails into his skin. Silent, unmoving on the drive to the VA hospital, she stared out the darkening window at rain and lights and pedestrians getting soaked on the sidewalks.

Hank ran his fingers around the cold steering wheel. The balmy days had been shoved out of the way by this cold, damp Pacific storm, as if Joseph himself were blowing in with it, bringing with him a searching despair.

Nervous, more nervous about meeting someone than ever before, Hank had only seen Joseph once by accident arriving early, a slim, red-haired young man, extraordinarily pale, striding down Susan's walk and turning north along the sidewalk. About to turn into Susan's driveway, Hank coasted, slowed, stopped, pretended to be checking something on his bike, and watched Joseph walk quickly, nothing like the way Hank thought a shell-shocked soldier might walk on his way to a visit with an Army psychiatrist.

Cars came and went while Hank waited, picking up patients and employees. He strongly wished for a cigarette. He knew there was a pack in the glove compartment, and he had Susan's lighter in his shirt pocket. But he had promised, when she gave him the lighter, that he would quit. Taking it out of his pocket, he flipped it open and closed, liking the soft metallic click it made. A moment later there was a tapping at the passenger window.

Susan was outside, gesturing for him to get out to help her. He did so, circling the back of the car, to where an orderly stood holding Joseph's wheel chair.

Hank saw the back of Joseph's head, red hair lank and un-washed. As he came beside the wheel chair, Joseph looked up at him.

"You're the friend. Nice to meet you—Joseph Chagall. My sister Susan of course, you know, and this is Sebastian, my manservant." His voice was smooth and quick. Red stubble coated his jaws and chin and he thrust out a white hand, thin and fine.

"Hank Cleveland." Hank took the hand gently, but the re-sponding grip was tight and sudden.

"Hank. For Henry? You do resemble Fonda, don't you think, Suze?"

"Let's get you inside the car, Joseph. It's cold out here." Susan held the back passenger door open.

"OK, Mr. Chagall, here we go," said Sebastian the orderly, if that was his real name. "If you would hold the chair please, sir."

Hank held the chair and Susan held the door as Sebastian

expertly lifted, twirled and settled Joseph in the car. Plaster casts encased Joseph's legs up to his calves, and he slid backward as Sebastian lifted both onto the seat.

Glancing at Susan, hoping to catch her eye and give her a comforting smile, Hank was disappointed. Susan wouldn't look at him at all, focused on her brother, her face masked with worry. She seemed genuinely concerned for her brother; a special love passed between them, the kind of love Hank never felt for his brother and sister. He had hoped to see chagrin or impatience on her face, but was not satisfied, and instantly felt bad about wishing to see it.

Joseph set up a constant chatter as Hank drove them home. Sitting sideways in the front seat, looking at Joseph over her shoulder, Susan listened, and even laughed at one point, a startling thing, because Hank very rarely heard her laugh out loud.

Hank listened to stories about other patients in Joseph's ward, fellow veterans like Joseph. Hank was a young teenager during the war years—he still was, technically, but he thought of himself as much older. Connie and Carl volunteered at the USO entertaining sailors from Long Beach. But Hank stayed remote—he didn't, like many of his friends at school, keep maps on the wall or track the movements of the forces scrambling for territory in Europe and the Pacific.

"So, sister, what kind of old battle-axe have you hired as my minder? A stiff-necked old maid with sponges made of porcupine quills?" Joseph had a cigarette, and to Hank's astonishment Susan lit it for him. The smoke smelled wonderful.

"Oh wait, I know, an over-muscled young man with the Charles Atlas course in his back pocket, and a gentle voice, and eyes like dried figs."

Susan shook her head. "I have no idea. It's a surprise. We shall both be surprised."

"Oh, I get it. A nurse in a tight white uniform jumping out of a cake, with two huge hypos, one in each hand."

Hank's irritation grew. He wanted Joseph to shut up, for the ride to be over, to get back on his bike and get home. Even the nuthouse atmosphere of his own home would seem like a beach in Hawaii compared to this.

Arriving at Susan's bungalow, the problem of getting Joseph into the house became apparent. The nurse had not yet arrived; she—or he—was expected any moment, the poor soul having to finish out a swing shift at the hospital before schlepping over to Susan's to care for a neurotic moron. Hank voted strongly for the porcupine sponges.

Hank understood why Susan needed him. It was not for emotional support or because she liked to gaze into his face. She needed muscle to get Joseph settled in in case the nurse wasn't here. No nurse was here, so, they settled on crossing their arms with Joseph sitting between them and stumbled up the stairs.

Joseph was surprisingly light, and Hank could feel bone under the emaciated muscle of Joseph's butt. The guy was as skinny as a broom. Having already taken the wheelchair into the house, they settled him in. The effort was fairly easy for Hank, but Susan looked wrought, her chin frozn with breath-less pain. She was fit, perhaps, but small.

Joseph expertly wheeled his chair back and forth over the braided rug, clanking into the coffee table.

"Hank, you are a paragon of youth. I would like you to be my nurse."

"Sorry, my duties lie elsewhere." Hank glanced at Susan as she flopped down on the sofa, and this time, she did meet his eyes. Her sharp little glance warmed him, and if Joseph saw it and drew a conclusion that was all too evident, Hank was glad for it.

Joseph said, "I fear, dear sister, that we shall have to make accommodation for this, my steel-wheeled assistant. Let's see, can I even get through the door into the kitchen?" Whirling the chair around, knocking into chairs and tables, he aimed for the dining room doorway and made it through, all the while talking about removing the walls with a sledge hammer.

It took all Hank had not to pull her to him, close, and lick her skin. Her hair had fallen over one eye, her eyes rimmed with a sadness he could not identify. Tipping his head, he gave her a questioning glance, but she shook her head quickly, once, twice, as Joseph wheeled back in.

"Mr. Atlas, I don't suppose you would bring in my small, inadequate bag of belongings, a mere toothbrush and razor, which as you see, I haven't used in days." Joseph gave him a friendly smile, lines deepening around his mouth, his eyes, the same chocolate-color as Susan's, self-deprecating in a way that might otherwise be engaging.

"Sure." Hank went to the car, his soul chewing on a chunk of jealousy that distressed him. Susan seemed to really like Joseph's company, enjoyed his stupid prattle. A paper bag containing underwear, the aforementioned toiletry items, and a book, one of those blank books writers use, was on the floor of the Packard. Curious to open its pages, Hank would have liked to see into the soul of this little brother. Maybe here was the key to Susan.

But he took the bag inside, set it down on the coffee table. Susan had gone into the kitchen, probably to get something pulled together for supper. Joseph lit another cigarette;

smoke enveloped him like a magician, and he smiled as he saw Hank.

"Thank you, my good man. A useful friend. Susan needs a good friend. I, unfortunately, am not it."

Hank didn't know what to say. He shrugged. He wanted to go into the kitchen to be with Susan. He wanted to go into the garage with her and let her show him what she had been working on, the horse and tiger and swan.

"I guess I better be going." He could pass through the kitchen. His bicycle was leaning against the back porch in its usual place. "Nice to meet you."

Joseph nodded, sucking on his fag. A weary grayness had flowed over his face, of pain and something else. Hank felt a little sorry for him. He had no idea what Joseph had been through in the war. And his ankles probably hurt like hell.

"Same here, Mr. Fonda. Hope we can repeat the experience under better circumstances."

In the kitchen, Susan was merely making coffee. Hank wondered if the nurse would be expected to cook meals, too. He slid his hands around her waist, felt her stiffen. She pushed his hands away.

"Thanks for the help, Hank."

A little stunned, but knowing the reasons, Hank stepped back. He glanced through the doorway to the dining room, the living room beyond. Joseph had not followed.

"See you Saturday," he whispered, half-expecting her to say no, to shove him even further away, out the door and into the lawn, maybe into the kiln.

But she nodded quickly, turned away to the cupboard to take down cups and saucers and set them on a tray--just two, Hank saw.

"The nurse will be here any minute," she said for explana-

tion. Her hands quivered as she moved the cups. Susan giving an excuse for anything was a new thing.

Without a word Hank left, but he looked through the back
door window and saw her standing motionless at the stove,
watching the coffee.

Getting on his bike soothed him, with the cold rush of the
wind, the occasional spatter of water from the trees as he
went down the driveway felt as soft and glorifying as Susan's
hair. It had fortunately stopped raining. As he flowed out
into the street, a taxi cab pulled up in front of Susan's house.
The nurse apparently had arrived, but he didn't wait to see if
this was Charles Atlas or the battle-axe.

Nine

DAD WIRED THAT HE WOULD BE HOME the next week-end and Hank again was designated to pick him up at the station. He was due to meet Susan Saturday afternoon at the Lady Windermere Hotel in Santa Monica, where a friend of Connie's had an apartment he wasn't using, but they would have to postpone the date for a later time, dinner time, which Susan didn't like, as she preferred to eat with Joseph. But now Hank was floating at the prospect for taking Susan out to dinner even though there was a chance they might run into someone they knew. Hank had few friends who hung out in Santa Monica, and the only ones who might recognize him were Connie's or Carl's friends, and they wouldn't give a hoot to know what the twins' little brother was up to.

As for Susan, she didn't seem to have many friends either. She rarely talked about Sam or the others at the Potteries. When she did talk, it was about her work, the figurines, glazes and clay, as if she was happier in the company of ceramics than people.

Hank didn't even know if she was happier in his company, either. But he tried not to care, eager for the hours she let him have, hungry for more, but knowing better than to ask for seconds.

But he did ask for money, from Mom, who refused, giving him the lecture about college versus getting a job. Connie slyly gave him twenty bucks, pulled from a stocking hanging in her closet stuffed with bills—her savings account. Carl too contributed, not even asking what it was for, assuming a big date, and gave him advice about the process of seduction for a good twenty minutes before Hank could make an excuse to get away.

When Saturday came, Dad was quiet the entire drive home from the station. A rain squall, rumbling from the Pacific toward the east, astonished everyone in LA with thunder and lightning. Making its appearance next, the sun became the star of the show, introduced by the grumbling storm. In the seat between Dad and Hank was a white box with a black ribbon: Grandfather Joel's ashes, Dad said in an embarrassed, almost off-hand way.

As Hank pulled into the driveway, Dad at last began to talk. "Wait a minute, don't go in yet."

Perplexed, Hank sat with his hands on the wheel, turned off the motor. The car smelled of Dad's last cigar, a crushed corsage left in the backseat after one of Connie's many dates, and motor oil. Hank inhaled familiar notes, and something else, a tang he couldn't quite place.

Placing one knee on the car seat, Dad turned to face Hank. "How is everyone? How is your mother?"

Not having seen much of anyone lately, Hank wondered what he should say. "Mom seems a bit run down, maybe. Working too hard, you know."

Dad nodded. He scratched an eyebrow. To Hank's observant eye, he looked well rested and well-fed. Aunt Hope and the relatives must have been cooking a lot out there on the farm.

"I wish I could get her to take a vacation. I've been think-ing about Havana, or Rio. Gambling. I think Bess would love that."

Hank thought Mom would like it too, if she could be pried away from her twins. As far as he knew, Mom hadn't ever set foot in a casino. He nodded in agreement.

"I'd better do it soon," Dad said, nodding, lips sticking out. His silver voice was almost wistful.

"She'll fight it. The twins are thinking of splitting up the act, did you know that?"

Dad's eyes widened in shock, followed by his eyebrows moving in opposite directions in anxiety.

"Are you kidding? Break up the Cleveland Twins? Now when they got their first big break in a movie?"

Hank was sorry he'd said it. No one had confirmed to him one way or the other, but he could tell something was in the air by Connie's breezy and forced manner, the amount of time Carl spent out, and Mom's diminishing weight and in-creased smoking.

Dad shook his head, back and forth. Hank thought Dad had actually come out of his world of voicings and scripts for a moment to think about his wife and children. Worry about them even, something he sometimes did not seemed capable of.

Sighing, Dad opened the car door. A wave of relief swept through Hank as he realized he would get away from all this angst and spend the early evening with Susan. He might, after Susan went home, spend the night in the apartment, walk Santa Monica beach after dark, and try to cadge a drink in the old Speakeasy. But all that would be so much more fun with Susan along. He made up his mind to break rule number one and beg her to stay with him.

Now traffic and Dad's lonely musings were making him late. He had planned to cycle out there—it was less far than Susan's bungalow—get there early and shower and dress, but now he gave thought to hiring a car, wondering if his meager amount of cash was enough for that and dinner too. And flowers.

Following Dad inside, he found the place in an uproar. Everyone was home as if they were all waiting for Dad. Connie, sweaty and flushed in a tennis outfit, Carl with not a hair out of place or a wrinkle in his knit golf shirt, and Mom in a forest green suit and a big yellow corsage, just in the act of taking off her hat.

If it had been staged, it couldn't have been better. There was something in the air, and as Dad walked into the foyer carrying the white box, everyone struck a pose as if the clapboard had been struck.

Hank didn't wait; dashing up the stairs he pulled together everything he had already planned to bring to the apartment, stuffed it into a small satchel and ran back down. Skirting the stairs and heading toward the kitchen where only his partner in crime Joaquin might make a remark, he hoped he wouldn't be noticed, but there was to be no such luck today.

"Hank!" Connie's best theatre voice, booming loudly through the house, stabbed him in the back.

"You have to help us. The driver from the studio is sick—this flu or whatever that's going around. Someone has to take us to the cocktail party at Cedric's."

A slow angry boil started somewhere deep in Hank's gut. Folding his arms, he leaned against the staircase.

"I have plans," he said slowly.

Mom separated herself from the twins and walked toward

Hank. Behind her, Dad disappeared through the living room arch with the white box. A searching look came over Connie's face as she gazed at Hank. Carl hung back, watching the entire exchange with an amused expression.

Smelling of Chanel and smoke, Mom stood before him. In her heels, she was as nearly as tall as Hank.

She said in a low voice, "If you will drive them, I will let you borrow the car for your 'plans'. I'm sure they can arrange rides home."

This was a tempting offer. Driving the twins into Beverly Hills to the Sigfried mansion would take time, but he could make it up by driving out to Santa Monica instead of cycling.

Connie had already bounded up the stairs like a mountain goat, and Hank could hear the water running for her bath.

Nodding, Hank tried to keep a smile off his face. Mom scanned his eyes, then turning away, clip-clopped along the tile floor toward the kitchen where Joaquin was already fomenting a volcano of interesting smells.

Carl twirled his sunglasses. "We should get you a little chauffeur's cap, with a patent leather visor. You would look great. Everyone likes a good-looking chauffeur."

"And with your new sunglasses, my look would be complete," Hank said, folding his arms. The angry broil still burned inside him, subdued by the promise of the Cadillac.

"Here. Catch." Carl flung the glasses. Catching them, he put them on, and Carl smirked. "They look better on you. Besides, I have a dozen more upstairs somewhere."

Oddly, as Hank walked toward the living room, he was disappointed not to be riding his bike out to Santa Monica. His body itched with lassitude, almost achy, and he was eager to push the bike to its limits. He hadn't taken the Peugeot out for a spin in a while. And Connie wouldn't be ready for the party for an hour.

But first he phoned Susan to tell her the change of plans. A feminine voice answered, young-sounding, barely accented with Spanish. She told him to wait while she called Susan to the phone.

Not a battle-axe or Charles Atlas. Hank wondered how things were going with Susan and Joseph and the nurse. She sounded professional and cool.

He found himself telling Susan he would pick her up at six, two hours later than planned, and she was silent for a moment, digesting this change of plans, Hank thought.

"What do you mean, 'pick me up?'"

He told her about the car. He pushed further, telling her she could eat with Joseph early, then have a late supper with him at the hotel. Stopping there, he didn't push his luck at implying she should stay overnight.

She was silent; Hank thought he heard a voice in the background, Joseph speaking impatiently to the nurse, or to Susan. He waited, not saying anything, listening to her breathe.

"OK," she said, and the line went dead

Ten

"OH MY GOD, WHAT IS THAT?" Carl's voice floated in an exaggerated way through the living room archway. Hank followed its echo, followed by Dad's best *Ten Commandments* voice as he proclaimed, "That, my son, is the sarcophagus of Joel Aloysius Cleveland, scion of the Oklahoma wheat fields."

Entering the room, Hank found Dad and Carl standing before the mantle looking at a garish blue and red urn, emblazoned with the image of Grandfather Joel in the frame of a gilt medallion.

"Hope chose it. By the time I got there, of course, the deed had been done. Pop cremated and the ashes divided between the two of us in matching urns." Stalking over to the drinks cart, Dad waved his arms, pitched down three glasses, splashed them liberally with scotch, and carried one first to Carl, and then to Hank, who took it, astonished.

"To the old man. May he come back as an ass." Dad threw back his scotch, and so did Carl, but not before turning a curious glance on Hank, who returned it, equally confused by Dad's sudden change in personality. Hank sipped the whiskey; it tasted brown and spicy and faintly of gasoline.

"Will it have to stay on the mantle?" Carl tipped his head, looking the urn over. "Will we have Grandfather Joel perpetually observing us from up there?"

Re-filling his glass—Hank didn't remember seeing his father drink this way—Dad flopped back on the sofa and toasted his father's visage again.

"For now. Just a reminder that even the most obstinate man on earth can lose his hold on life."

Exchanging another puzzled glance with Carl, Hank finished his glass of scotch. Carl shuffled ice into his glass, poured more, offered to Hank, who wanted it, but shook his head.

Carl said, "I didn't know you hated him."

"I don't hate him." Dad undid his tie, flung it down on the floor. "I loved him. I just spent my entire life trying not to be him."

Hank thought wisely that Dad had succeeded at that, but he wondered what Grandfather Joel thought of it all. Dad certainly had not involved his father in his life in Southern California. The two seemed to be living in separate neighboring countries, lives bordering each other, but neither spoke the other's language.

Approaching the urn, Hank looked at the photograph etched in it. He wondered how it was done, and by whom. He had never seen this photograph of his grandfather before; indeed, he had seen so few photographs of the old man, just the handful in the box up in his room. Aunt Hope must have the rest of them.

"Don't touch that," Dad said, "we don't want another accident."

Irritation swung through Hank. People were always telling him not to touch things, as if he was an ungainly klutz. But he noticed something, reminded now of the shattered marquis. Dad had placed the urn in the marquis' old place. The little marquess faced away, holding up her skirts as if she were stepping in something unpleasant. Turning, Hank glanced at Dad, who was staring into his empty glass.

Carl approached, and seeming to comprehend the irony, turned the marquess so that she had to look at the urn.

"She doesn't look happy, does she?"

Setting down his glass, Hank stretched. "I'm going for a ride."

Looking at him with one eyebrow raised, Carl said, "Don't get lost. You have to drive your sweet little *familia* to the great lord's castle so he can have his ass licked by the prettiest women he can assemble into one room."

"Carl, don't talk that way," Dad murmured. His head was back and his eyes closed.

The sun was in Hank's eyes as he followed the switchbacking road to Griffith Park. His breath blew in his ears and his thighs burned as he stood on the pedals, keeping his cadence steady. Cars brushed past, barely missing him, some with pretty girls who stuck their heads out the windows to watch him.

Once in the park he followed winding drives, going hard, keeping up a good speed. But as he circled and prepared to return home, fatigue laced his muscles and he ached with weariness. As he coasted along Sunset, he wondered if he had pushed himself too hard, pressured by having to be back home at a certain time.

He could, right now, follow Sunset all the way to the shore and buzz south to the Lady Windemere where Susan would be waiting or about to arrive. But he was to pick Susan up at a certain time; he obeyed, today, the rules of the grown-ups, and despite his need to escape his mother's worn uneasiness, his sister's careless egotism and his grandfather's ashes on the mantle, he had to get back to the house.

Connie, annoyed that he had gone for a bike ride, stormed around upstairs, bemoaning lost articles of make-up, whining about her clothes, and tap-dancing, at one point, in the hall just as Hank came up the stairs.

In nothing but white silk panties, she grinned at him as he stopped at the top of the stairs. Wiggling white, pink-nippled breasts at him, she twirled and vanished back into her bedroom.

"I have to get out of this nuthouse," Hank whispered to himself. If he got a job he could move out, get a room in Venice near Susan. Maybe the Potteries would have him, hire him to sweep up shards of broken piglet cookie jars and dump them into the trash.

Not bothering to shower, just to annoy Connie, Hank waited in the hallway in a white shirt without a tie, corduroy trousers and the sunglasses Carl had given him. Carl waited with him, wearing the same clean golf shirt and slacks, but now with a tan dinner jacket. They waited for Connie so she could make her entrance.

And she did, coming down the stairs in a flared black dress of rustling silk, black gloves, black handbag, and a red heart-shaped pin over her right breast. The neck line plunged and picked up her boobs nicely, and she had little poufy sleeves. The dress was a far more subtle and attractive version than the one she had impulsively shown to Hank. She was smashing.

But Hank said nothing, allowing Carl to sweep forward and take her hand, just as they did in countless dancing scenes in countless rehearsals. Her hair flowed across her shoulders ala Veronica Lake, and she wore tomato-red lipstick.

"You are a dear for driving us, favorite brother. And you look so devil-may-care—wait a minute, did you take a shower?" She sniffed him, wrinkling her nose.

Hank made no reply, turned and walked toward the door, Connie grizzling to Carl about the general untidiness of baby brothers. The sun hung near the horizon, showering attendant cloudlets with gold and pink; girl clouds, Connie used to say when they were little and she would take Hank for an enforced march around the neighborhood, *let's go find some girl clouds*.

A cool breeze swept up the canyon bringing with it the hint of sea and mud. Throwing his valise in the front seat, Hank opened the door for the Cleveland Twins, bowing with a flourish.

"Don't you dare do that when we get there," Connie hissed as she crawled in.

Maybe it was the scotch whiskey. Maybe it was the euphoria he always felt after a long ride, but Hank felt buoyant and perfect, and it was really because he was going to see Susan. He was going to dance with her, he was going to see her dance naked in their room and then he was going to fuck her.

From Sunset they descended into Beverly Hills. Carl gave apt directions to Cedric Sigfried's mansion, which supposedly once belonged to Charlie Chaplin. Hank eased the Cadillac into a line of cars pulling up the drive and stopped near the door, not right at the door reserved for the truly famous, but close enough for Connie to feel appeased.

Without a word, he hopped out, ran around the car,

opened the door, and bowed with a flourish. Connie slapped his hand as she got out. Murmuring and careful laughter filtered to Hank's ears as he dashed around the car and opened the driver door. People in furs and tailored sport coats glanced his way, stopped to look. With one more wave, he slid into the car, watching for a moment, while Connie and Carl were swept into the line of people heading for the main entrance, Connie smiling and mewing, Carl happily absorbed into a clutch of beautiful women.

As soon as the way cleared, Hank got out of there.

By the time he got to Santa Monica his entire body ached, but it was a good ache. The only hitch to it all was a nagging headache, brought on, he supposed, by Carl's dark glasses. Throwing them onto the dashboard, he left the car in the apartment owner's parking space and rode the elevator to room 818, top right, overlooking a panorama of Pacific, palms and beach safely hidden behind a veil of night. Except for the sweet salt smell and the thump of the waves, he could be looking through the window of a rocket into the lost reaches of space.

Funny, his mood, he thought, as he ordered a bottle of wine and showered and shaved, realizing his black stubble was noticeable—maybe that's why people at the party were staring at him. Ensconcing himself the window, dragging a chair close so he could put his feet on the sill, he filled one of the glasses and drank. He was not sure he liked wine, but he knew Susan did, and she liked French wine, even though the one he ordered came from some obscure region in Northern California.

He found himself thinking of the Girl, not Susan, and Mom's face when he asked her about it. Maybe this was the origin of his strange, reckless mood, but he knew that thoughts of her intruded into his mind at the oddest times, and it was ever since Grandfather Joel died and he thought about the photo of Grandmother and Grandfather Cleveland and what the Girl, then Susan, had said about them.

That the woman despised the man and was bitter than she had not outlived him. How could anyone know that from a photograph, one taken before the person died? Was it the way Grandmother Annette leaned toward Grandfather Joel smiling stiffly as he rested his hand on her shoulder? Grandma Annette was not a pretty woman, Hank could see, and Dad rarely spoke of her, so Hank had nothing to go on except the crazy dream-speech of two women, or one a girl just sixteen, and the other a woman wholly mature.

Now he remembered liking the Girl a lot the afternoon in his bedroom; now he could recall at least one walk along Sunset Boulevard, meeting after school for sodas down in Hollywood. He knew her—she was a good friend and funny. He liked her company. But he had nearly forgotten her existence. How as that possible? He wondered where she was now. Probably married, with five kids and a fat husband. Hank didn't like the idea, even though there was no way she could have five kids in three years. The Girl, he knew, wasn't going to do anything like that.

He'd forgotten his watch and couldn't see the clock from where he was sitting, but he was too tired to get up to see if it was time to pick up Susan. Maybe it was the wine or the droning chant of the waves that sounded like Susan breathing that made him fall asleep.

When Hank woke up a minute later, he couldn't remember where he was. His body stiffened and shook with rigors, and he stumbled out of the chair to the bed and wrapped himself in blankets. The window stood open, the bottle of wine empty and he felt queasy because of it; his head poun-ded and he wondered where the hell Susan was.

Then he remembered. *I'm supposed to pick her up*.

Cursing, he grappled for the phone and held it, trying to remember her number. Was it five-two or two-five? But he was too cold. In a minute, when he warmed up, he would re-member. Waiting to be warm, he thought for the first time that maybe he was sick. This flu was going around, they said, lots of people sick, lots of people in the hospital.

His mouth felt drier than his grandfather's ashes. He thought of going for a drink of water, but the bathroom seemed impossibly distant. The light from the bathroom through the open door was the only light in the room. That and blinking neon of Santa Monica Boulevard, a river of color streaming into the sea. The dizzying, shushing sea. His ears burned with the sea.

Finally, finally, he was warm. The shivers eased; warmth crept over him in waves, burned his skin, and he threw the covers off, tore off his shirt. He lay on the bed in just his slacks, stared at where the ceiling or the sky should be, and wondered about the Girl. Where was she? Why hadn't she come? They had reservations at nine. He was going to wine and dine her. He was going to bring her back here and suck on her skin and taste her and press his fingers into her breasts.

Eleven

THE ROARING IN HANK'S EARS sounded as if he had somehow gotten down to the sea. Sand scraped his neck and chin; he was cold again, very cold; the rough wool blanket wrapped around him wasn't enough.

A moment later he understood he was in the back seat of a car, covered with sand and a wool blanket, and the roar was the motor, purring and loud. He looked up and saw the driver in a printed scarf. The car shifted around corners; he saw colored lights dance their reflections across a ceiling of quilted fabric torn in two places.

Dozing again, Hank woke up when someone said his name. He was still in the back seat of the car, but it was no longer roaring. Whispering, shoving, someone crawled into the car and said his name again.

"Hank, you have to get up and come in the house. We have to get you to bed."

Was this his mother's voice? Ragged and grief-stricken? He didn't think so. Trying to focus, he thought he saw Susan's pale face, watching him. She pulled on his arm, forced him to sit up.

Someone else reached in and grabbed his other arm,

pulled him with a strong purposeful grip. Dad? Carl? What was Susan doing at his house? Had she driven him home?

But when he was in the car door and trying to stand up, he saw a familiar expanse of black lawn and a beehive-like structure along a fence. Looking up, he saw Susan, her face urgent, hurried. "Hank, we have to get you into the house."

He forced himself to his feet, and a wave of dizziness took him, and the next moment he was leaning on the Girl; she helped him, strong and sure footed, his arm across her shoulders, toward Susan's house. He looked for his bike, but it wasn't there in its usual place beside the steps.

When he woke again, people filled his room, and voices rumbled, eager and clipped, whispering (Susan) shouting (himself). They bored into his head, planted bombs there, set them off in little explosions of pain. Ken Cleveland, intoning about the Holy Lands. Constance and Carlisle Cleveland, singing and dancing, their voices speeding up and slowing down. But the worst was his mother, her voice halting, words misspoken as if the muscles of her jaw and lips misfired. He pressed his hands over his ears, so as not to hear her; she sounded like grasshoppers rasping.

But there was one soft, soothing voice. It sang to him in Spanish. It was the Girl's voice, a luscious contralto, accompanied by cool hands when he was fevered and warm hands when he was frozen.

Then the nightmare ended Hank opened his eyes, swimming up from a dream where he was on a bus crossing a bridge, but the end of the bridge was gone and the bus slid backward into the water and he held on to bare branches and tried to scream.

He lay in Susan's bedroom. Outside her windows night hung. A shaded lamp burned on the bedside table covered with a towel and a neat array of medicines, hypo tray, a blue liquid in a bottle, a pile of wash cloths in a basin. His body felt like lettuce left out in the sun, limp and moist and transparent. But the headache was mercifully gone.

Looking at the window he always looked at after making love with Susan, Hank considered the lost time, how much lost time? And how did he get here? And what the hell happened to him?

Through the ajar bedroom door he could see the soft light of the living room. Voices murmured, the radio was on, and ironically, he recognized his father's voice extolling the virtue of Brylcreme. It felt good, light, ethereal, as if he had just cycled a century.

A shadow moved in the doorway; it widened and Susan peeked in. "Hank?"

He nodded, watching her. She wore her hair wound up in a scarf, and a lose flannel shirt and capris. She came across the room and knelt on the floor next to him.

"Hank? How are you feeling?" Her cool hand brushed his forehead. His head itched.

"Like a toad run over by a truck."

"You were very sick. The doctor said you had meningitis."

A cold uneasiness swept through Hank's chest. How could he have meningitis? How did he get it?

"You're kidding."

She shook her head. "We were getting ready to take you to the hospital when you started to improve. The doctor didn't want to move you."

"How long? What day is it?" A number of concerns fluttered into Hank's mind. His parents. The car.

"About two days. I found you Saturday night, late. You weren't making any sense and I knew something was

wrong." A half-smile crimped her lips, and she looked embarrassed. Hank felt mortified. What had he said to her?

"It's Monday evening."

Closing his eyes, Hank felt grateful for the soft coolness of
the bed. He was tired already, but questions swirled in his
mind and he wanted to ask them.

Susan answered them, without his having to ask. "I
phoned your parents. The doctor didn't want them coming
here, in case, you know, they got infected. The nurse and I
have been taking turns, taking care of you." Her voice moved
on, soft and luxurious, like a bath of satin. He listened, questions came and went, and then sleep came too.

When he woke again daylight filled the room, and Hank
could see, from his place on the bed, the rectangle of familiar
sky becoming blue as the sun ascended. The room was tidy,
dresser drawers closed, clothes put away, the top of the
dresser piled with towels and sheets and a bed pan. Hank
worried for a moment about that function, and what was
done about it while he was delirious. Rubber sheet underneath, he thought, and his face warmed at the thought of the
nurse cleaning him up each time.

The door was still ajar. The house was quiet; he wondered
what time it was, and whose shift it was to look after Hank.
He was thirsty, and saw to his relief a half-full glass of water
with a glass straw in it on the bedside table.

Getting up on one elbow, he was astonished at his weak-
ness. His hand shook as he grasped the glass and sucked all
the water from it. Breathless, Hank lay back, thinking, remembering how irritable and tired he was a day or so before
he became sick.

He thought he would experiment with sitting up, test his
strength. Pushing on the bed, he strained to raise himself,

was able to at least lean back against the headboard, and feeling it behind him remembered Susan's hands gripping the head board as she came.

Hank felt a stirring in his groin but nothing happened there, and he didn't worry yet. He was still very sick, he presumed. Leaning against the head board with a better view of the room felt good.

Susan came through the doorway again. She was wearing the same outfit of last night, face looking crushed as if she had just woken up. She must have been sleeping on the couch in the living room.

"Oh, you're awake. You hungry?"

Hank shook his head, although he could feel a mild interest in food stirring in his stomach. "Thirsty."

She vanished, returning with a pitcher of water and filled the glass. He drank greedily, watching her.

This time she sat on the bed, glanced back at the open doorway, then touched his forehead again. "We need to get you into the shower. Your hair."

Hank could feel the oily itch of his head, but he didn't care. All he wanted to do now was kiss Susan, taste her lips and the pale skin of her face.

As if she could read the wish on his face, Susan shook her head, and gave him an indulgent smile.

"Poor baby." she lowered her voice. "We can't. The nurse, and Joseph."

Her reluctance disappointed but it was enough that he was here; she had found him and brought him to her house, not home to his crazy family. And the thought of home and Dad and Mother brought a fresh set of worries.

"Don't worry about the car. Your brother picked it up Sunday."

Hank gazed at her, wondering. She didn't have to do all this. She could have just cut him out of her life. But she was making him a part of her life, a secreted, compartmentalized room for him and him alone.

"You talked to my parents?"

Nodding, Susan rubbed her neck. Crescent lines formed under her eyes, cupping them with weariness.

"Your mom. She wanted to come down here, to nurse you, but the doctor talked her out of it. You were contagious, you know."

Numerous thoughts shifted through Hank, and he couldn't concentrate on one before the other fled away.

"She wanted to come here? My mother?"

"She sounded very upset, on the phone." Susan tilted her head, narrowed her eyes. "She was very nice and listened to reason."

Hank wondered if Susan was secretly relieved that his mother, my-god-his-*mother* didn't show up on the doorstep of Hank's 32-year-old lover. He wondered what Mom, Connie and Carl, even Dad, were thinking about where he was recovering from his illness. Carl and Connie would dope out that Hank was with the girlfriend he was shacking up with at the Lady Windemere, but Mom—she might think that too, but Hank was utterly relieved to believe that Mom could have no idea about Susan's age.

They spoke no more of that. Hank reached, took her hand. Her cuticles were still stained with red and yellow. He wondered if she had time to work in her workshop with himself, the sick asshole, in the house. It was logical that he be here, more than appropriate. There was a nurse in the house, too. Settling back into the pillow, he felt his body relax into the sheets as if he were being absorbed into the mattress.

He must have fallen asleep because time again slipped away and Hank could tell that it was afternoon from the slant of the sun. Twisting, he could almost see the front yard, Bermuda grass and palm, golden from afternoon light. Someone had come in the room while he was sleeping, he thought he remembered, and placed a pill on the bedside hypo tray. And someone had gently shaken him, turned him, and gave him a shot in his butt. Penicillin, he presumed, the miracle drug.

Now he saw the nurse walking on the lawn, a woman in white with a little round white cap on her head, black hair massed underneath, pulled into a tight bun. She was slender, small, but he could tell she was strong, by the way she stood, holding a fan of pampas grass heads.

Why would she be out on the lawn in her uniform, standing to face the setting sun? From the yard, if one stood on tiptoe, one could catch a sliver of the silver sea, always present and breathing. Perhaps she was looking at the sunset.

Wondering where Joseph was, where Susan was, Hank got his answer. Into view came the wheelchair along the buckling sidewalk under the palm. Joseph's two white casts stuck out as he wheeled himself along. The nurse watched him, her back to Hank's window. Joseph waved an arm and made a face at her. She nodded, encouraging. Maybe this was the first time Joseph had gotten out of the house since he was discharged from the hospital.

Hank drifted off to sleep again, and when he woke it was night time. Susan came through the door with a tray.

She set it down on the bed—it perched uneasily on Hank's knees, and she had spilled the soup. It looked like canned noodle soup, beside it a handful of saltines. It smelled wonderful, and Hank was hungry for it.

He sat up, leaned against the headboard, sipped the soup.

The strange thing was, after a few bites, his appetite vanished completely. Nibbling on crackers, he watched Susan as she walked around the room, dropping used towels on the floor, making straight lines of things, shifting things into orderly rows.

The door opened and Joseph shoved his way in, banging the doorway, cursing.

Susan said, "Joseph, you shouldn't bother Hank. He's not anywhere up to visitors yet."

Hank wondered if his mother knew the crisis over and he was, no longer, according to Susan, contagious. Everyone in the house seemed healthy—the doctor was more worried about workers at the hotel, and Hank's family. But fortunately, no one at home was sick, either. Sadly, the driver whose place Hank took that evening had died.

"This is nothing to sneeze at," the doctor had told Susan.

"The doc's coming tomorrow to check on you. Better behave yourself." This from Joseph, who wheeled closer. His chair made a rhythmic squeak. "Have to speak to that nurse about oiling this. Nurses have a specialty in wheelchair engineering, did you know that?"

Shaking her head, Susan left them alone.

Joseph had gained a little weight, and his color improved. Hank wondered what he looked like himself, after this Victorian illness, being cared for at home by his mistress.

"You look like shit." Joseph leaned forward, squinted as he looked Hank up and down. Fiddling in his robe pocket, he produced two cigarettes. "The old doc will kill us—loses so many patients that way—if he catches us smoking."

He handed one to Hank, who took it. Hank ran it under his nose as an executive would a cigar. The odor of the tobacco made his throat ache.

Joseph said, "I know you quit, but after what you've been through, you need this."

Hank wondered where his special lighter had gone to. His clothing seemed to be nowhere in sight—he wore a regulation hospital gown and cotton draw-string pants, probably procured by the nurse. But Joseph produced a polished Zippo and had it glowing under Hank's cigarette.

Susan didn't like smoking, and while Hank obeyed her demand, Joseph showed no signs of quitting any time soon, which must have been an irritation for her. Hank drew in the smoke, feeling his body come alive, as if strength pumped back into his muscles from wherever it had leaked to.

"Meningitis. Just after I shipped out, I heard it went through Camp Hood. Three guys died." He squinted as the smoke licked his face. "Of course, if I hadn't shipped out, maybe I'd be dead now too."

He said this in a conversational way, and Hank tried to smile, but he didn't think it was funny.

Joseph continued, "Instead I checked out. That's what one of the orderlies used to say to me, back at the hospital. Here I was in a ward of a whole bunch of guys who 'checked out'. You know, lights on, nobody home. Only I didn't belong there. Nothing was wrong with me. Nothing that a memory eraser wouldn't cure."

"I could invent one for you."

Joseph's eyebrows went up. "What are you, a boy genius? If so, what I need is this: a time machine. That's the only way I think it could be done. Send me back in a time machine. I could assassinate Hitler, and things would be different. But I'd have to get Hirohito too."

Hank waited, not sure what to say. Joseph stared at him, and Hank got the feeling that he wasn't really seeing him, that he was off somewhere else.

"I had this lieutenant. I was just a corporal, you know? Little better than snot. This lieutenant, he had seen a lot of action. Battle of the Bulge and all that. I was a driver, you know? I wasn't that good at gunnery, but I knew how to fix cars and I could talk my way into anything, or out of anything."

Hank had no doubt this was possible.

"So we're in Italy, right? Where there are old castles, and churches, still intact. Not much bombing there, and the resistance to the Krauts was strong, you know? Women walking into barracks with grenades under their skirts. Stuff like that. We'd heard about a rogue group of Germans, still fighting, underground-like, very unlike Germans—no marching or rules, but sneaking in and blowing up allied ammo dumps and booby-trapping train tracks. This lieutenant, he wanted to go up there, even though his squad was supposed to be going home. But he wasn't done, this guy, I guess, and his squad would walk barefoot over burning coals for him, so he commandeers my jeep and off we go with two of his buddies, to see if we can get these Krauts."

A nervous itch started someone under Hank's breast. Joseph was talking easily, telling a war tale, but Hank worried there would be a real punch-line somewhere. Maybe it would be the *Thing*, the Thing that had tipped Joseph over the edge of sanity. Hank didn't know what behaviors had gotten Joseph hospitalized in the crazy ward, then discharged with a Section Eight into his sister's care, but he wasn't sure he wanted to know.

But he did want to know. His head was starting to ache again, and he tried to ignore it.

Joseph smiled at him in a lopsided way. "Only little bits at a time, Fonda. Not to tire you out. Installment 2 tomorrow night. You look like you need to sleep for a year. Later." Backing up, he expertly whirled the chair around and slid through the door without knocking into anything. Hank leaned back on the pillows, eyes burning with weariness. He drowsed, heard the phone ring. A moment later, Susan was there.

"You up for a visitor? Your mom wants to see you."

Hank shook his head. "Tell her I'm too tired. I need more rest. Tell her I'm getting better, but I can't, Susan. Not yet."

Susan nodded, left the room. Hank heard her talking softly in the hall. She didn't come back.

Twelve

TEN MORE YEARS had been added to Mom's face, Hank thought, as she rushed into the room with a breath of cool air and tobacco and perfume, the constant mix of his mother's curious scent. He had known she would come, even though he told Susan he didn't want to see her. At least she waited until the next morning. He wondered, as he felt her dry kiss, if the real reason he didn't want her to come was that he didn't want to have to explain, make up a story about how he knew Susan.

All he had to do was say, if he was asked, that he was a friend of Joseph's, and Susan was the sister who was helping to take care of him.

Leaning back in the chair beside his bed, Mom closed her eyes. Her lids were like transparent shells, her lashes long and combed. She wore a tan suit, the perpetual corsage; the impeccable hair.

"You have no idea what you put me through. When Miss Chagall called me, I was certain you were dead."

"Just a little touch of meningitis."

"That poor driver died, did you hear that? Ten other people are sick. I don't understand where you were that you got infected with it. It was all studio people."

Shrugging, Hank wondered about that, too, but he didn't feel like speculating about it. Leaning forward, Mom shook her head, opened her purse, took out a pack of cigarettes, put it back as if realizing this was a sick room.

"This is a nice little house. These people seem to be artistic. You know the brother? Mr. Chagall?" Again, Hank noticed hesitation in her voice, and a curious lateral movement in her jaw that he had seen before.

Hank nodded, deciding not to elaborate unless he had to.

Mom looked down at her hands. "I miss you at home, Hank. Now that you're better, you can't impose on these people any longer. I've got a taxi outside to take you home and recover there."

A cold fear sliced through him at the thought of leaving. He knew Mom was right—this wasn't his home, but he wanted it to be, to stay here with Susan forever. He could even put up with Joseph. The guy was growing on him. He wanted to hear the end of Joseph's war story.

"But I've barely been out of bed. I'm not sure I can walk even to a taxi."

Mom straightened her gloves. "I've spoken with the doctor. He is a very good man. He says you're out of danger, but you need a long rest."

Hank knew he lost the argument. Mom had made up her mind. He watched the set of her jaw, recognized that she was fighting with herself over her decision. He knew where he was concerned she tended to indulge, but this time, she was firm.

They waited for the doctor, who would confirm that Hank was able to travel home. Mom sat quietly in the chair, but she fussed with her clothes, swallowed a lot, a nervous shivering seemed to course through her. This was more, Hank thought, than fear for her son's life. She still hadn't told him the thing she was going to tell him, but maybe it had blown over, whatever it was.

Susan brought her a cup of coffee. Hank's heart skipped a beat when she came into the room carrying the cup. She introduced herself, saving Hank the unpleasant task; Mom thanked Susan again and again for caring for Hank, wanted to help in some way, and Hank prayed she wouldn't offer Susan money. Luckily, she didn't. Standing beside the door, Susan said she was happy to help a friend of her brother's.

"But what happened, exactly?" Mom wanted to know. "How did he end up here?"

Hank stiffened again, glad the question was asked of Susan, with him present, so they could get their story straight.

"He came over to cheer up my brother. Joseph gets so bored, having to stay at home and play Scrabble with the nurse all day. He sort of collapsed. We called the doctor Saturday night."

Mom nodded, accepting this. "You looked fine Saturday," she said to Hank, sipping from her cup. "Was that your big date, coming here to play Scrabble?"

Hank remembered wanting the car, the money—he was going to wine and dine Susan. He smiled in what he hoped was an embarrassed way.

"Well, that wasn't all." Susan gave Mom a smile, crooked, knowing. "You saw how pretty the nurse is. I think he had an idea to ask her on a date."

Mom tried to hide her dislike of the idea behind her coffee cup, but Hank saw that wary look again, the same look as when he asked her about the Girl.

There was the problem of the car—and Carl having gone to pick it up. Hank hoped he wouldn't have to try to match his story to Carl's without finding out what it was. But he was saved from further explanation by the arrival of the doctor, who, unfortunately, agreed that Hank could be moved.

There was little to pack, Hank's clothes that he had worn to the hotel, items brought from the hospital by the nurse; Hank could borrow one of Joseph's seemingly multiple robes to wear to the taxi. And, to top off the humiliation, he would ride to the car in Joseph's wheelchair.

Finally it was time to go. Hank sat on the edge of the bed, feeling weak and flustered, and wishing Susan would insist he stay, not let him go. But she expertly helped to pack his things while his mother directed her actions, which she obeyed without a word.

"It's best you are home, Hank, with your family. Nothing is the same around there without you," Mom was saying, shaping and wiping her hat. "Your dad really misses you, isn't that odd? But Ken is a softie through and through. Not a strong man at all."

Mom touched the edges of her hat in Susan's mirror. "Well, let's get going. Hank, we'll get you into the chair."

"I think we should wait for the nurse, Mrs. Cleveland." Susan stood near the foot of the bed, one hand rubbing the other. To Hank she looked as if she were quivering.

"Oh, but she's probably busy. And, we can't impose on you any longer."

"No, we should wait." Susan's voice was darkly edged. "I'll let her know we're ready."

One of Mom's eyebrows rose up. A cat-prick of wariness caught Hank but it felt good hearing someone talk to Mom like that, as he watched Susan leave to find the nurse. Personally he hoped Susan would help him but he knew that would look weird to his mother, and so did Susan.

Susan returned minutes later, alone. "I can't seem to find her. Joseph doesn't know where she is either." Her eyebrows closed down over her eyes, and she looked more annoyed than Hank liked to see.

"That doesn't seem too professional." Mom turned around, faced Susan. "She is here for your brother, as you said. Well, we don't need her. I can help Hank."

Joseph's voice floated from the living room. "Check your garage, Suze. She likes to go out there and look at your stuff."

Her lips thinning with irritation, Susan turned and left the room. Mom sighed sharply. "She's a bit edgy, isn't she?"

Hank shrugged. Sitting so long made his head ache. "She's an artist. They're fussy that way."

"Don't I know how fussy, as you call it, artists can be."

No doubt, Hank thought, she was thinking of the twins.

Hank leaned back on the bed, weary and weak, closed his eyes. A moment later there was the sound of someone coming into the room.

Mom's voice, "Thank you for helping. It's just that Miss Cleveland is afraid I'll drop him."

A hand touched Hank's shoulder, colors cycled across his eyes, and he saw for a moment, glinting wheels, the wheels of a bicycle catching the sun and sparkles of the sea. He opened his eyes, expecting Susan to be kneeling beside him, her pale hand drawing up his neck and into his hair.

But it was the nurse beside him, sheer cap on her head, uniform white against skin the color of chocolate milk. With her touch, she seemed to raise him, gripping his legs, expertly sitting him up.

Hank was dreaming, he was in delirium again, he had fallen back into the arms of sickness. He looked, astonished, at the nurse who now stood, turned to move the wheelchair beside the bed and faced him.

This was the Girl.

Thirteen

HE REMEBERED SAYING GOOD-BY to Joseph waving from the couch with his white legs gleaming, two stumpy casts on pillows. He remembered going down the ramp he had helped build for Joseph, in Joseph's chair, behind him the sure, strong step of the Girl in her heavy nursing shoes.

Later, at home, as Hank lay in his bed surrounded by the scents of his own room, leather oil and shaving cream, broken bits of memory floated in and out of his mind. He faced the setting sun, the colors under his eyelids blood red and pink.

She remained compact and strong, even three years later. He could see that her figure matured, filled out; even under the starch of her uniform he could see her breasts as she tucked a blanket over his legs, leaned down to unlock the chair, and he looked over the line of her hips.

The Girl called him Mr. Cleveland. She gave no indication that she recognized him. She recognized him, all right, she had to have recognized him when Susan had brought him home. She had been taking care of him, giving him shots, wiping his butt. His cheeks flamed again as he thought of this. He knew her better than anyone else for that moment when they glanced at each other.

Lying here now, Hank wondered if this was enough to ignite a memory in Mom's mind about the Girl who came to visit Hank that day, the Girl he had once known so well, but had someone, irrationally, forgotten. And he still, as much as he sweatily, head-achy tried, could not remember the Girl's name.

Also, he couldn't remember saying good-by to Susan. He couldn't remember even seeing her on the porch, waving good-by. No one stood on the porch as the taxi pulled away and Mom tucked up the collar of his robe and fussed at his blankets. The Girl was gone, Susan was gone; pale blue bungalow stood lonely in the golden sun, only a handful of starlings on the lawn picking at the Bermuda grass.

Mom had set up Hank's room. There was no question in her mind that Hank was coming home today. There was even a commode. Basin, liquids, magazines. A bell to ring if he needed anything.

Whispering, *Don't bother him now, he needs to rest. You can see him later when he wakes up.* They would all want to see him of course, but he didn't want to see them. Pretend to be asleep, and think of the Girl.

Nursing students couldn't be married, he thought, although maybe that changed because of the war and so many nurses were needed. The Girl was too beautiful not to be taken. But then there was Susan. Susan was beautiful too, in her pale, red-gold way. She was not taken either.

And the Girl was delicious, chocolate brown eyes and huge lashes, and smarter than any of the other girls in her class, but not in the same ways. Maybe that was because her teachers, underneath their stern politeness, despised her for what she was, a Mexican upstart student in a rich kids' school.

He couldn't believe he had seen her again. Memories broke open, one by one, in tantalizing scraps. Sighing massively, Hank opened his eyes, forgetting about his audience.

Connie stampeded to his bed. Circling it like a wary mustang, she came around to the side he faced, yanked his desk chair forward, and sat between him and the window.

Leaning forward, she examined his face, reached for his hand, counted his fingers. "All there," she announced. "Nothing missing. Except maybe half your capacious brain. Meningitis!! Of all things."

"Gadzukes!" This from Carl, imitating Dad. Carl sat himself on the foot of the bed. "You are a long way from the healthy boy you once were."

Hank rolled his eyes to let them know he was not amused. He sat up, his arms like two saplings, and Connie bustled the pillows, patting and shaping. He slapped her hand away.

"OK, Nurse Cleveland. I am well situated."

Connie leaned forward again. She wore a tight white sweater and a tight tweed skirt. She said softly, "So I hear you were at your girlfriend's" She cast a glance at Carl, who nodded.

What could they know about Susan? Would they care if they knew? Would they tell Mom, whom they used to, at any rate, tell everything?

He sent both of them a glance, saying it was none of their business.

"Dear Hank, always the Sphinx, saying nothing, knowing everything." Carl's glance shifted to Connie, back to Hank. Connie ignored it, but Hank saw the thing he had wondered about. Between the twins there was secret information. Even though they were fraternal twins, they had always been close.

Hank looked down at his hands, remembering the time he had walked into Carl's room, when he was ten and learned how to knock.

The atmosphere grew serious. Talk faltered, as if each remembered something unpleasant. Then Connie said, "She's very pretty, your girlfriend."

Hank stiffened, narrowed his eyes, cocked his head. Was she bluffing? Would she just have assumed any girl Hank was with was pretty? He wondered if Connie and Carl remembered the Girl. They were so busy then, school and lessons and auditions.

Straitening his legs, Carl leaned back on his elbow, striking a pose. Everything he did created a photographic opportunity, and he did it, even unconscious of it, as if he were training his entire life to be in front of a camera.

"OK, I told Connie about your big date. But I was too late. Seems she already knew what you were up to. And as usual, knew before I did and a lot more, besides."

Now Hank was tired. Really tired. He didn't want to hear about it. He closed his eyes.

"You're boring him, Connie."

"He closed his eyes while you were speaking."

"And you started this mindless conversation."

"It's not a conversation, it's a monolog as usual. You and me doing all the talking and Hank just being Hank."

When he woke up again, Joaquin was bringing him a tray. Chili-flavored chicken broth and hand-made tortillas. Night lay a hand outside, the clear expanse of Hollywood flowed out in colored bands beyond the palms. Hank actually felt hungry as he sat up, and Joaquin placed the tray in front of him.

"Dinner in bed. Like a king." Joaquin unfolded the napkin with a flourish and began to tuck it into Hank's collar.

"Whoa there, Joaquin. I can feed myself."

Joaquin's heavy eyebrows went up and down. "Good you are home, young man," he said and marched out of the room. "Someone has to repair the cracks.

Hank wondered about that as he finished his soup and the tortillas. He managed to make it to the commode and back, sitting down like a girl to pee, praying no one would barge in on him. But the trip wearied him, breaking sweat on his skin, muscles quivering as he got back into bed. He lay there, exhausted, thinking of the Girl, and Susan. Connie, and Carl. Mom, Dad, and oddly, the ugly urn of Grandfather Joel.

Hank was trapped in the house for an entire week. Outside the sun gleamed, the days were breezy and fine. Hints of spring blew through the open window. Mom spent a great deal of time with him, helping him bathe, washing his hair, reading the papers to him; even shaving him. When she read to him, that halting jolt to her voice he'd noticed lately seemed to go away.

He wondered what the twins thought of Mom spending so much time with him, and not with them. But they too visited him daily, never seeming to grow bored with the sickroom. And only spoke of trivial things, funny stories from the studio, Carl's latest conquest, Connie's photo shoot, as if instructed not to ask about Susan, what he was doing there, how he knew Joseph. *Don't upset him, don't get him excited. He nearly died, you know.*

And he noticed, as his strength returned and he could sit in a big chair brought up from the living room and situated near the French doors, that Mom's running, wire-hot tension cooled; she would come into his room, kick off her shoes, undo the top buttons of her blouse, turn away phone calls.

Dad was the less frequent visitor. It was as if after the death of his father, he spent more time at the studios. Recording, taping—his velvet, deep tones were in more demand than ever. Dad had come into Hank's room while he was sleeping, Hank was told by his mother. And a couple times while he was awake, only to stand awkwardly in the doorway, or at the foot of his bed. A man with the voice of God in the movies was incapable of making small talk to the sick.

After a week of tentative walks around his room, up and down the hall, Hank was able to go downstairs. At first astonished at how his body failed him, now he could feel it resuming itself. He had a goal, however, and worked to achieve it.

He wanted to get downstairs to the telephone.

Fourteen

IT WAS A PERFECT OPPORTUNITY, more perfect than he could ever hope. Everyone, even Mom, was out, Connie and Carl at rehearsals, Dad at a recording, Mom at the hair-dressers. She had been focusing all her attention on Hank, occasionally leaving to deal with a crisis about wardrobe or copyright, but always returning early to be with Hank. But she had finally lost her courage about letting her hair go, so she had left, promising to come right home. Hank felt a mountain of relief. Only Joaquin remained behind the closed door of his room on the first floor near the kitchen, ready to respond if Hank ran the bell, which he never did; the luncheon buffet cleared away, dishes done, an hour or so before starting dinner.

The house was blessedly quiet. No voices, radio, footsteps or crinkling of papers, tap dancing or humming. Eerily quiet, as Hank came softly down the stairs in his slippers and robe, holding onto the bannister, not quite sure of his balance.

The trip down the steps did not tire him. He did not anticipate the return trip would be an easy one, but at least he could sit in the hallway chair beside the phone table. This was the main phone—they had extensions in the kitchen, living room, and Mom and Dad's room upstairs. This phone was generally used by Connie, while Carl preferred the living room phone.

Hank dialed Susan's number, his hand sweaty. He felt like a kid again, torturing himself about dialing up a girl to ask her for a date, a girl he barely knew or had just met.

He didn't know who he wanted to answer the phone as it rang. Any of them, or none of them. Joseph? And then have to ask him to speak to Susan? He hoped Susan would answer —but what if it's the Girl—his last thought as he heard her voice in his ear.

For a moment he couldn't speak, wondering what to say— he fought not to hang up, it was a fierce urge. But he managed to say it, to calm himself.

"Hi. It's Hank Cleveland."

A momentary hesitation. "Hello, Mr. Cleveland. How are you feeling?"

Hank almost felt like laughing, if he wasn't so irritated. "I am fine, Nurse. How are you?"

"You sound well. Are you out of bed? Walking around? Getting your strength back?"

Sighing, Hank gripped the phone, pressed it to his ear, as if he could feel her ear through the hand piece.

"I'm fine. I'm so bored." *I can't believe it's you. What is your name? How can I ask that? I should know.*

"Mr. Cleveland," she interrupted him, her voice rushed, unsure. "Perhaps I should let you talk to Miss Chagall. She would like to know how you are."

"Wait a minute, don't go." But he knew it was too late, and he knew Susan heard him as she spoke seconds later, as if she had been standing right there beside the Girl.

"Hank, how are you? You feeling OK?" Her voice was

conversational. He imagined Joseph in the living room, maybe the Girl was still there too; Hank could hear the radio, Joseph's laughter.

"Susan, I miss you." He had never said that to her before. It was out before he knew it.

"That's good to hear," she replied, and he wondered furiously what she meant by it, if anything at all. "Hank, you looked terrible. We honestly thought you were going to die,"

Snorting, Hank couldn't believe this. "If I don't see you soon I will die."

He didn't care about preserving her reserve for her. He loved her. He wanted to be with her. He wanted to come to her house now, this instant, get on his bicycle and ride over there. But he knew he probably couldn't even lift the Raleigh, much less ride it.

"Well, that's too bad. You know, you will get better. It just takes time, is all."

He knew she said that because of Joseph nearby, but it made Hank want to slam the phone down. Shake it, shake her, grab her around the waist and mash his body into hers. In response to this, he felt a meager stirring in his groin; maybe he was getting better.

"Hold the phone, I think Joseph wants to talk to you."

"No, wait, don't go—" but she was gone, just as the Girl was gone. Why was he even more desperate for Susan than ever before? Leaning his head against the wall, he sighed fiercely again. *Hang up, hang up before Joseph gets on the line*.

"Hey, Hank, how are ya? You getting out on your bicycle yet?"

Resigned, Hank told him about his progress. Joseph sounded appropriately impressed.

"All the way down the stairs to the phone, huh? Magnificent! So, I won't run up the phone bill, but you need to get well and come visit. I want to tell you the end of my story." Joseph lowered his voice—static bloomed around it, making it, in Hank's mind, sparkle into tiny little shards of sound.

"It's better told face to face, I think. Especially since I never told anyone before."

Hank could barely believe it, but Joseph sounded, to his surprise, as if he was awed and puzzled by wanting to tell Hank his story.

Joseph said, "When I jumped off that streetcar, because I really did see that old lady go under the wheels, when I did that, I knew that something was changing for me, something I couldn't stop.

"And I feel bad about it, you know? Messing up Susan's life this way. She was happy. She had you for a lover. Yeah, I know what's been going on. I could tell she was really enjoy-ing herself with you. I could tell. Even though I never met you, I could feel you around, you know what I mean?"

Hank's hand began to quiver. His ear grew sweaty. Joseph sounded a little too wound-up for his taste. And gratefully Hank heard the Girl's voice in the background, urging Joseph to get ready to go outside, it was time for his walk, and yes, not to run up the phone bill.

"Yeah, OK. Bye, Hank. Call again soon, will ya?"

And he rang off before Hank could ask to talk to Susan again. Hank could have, he thought, as he listened to the empty hiss of the line in his ear, and he also could have asked to talk to Nurse Girl again, pretend to have a medical ques-tion to ask her. But it was too late. And now he had to get up-stairs again.

To postpone that unpleasant task, Hank went into the liv-ing room to look at the urn, as if to make sure it was still there. It stood next to the marquess, who had turned away again, probably moved by Carl who had taken an interest in the figurine, probably wondering how much he could get for it. Perhaps she was worth half as much now; having lost her partner, her worth plummeted. She was angry about that, Hank thought. And now she had to stand next to the one who had caused the destruction of the marquis.

Hank chided himself. Here he stood believing that Grandfather Joel's death caused the marquis to fall from the mantle.

Maybe the illness had changed his brain somehow, like Connie joked, so that now he could see and feel things that others could not. He did notice that he was more sensitive to noise; thump of a shoe dropped to the floor, phone ringing in his parents' bedroom, Connie practicing a step in her room—shoes tapping like nails driven into his brain.

Looking at his grandfather's image etched in the urn, encircled by an ornate gilt oval, Hank thought of Susan's work and how different it was. He could see the vase was sloppily produced; the edges of the different glazes met imprecisely. They were not as vibrant, pulsing, alive as Susan's were.

Next he turned to the marquess. Boldly he picked her up, upended her, and looked for the mark Susan said should be there.

Tearing off a corner of a magazine lying on the coffee table and picking up a pen his father had left behind, Hank wrote it down, not trusting to memory. The marquess felt solid in his hand, details precise and intricate, carefully placed, each layer of glaze perfectly set, chin lifted haughtily, wig roped with rosettes. Carefully he replaced her, back to the urn, knowing she didn't want to look at it.

Knees quivering, Hank knew he should lie down. He hadn't been out of bed, standing, walking, for this long a period of time since he had fallen ill. The torn paper in his robe pocket, he crossed the living room to the door, looked back at the marquess one more time, as if he half-expected her to rotate back so she was facing the urn again. But she re-mained stonily turned away.

Fifteen

ANOTHER WEEK PASSED before Hank felt well enough to go out to Susan's again. He had enough money for a cab ride, scrounging what he could find and borrow from his brother and sister who seemed happy to oblige him. Connie in particular showed interested in Hank's plans, but she had little time to bother him about it. The film was behind schedule; hours of rehearsals and filming stretched late into the day and into the weekends, keeping her, to his pleasure, out of his hair. It was as if no one was around much at all anymore. He had the house to himself more often than not, and he loved the quiet roaming.

But one thing had changed; his mother was home more often. Now that he was well again, she had retreated to her bedroom. He could hear her speaking on the phone; she was on the phone a lot, he thought.

But this morning as he dressed and went downstairs, venturing out to the garage to look over his bikes, he realized she couldn't be on the phone that long. And, times when he thought she was on the phone, a call would come in and Joaquin would answer.

He spoke with friends and relatives inquiring after his

health; they sent letters and cards and boxes of chocolates, but the only time he spoke with Susan was when he called her, and more often than not, especially lately, Susan, not the Girl, answered the phone. Disappointed because the calls that did come in were never from Susan who had not once called him to see how he was, it took him two weeks to puzzle out that something odd was going on with Mom.

Squeezing one of the Raleigh's tires, Hank remembered Dad's concern about Mom, wanting Hank to keep an eye on her. Hank, wrapped up in his own difficulties, had sort of forgotten that demand. So, he made up his mind that today, the day before he planned to go to Susan's blue bungalow, he would knock on Mom's bedroom door.

He could hear her talking, but at the sound of his voice, she stopped. Then, instead of shouting "come in," she opened the door.

Seeing it was him, she turned away, leaving the door open so he could trail in after her.

Mom's and Dad's room was huge, larger than Susan's living and dining rooms combined. Their private bath was also large and the door, draped with robes, stood open to show towels hanging off the sink and tub. The room stretched to the back of the house with the same view Hank had, looking down on Hollywood through a larger set of French doors opening out to their own private balcony. Papers, manuscripts, books littered the bed and Mom's dressing table in the corner between the bathroom and the windows. Closet doors stood open, gowns and suits and ties flung over the doors and on hooks, open boxes of shoes scattered the floor of the closet and out onto the plush pale rug. The room smelled of floral perfume, well-worn shoes, and oranges.

And cigarettes. Walking back to her dressing table that

doubled as a desk, Mom stubbed out the one she was smoking. The doctor had forbidden smoking in Hanks' sick room. Mom picked up her little pink pig lighter and another smoke, but seemed to catch herself and put them down. In a white cotton blouse and slacks, her blond hair coifed and rolled, she looked as casual as she ever looked except when getting out of bed in the morning.

Moving a stack of documents out of the way, Hank sat on the foot of the bed. Mom turned, looked at him, reading glasses pushed back on her head, a pencil stuck in her hair over her right ear. She looked well enough, but he thought he saw new lines, fine, like crazing in old porcelain, around her mouth.

"You look so much better," she told him, leaning back against her dressing table, even smiling a little. "God I was so worried about you."

She had told him this many times, so he made no response except to shrug. Glancing over his shoulder, he saw the telephone on the bed, had not heard her hang it up when he knocked or the necessary end-the-call words to the other party.

"Quite a mess, isn't it." Pulling the pencil from her hair, she twirled it in her fingers. "I've been working at home more. No point in me hanging around getting in the twins' way. They can always call me if they need something."

This was a real change. Hank wondered what she was doing, exactly. "I heard you talking when I came in. Sorry if I interrupted a phone call."

Mom touched her glasses, put the pencil back into her hair. Walking to the French doors, open to bring in the hint of spring, she stood still for a long moment, statue-like. Turning, she walked to the bed, sat down beside Hank. To his astonishment, he saw that she was barefoot, her toenails painted pale pink.

"I wasn't on the phone, Hank."

He had known this, but there could be any explanation.

"And no," she continued, her jaw working sideways in the strange tic he had noticed lately. "I'm not going back to the courtroom, nor practicing for a case, and I'm not auditioning as a sudden urge to become an actress."

She smiled at this, although it was not a happy smile, nor a sardonic one. It was an angry smile, Hank thought, Mom's eyes narrow and dark.

"I'm just trying to get it all said, to get the words out before—" She stopped abruptly, and Hank waited. But her face was stony, grieving, bereft.

"Before what?"

"Before I can't anymore." Turning toward him, Mom took his hand, looked it over, touched his knuckles one by one. "You are the quiet one. You are my sweet, quiet son."

A wary stiffness settled into Hank's muscles. He saw in his mother's face a rigor of sorrow he had never seen before.

"What's the matter?" This fear was new. His confident, strong, guiding mother, the tornado force that kept the family together, was melting away before his eyes.

Swallowing, Mom laid Hank's hand onto his knee and patted it. "He says it might be a tumor, but probably isn't, but a rare nerve disorder." She looked at Hank, her eyes wide, sighing, anxious. "It affects the nerves that work my mouth and jaw and larynx; it's degenerative. There is nothing to be done, at least, maybe a few things, a new drug, but eventually, he says, I will lose my power of speech."

"No, that doctor's crazy," Hank heard himself say, standing up.

Mom looked at him, shook her head in a resigned way.

"The tests, they're not perfect he says, but my symptoms—" She folded her hands. "My doctor sent me to a specialist in this sort of thing, a neurologist. They specialize in nerves and the brain. He says my symptoms indicate this disease. He suggested tumor, but he doesn't really think that is what it is. They did x-rays, but that didn't reveal any clues."

Frozen, Hank looked out the windows where a meadow lark called into the brightness of the day. A spear of grief went through him, followed by a heavy dose of guilt. Turning back to her, she looked old, stricken, her hair out of place, her hands mottled as they pressed against one another.

Hank said, "Is that why you read to me so much, while I was sick?"

Nodding, she turned her head away, brought a hand to her face. As she sobbed noiselessly, Hank stood, uncertain, frail. Should he touch her, should he leave her alone to cry?

Her voice was ragged. The hesitation in her voice that had never been there before, garbling of words.

"Don't tell anyone, Hank. You hear me?"

Talking, talking, talking. Jaw and lips and teeth and tongue making words, failing to make words. His towering mother shrunken into a fragile figurine of herself.

Uncertain, Hank stood, slightly turned away. She had trusted him with this knowledge, him alone, but then she always leaned on him, told him things he wished he didn't know.

Keeper of the family skeletons. But this was different. He saw now, how alone she was.

He should leave her alone. Maybe she didn't want him here anymore.

But instead, he sat next to her on the bed and put his arm around her. He hadn't voluntarily touched his mother in three years.

Scrabbling for a handkerchief in the pocket of her slacks, Mom smelled like peaches. She gave a short laugh, blew her nose.

"He says I should quit smoking. Fat chance. Maybe you could hide all my cigarettes, lighters, and take away all my cash, Hank."

"You could try," he said, knowing how hard it was.

"And pigs can fly." She looked at him, her eyes bright and red-rimmed. "We won't talk about that any more, but there's one other thing."

Wariness went through him again as he wondered what she was going to ask of him. He still didn't know what was bothering Connie. And he wondered what he would say to Dad when he asked Hank about what might be wrong with Mom.

Silent for a while, Mom crushed her fingers together, and Hank grew more nervous. She got up, went to her dresser, picked up her cigarette case, put it down again, and turned to face him. The old Mom was back, the sick one tucked away as she folded her arms and leaned on the dresser. The only clue that the veneer was cracking were two splotches of wet on her blouse.

Hank remained on the foot of the bed, although every fiber in his body was telling him to get out of here. Make the phone ring, Connie come home early, another figurine to crash to the floor.

Mom sighed, her glance darting toward the open doors and then back to him. "When I came to pick you up at the Chagall's, I could see that Miss Chagall had taken very good care of you."

Stay neutral. It's all nothing. Whatever she says doesn't

matter. Hank stared back at Mom, who wore her best courtroom face, decisive, stern. I'm innocent, he thought. An innocent guy pulled in for a crime I didn't commit.

But in good lawyerly fashion, Mom redirected, made a right turn from the thing he thought she knew.

"The nurse. She looked familiar. Did you recognize her?"

Mom's voice was too casual, which made the hair on the back of Hank's rise up.

"Yeah, I think so. I think I knew her in high school."

"Yes." Mom said from where she leaned against the dresser, playing with her lighter. "I remember her. She was a very cute girl, a very lovely young woman. But, you didn't seem to be friends with her long, right?" Mom swept her hand down her blouse, as if wiping something off. Hank couldn't see anything there.

"No, not very long. I saw her a few times, that's all." He tried to remember, thinking there must be more. He had felt really angry about something when the Girl was his friend. And when he tried to bring up the memory associated with it, he failed.

"You know, Mom." He had to ask. He couldn't help himself. "I can't remember her name."

Mom's lips moved slightly, but nothing else in her face. A good lawyerly visage, revealing no reaction. Mom has prepared herself for this. She's been waiting for this.

"I don't remember either." She was very still, arms folded, leaning against the dresser. "She was just one of the girls who hung around you."

Mom sighed. "Well, I have a lot to do." But when Hank turned to go, understanding he was dismissed, she said

"How does one get another voice? Do you suppose they can be grown or purchased?"

Hank heard the snick of her lighter behind him as she lit the cigarette she had been playing with the entire time. He turned to look at her as she inhaled the smoke, a small seed of anger lodged under his ribs.

"Maybe you should get a parrot."

She smiled at him crookedly, lifted her chin. "Maybe I should."

Sixteen

HANK LAY ON HIS BED, staring at the same crack in the ceiling. He might have dozed, but all he could think about was finding out the name of the Girl. And he knew Mom knew it. And he wondered why she pretended she didn't, and why he had forgotten that he had been deeply, obsessively in love with the Girl.

Connie was singing, something she did when she was nervous, her voice winding through the voices of Carl and his parents. They were all downstairs in the living room, and the conversation sounded pretty wrought up.

Drawn to the vocal spectacle below, Hank wanted to sit a moment in the growing dusk as cool air flowed through the French doors. When he had come back to his room after listening to Mom, his body propelled him directly to the bed, requesting rest. The moments had stretched into hours, and someone had closed the doors to just a crack and turned on the lamp on his desk, the bright bulb angled away from his face like a night light. Mom must have walked noiselessly through the room; she might have touched his hair, pulled the bedspread over his shoulders.

Hank pushed himself off the bed, went to his desk chair,

sat staring into the dusk. What would it be like, knowing you were losing an essential piece, half of a matched set like the Meissen marquess and her husband? A leg, an eye, a kidney. You would not be yourself anymore, especially not Mom, who used her voice to persuade, cajole, influence. A voice inside his head all his life. Would it still be there, after it all was gone?

Hank still felt a faint, twisting fury at something he could not recall. He had not thought about the Girl for years, yet now that he had seen her, he hungered to remember.

Getting up, he went to the bathroom and splashed water on his face. He looked terrible, he thought, needing a shave, black stubble contrasting against pearl-gray skin. He needed to get out on his bike. He needed to be in the sun. He needed Susan. He wanted to see the Girl one more time.

Sharp, angry voices beckoned him into the living room. When Hank arrived Carl was on the sofa belting back scotch, Dad stood near the drinks wagon, Mom at the mantle, opening and closing the evening paper as she shifted through the stories.

Only Connie noticed Hank enter. In the dining room archway, behind the table set and ready for supper, she hummed and stretched. Seeing Hank, she rolled her eyes.

He took his place in his favorite chair in front of the French doors. A fire burned in the fireplace against the chilly night.

"What I don't understand is," Carl was saying, "why this girl is going after me? I'm nobody. I don't even know her. Not really."

Mom crumpled the newspaper edges. "Because you are getting known, Carl, that's just the thing. You and Connie are being talked about. You've been mentioned on the front page of Varsity. There's talk about a picture featuring you two in major roles. And television, this new thing, television."

"Oh that," Dad said, returning from the drinks cart empty-handed and sitting down on the sofa next to Carl. "That's going nowhere. Tiny ugly screens? How can that compete with the sound and glamor of the big screen? People aren't going to want to stay home and watch our Connie and Carl dance and sing in miniature. And the sound! Horrendous!"

Mom ignored him. Hank wondered if he was the only one who noticed her fumbling over words. What if she invented this whole nerve disorder thing just to reel him back in?

Carl waved his hand. "I'm not going to hide under a rock this time, Mom. This is different. This girl says I raped her!"

This *was* interesting. Getting off his chair, Hank moved closer, leaned against the mantle, looked at Carl.

"You're joking," he said.

"No I'm not. Look at what the bitch told the papers." Getting up, Carl snatched the newspaper from Mom and handed it to Hank.

"Carl, you have to ignore this." Mom tried to touch Carl's arm, but he pulled away. "You can't dignify this with a response. We know it isn't true. You might have stayed with her, mutually agreeing to sexual intercourse, no strings, and now she's claiming rape. Let the authorities unravel her lies. It's only a matter of time."

Hank looked at a photo of the girl, a pretty blond, a starlet at some studio. She related, in lurid detail, how Carl lured her to a room at the Roosevelt and attacked her. She claimed bruises and scratches, but by the time she got up her courage to go to the police, they were healed. Didn't sound too good for the girl, Hank thought.

Connie twirled in the corner of the room. Mom rattled on with plans about how Carl should conduct his life in the next few weeks, staying away from the Roosevelt, laying low. Dad picked up a script and murmured the words, occasionally gesturing. In her corner, Connie began to sing a nonsense song, and Hank could pick up words like 'house' and 'insane'. He had to agree.

"Connie STOP THAT!" This from Mom, her voice perfectly clear without a hitch. Everyone stared at her and the room fell into blessed silence.

Hank watched Mom. A flush covered her cheeks and her hands were shaking. He noticed, too, and wondered if anyone else did, that she was not smoking.

"Oh fuck you! Fuck you all!" Connie whirled, stomped through the archway and up the stairs just as Joaquin came into the dining room doorway to announce supper was ready.

Mom squeezed her knuckles, turned her wedding ring. Getting up, Carl sent Hank a perplexed shrug and walked toward the dining room, hands in his pockets, followed by Dad, who glanced back at Mom over his reading glasses, but didn't say a word to her.

Hank waited. Mom was shaking her head, as if to clear it.

"Maybe you should have one, just to calm down," he said, picking up the cigarette jar from the coffee table.

Shaking her head fiercely, Mom looked up at the ceiling, and then at Hank. "Tell her I'm sorry. I can't just now, I can't."

"She's such a bitch sometimes," Connie said after Hank knocked and came through the door. She lay on her back, staring at her blue print canopy.

"She's trying to quit smoking. It's making her crazy."

Sitting up, Connie smiled at him and sighed. "Why would she do a crazy thing like that?" Shifting, she reached into her bedside table, pulled out a pack, offered one to Hank who refused, and lit up.

She inhaled. "You know, I think Carl did rape that girl."

Leaning against the chest of drawers, one elbow on top, Hank felt a cold wave go through him. He looked at his sister, wondering why she said that.

"Look, little brother. You know him. He never has a girl-friend for long. He's had hundreds of girls, probably. He gets rough with them, sometimes. I've seen it. I know." Her mouth set firmly; her lipstick was rubbed off and she looked like she was fifteen again. Hank wondered what she did know. He knew what had happened at least once between Connie and Carl. She gazed at him through the smoke, squinting.

She said, "OK, I think she was willing to go to his room and go all the way. Tons of girls make that decision. They, or at least most of them, know what they are doing. But maybe she changed her mind, Carl didn't like that, and he went ahead and now she's miffed about it. Maybe she was stalking him and he ignored her. Maybe she thinks she's pregnant. End of story."

Hank watched his sister. She gazed out her window, a square of black, curtains open, facing the windows of the house next door. He wondered if she left them open when she undressed.

"I think Mom's right. He needs to stay underground for a while."

"Oh, that's a laugh. Carl keeping his dick in his pants for two weeks? Not likely. And I don't want to be around him 'under the ground'."

He looked at her, still thinking about the time he had walked into Carl's room without knocking, and there they were, Carl and Connie, on the bed together, doing something he had only a glimmer of understanding. As if she could read his thoughts, Connie smirked, stubbed out her smoke, and slid off the bed.

"Yeah, you know what I mean, little Hank." Approaching, she chucked him under the chin, then rubbed her hand.

"You need a shave, little man." A moment later she crossed her arms, rubbed her elbows. "I wouldn't want to be that girl right now, either."

Hank looked at her, wondering what had spooked her.

"It's Mom you silly. She'll get her machine going and that girl will be no bigger than a greasy spot." Connie's mouth sagged, all pretense at sardonicism drained away. "She's done it before. She can do it again."

Hank had no doubt she had done it before, manipulating the timing of the world to protect the family's good name. But he wondered which time Connie was thinking about now as she gazed past him and out the window. He thought he knew every bone in all the Cleveland family skeletons, but now he wasn't so sure.

She looked at him again, one corner of her mouth lifted in a smile. "And by the way, Carl and I don't do that shit any- more. That was the only time, I swear. We are a nice little brother and sister act. He has his friends, I have mine. But I wouldn't want to tempt him. Let's eat. I'm starving."

Part II

LUZ

Seventeen

HANK PARKED at the end of the block. He wanted to walk to the house and look at the blue stucco from across the street. It was nearly three weeks since he had been here, an eon of time, and his body thirsted for the place, as if every wooden beam and rag rug were becoming a part of him.

The day was glorious, broadcasting spring with sun and mild breezes off the ocean and a clear sky matching the colors of Susan's bungalow. The palm twitched lazily in the breeze, the Bermuda grass took on the barest sheen of green. The salty spice of the sea came into his nose. He yearned for a hundred mile ride along the coast, but was far from that glory at present. For now, he had just been riding up and down Sunset, teaching his muscles to stretch and grow.

But today he had the car. A luxury, a waste. He could have taken a Red Car, transferring at Venice and walking six blocks north to Susan's, but he was too anxious to get here. And now that he was here, he lingered across the street from her house.

The neighborhood was busy. Children played ball in the street. A woman mowed her lawn, a man washed his car.

Hank was among people who lived and worked and raised families. So unlike his cold, tidy world, where Mexicans did the mowing and washing of cars, and neighbors barely knew each other.

Finally, Hank crossed the street. Susan's car was in the driveway. He had told her he was coming this afternoon. Anticipation stirred in his stomach, and he felt his heart beat rise in tempo as he walked up the driveway and into the back yard.

The kiln stood in its corner under the trees. The garage side door stood ajar, and Hank knew Susan would be in there, painting or sculpting or making molds. A headache touched his scalp with tiny fingers and he was annoyed. Nothing could spoil this moment.

Stepping through the open door, he saw her at her workbench, working a figurine with a curved knife. It was of a donkey, or mule, raised on its hind legs, and it was dancing. But as he watched her, fascinated at her deft molding and scraping, he realized something was not quite right.

It was the room itself, or the light. Someone had painted the walls yellow, with blue trim around the windows. The closed garage doors were framed and inside was a mural of a cave, trompe l'oeil style, with beaded hangings and niches filled with skulls.

Susan had done all this while he was recovering? It was amazing and smelled different, not of solvents and oils, but of damp earth and incense. He stepped in, wondering what to say, and could think of nothing.

Hank waited until Susan was done; he knew how she hated to be interrupted at her work, but he wanted to see the look on her face as she turned around and saw who it was.

But something was wrong. Hank blinked, squinted, trying

to clear his vision. The woman sitting at the workbench had black hair, caught in a blue scarf. Had Susan dyed her hair? And then it hit him, hard and miraculous. This was not Susan at all. This was Luz.

Her name. That is the Girl's name. Luz del Mar.

His heart did a back flip and a sweat broke out on his hands. Holding his breath, he waited for her to notice him. He fought an urge to run away, to back out of the room, go into the house and look for Susan, but he was rooted to the spot, his shoes nailed to the boards covering the earth.

She worked quickly. He watched the turn of her shoulder. She wore a blue work shirt, dungarees with the cuffs turned up, shoes with no socks. He stared at her ankle. He remembered Luz being clever with her hands, getting A's for her craftwork and designs, but he could see she was better even than Susan as she sculpted the dancing donkey, giving the animal a smile, sombrero, a garland of lilies.

Hank's knees trembled. He thought he should sit down, but he fought it. He was well, cured, and stronger every day. As he was considering moving to a chair, like a coyote catching his scent, Luz turned and saw him.

A quick intake of breath, and then she was out of the chair and moving toward him, quickly, and caught him in her arms.

Cinnamon and coconut filled his nostrils, the real and familiar smell. And the voice that nuzzled in his ears familiar as well.

"Hank, Hank. I missed you so much."

Susan's voice. Hank pushed her back, cupped her face in his hands. *Susan's face*, moist chocolate eyes, freckles, and lips full and wanting. Her face shifted, changed, and she stared back at him.

"What's the matter? Hank?"

He didn't understand what had just happened. Pulling Susan to him, he felt her breasts against him, and grew hard for the first time in weeks. Pressing her lips into his neck, her hands crawled up and down his back. He grasped her hair, tore at the scarf holding it in. As he did this, he looked over her shoulder. The garage door was blankly white-washed, the oil smell in his nostrils, the statuette on the bench a swan, not a donkey. Where was the mural? *Where was Luz?*

They made love in the garage, on the floor. His muscles took on a new strength as he molded and placed her body, and she moaned in a new way, he thought, as he buried his lips and tongue in the warm, moist place between her thighs, and she bit her hand as she came. Then, he was inside, pleasure climbing and building, and she watched him, her face eager and pleased as he came and closed his eyes to bite back shouts of love.

After, they held each other and he nuzzled her hair, ran his fingers over the curves of her breasts and hips. Occasionally, her hand would find him and she would trace the skin around it, avoiding its tender tip. Then he was hard again, and she was ready, and they did it again.

Finally, after, they said few words, sorted out their clothes, dressed and Hank followed Susan into the house. He said nothing about the vision, knowing it was a crazy dream, a remnant of illness that his brain fired off. But as he entered the kitchen, where breakfast dishes still sat on the table and in the sink, where the floor needed sweeping and the smell of coffee was heavy in the air, Hank worried again. What if Luz walked in right now and saw the film of sex that covered them both?

And yet, he wanted to see Luz more than the peanut butter sandwich Susan was making him.

But the house was silent. Not even the radio was on. It felt utterly empty.

"Where is Joseph? How are his ankles coming along?"

Piling up the dishes—two plates, he saw, half-eaten toast, a yellow smear of eggs—and setting them on the counter, giving the table a lazy wipe, Susan laid the sandwich in front of Hank.

"Casts are off. He's walking now. On crutches." She pushed back a hunk of red hair, her cheeks flushed, eyes bright. "I think he's taking a nap."

Hank wondered how to ask, how to make it casual, when his heart was racing. "And the nurse? She still around?"

If Susan thought his interest in the nurse out of line, she made no indication. "She left yesterday. She said she had another assignment that was more urgent, and she and the doctor thought Joseph was able to look after himself pretty well."

Hank knew he should be happy. Susan would think this would make him happy, they could meet here now. They didn't have to arrange a place. Something had changed; Susan didn't seem to care if Joseph was home when they met.

So he tried to be happy, but panic engulfed him. He wanted to be away, he wanted to look for Luz. He had seen her, in the garage. He had seen her as she helped him get ready to go home. He had seen her in his delirious nightmares, felt her cool hand on his forehead, dragging an icy cloth against his fever.

If she noticed this, Susan said nothing about it. She watched him eat his sandwich, and he talked about his recuperation, family dramas, how he missed her. She listened saying nothing. Susan knew everything about him, but Hank only knew the white geography of her body, and that her

133

mind was private, peculiar.

A thumping noise signaled that Joseph was up. Hank could see him pass through the living room in an open robe and white pajamas to flop onto the couch.

"Susan!" He called for his sister in an imperious way. "Where is my hypo?"

Susan got up, not looking at Hank, and left the room.

Following, Hank came into a chaotic mess; used dishes on the coffee table, disordered newspapers, reek of multiple cigarettes, empty, sticky glasses, a couple green with mold.

"Well, hello, stranger! The prodigal. Susan's teenage love —come in, come in."

After taking in the mess, Hank gazed at Joseph, and could not keep the shock off his face. A ragged beard had appeared on Joseph's face, and the bones of his face stood out in fierce angularity.

Joseph said, "Yes, you see how I mourn the loss of the lovely nurse. She left abruptly, it was my fault, I suppose. Ah, here we go."

Susan entered carrying a plate. On it was an ampule and a syringe. She expertly cracked the top off the ampule, drew the liquid into the syringe, and as Joseph turned to reveal a hip bruised and mottled with evidence of many shots, injected the morphine.

"The nurse showed her how, marvelous, isn't it? These damn ankles, they hurt me all the time."

Done with her ministrations, Susan got up, went into her bedroom, shut the door.

"She hates me, "Joseph said, his jaw tight. "What can I do? No good to anyone this way. But I am walking."

"I see that." An uncomfortable rage grew in Hank, that Susan would let Joseph destroy her house, her life. How could she have let Luz go, he wondered, angry that he couldn't have been here in a clean living room and see Luz and try to get her to talk to him.

"I better go."

"No, wait. How are you, young man? You look the picture of health considering the death's-head you resembled when they wheeled you out of here." Joseph waved his hands, his fingers extraordinarily long.

Hank gave him the standard answer, that he was coming along nicely. "Better than you, apparently," he couldn't help adding. But it was not out of sympathy, and Joseph noticed the edge to his voice.

He spread his hands, knocked a pile of magazines to the floor, and with them, a plate and fork. "The help around here. Really, it is too bad you can't get good assistants. How about at your fine house, Hank, up in the hills of Westwood? Do the Mexicans clean your house and your butts?"

Hank closed his hands into fists. Turning away, he walked to Susan's door and knocked.

"Oh, she won't be out for hours. She's sulking. Her big bad brother is an abusive asshole." Joseph's voice was louder now, so Susan could hear.

But Hank thought he heard her, and could see no light under the door.

"Go away, Hank," was she saying? "Come back tomorrow?"

Turning back to Joseph, Hank looked him over. No wonder Luz had left him. He must have muttered this aloud, because Joseph squinted, ran a hand through his greasy, unwashed hair.

"Luz? Who is this Luz? That nurse? Oh, was that her name?"

Sarcasm ringed his voice. Hank was stung. Joseph was mocking him. Mocking Luz.

The next thing he knew, Hank was on his knees beside Joseph, clutching the lapels of Joseph's robe, got his face real close in. Joseph's eyebrows rose in surprise.

"Yes," Hank hissed. "Her name is Luz. Luz del Mar. She cleaned your house and wiped your ass. And thank god she had the good sense to get the fuck out of the hell hole that is your life, Joseph."

"Leave him alone!" Susan's voice, brittle, quick. She was at their side, prying Hank's hands from Joseph. Heat burst on to Hank's face as he got to his feet, stunned that Susan had come to his rescue, in a way, even though he knew he was perfectly capable of handling himself.

But it was not Hank she came to rescue. Pushing herself between them, she smoothed Joseph's lapels and ran her fingers down his face.

"Are you all right?" she said, not to Hank, but to her brother.

Watching them, Hank saw something he didn't want to see, that he hated to see, that filled him with dread. His throat tightened with anger and turning, he headed crazily toward the kitchen thinking he would get out of here on his bike; then he remembered there was no bike, only the car.

Joseph's voice stopped him. "Wait, Hank. Don't go. I'm sorry. Please, stay for a while."

He sounded truly sincere, otherwise Hank would have kept going. It was Joseph, not Susan, who urged him to stay, who apologized.

Turning in the doorway, Hank looked back. Susan stood a few feet away, arms folded, face turned away. To his astonishment, Hank saw Joseph's eyes red with tears.

"I'm an asshole. I'm sorry for what I said. I didn't mean it."

Hank could only suppose this apology was for both Susan and himself. Joseph swiped a hand across his eyes.

"I need to get back to work, but these damn ankles. Susan needs the money. I'm just a shitbird, sitting here, a wart, a parasite."

"Joseph, stop it." Susan's voice was fierce.

"Yeah, I'll turn off the 'I Hate Joseph' show." He leaned back, closed his eyes, opened them again a moment later.

Hank stood in the silence with them. No one moved for a moment.

"Sorry I grabbed you." He thought he sounded like a child, apologizing via coercion.

"Good, good. I deserved it. He's a good guy, Suze. He's an honorable guy." Joseph lifted his arms, motioned at them, like a priest urging the marriage couple to kiss.

Susan walked past Hank without looking at him, and he followed her into a setting sun sending a cool shadow over the backyard; birds flicked away from them as they emerged.

Passing the makeshift patio, where a pottery monk, missing one arm, adorned the little table, Susan led him down the driveway, then stopped. He looked at her face, clear and dry, her eyes wide with anxiety. She kept her arms around herself, and he didn't touch her.

She said, "I don't make excuses for Joseph. But nothing, nothing in all the world, will make me choose."

Hank looked at her beautiful face, golden from the slanting sun. They stood on the driveway, almost to the street. A passing couple out for a walk with the dog glanced at them curiously. He wanted more than anything to kiss her, pull her skin next to his, feel her curves. But something stopped him, and it wasn't propriety.

"It's not like that and I don't care what people say about us," Susan said, and Hank remembered Connie and what she had admitted to him yesterday about her and Carl. "But I have to take care of him Hank, and you have to understand."

"I don't have to understand," he heard himself say. "How can you live like this, Susan? What crazy thing is he going to do next? You have your own life."

She stood, her hands opening and closing like his. She shoved her hair from her eyes. "I made a promise to our mother. Joseph has always been fragile. You see, he was five years old, walking with our Dad, when a freak accident happened. The limb of a big tree fell. Just fell on Dad, killed him on the spot. Ever since then, he's been an edgy guy. I was hoping the army wouldn't take him because of his history, but they gave him a jeep to drive."

Listening, watching her move her hands up and down her arms, looking everywhere but at him, Hank fell even more in love with her.

"You see, Hank, this is my life." She gestured toward the house. "This here."

Now she looked straight at him, searching his face for a re-action, he thought. Defiant. Hank saw inside her, through the chocolate eyes and saw love there. And it wasn't for him.

Eighteen

IT WAS FRUITLESS to telephone all the del Mars listed in the book. There were dozens of them, and Hank didn't know if Luz's parents even had a phone because he never called Luz because she never gave him a number. But he did remember where her father worked.

Various telephone ruses, discarded, resurrected, discarded again, came into his mind. *Luz won a contest!* No, she probably never entered contests. The hospital was short handed, needed her to return to work. But what if the hospital had already called, or called again? High school reunion? But they had only graduated two years ago.

Finally determining a fool-proof excuse, Hank realized he would have to enlist Connie. But when he got up Sunday morning, the day after his quarrel with Susan and Joseph, he found that both Connie and Carl had been called to the studio.

Dad and Mom were off somewhere, too.

"What's your hurry, *cuate*?" Joaquin picked up Hank's empty plate as he pushed it across the table. "Is there a special mass today? A holy day? The *padre* got sick and they called you in?"

"Yeah," Hank said, wiping his mouth. "I'm saint-of-the-week. St Hank, repairer of flat tires."

"You be careful out there, *San Enrique,*" Joaquin said, completing his sentence in Spanish, which Hank barely heard as he ran out the kitchen door.

Looking longingly at the Peugeot, Hank pulled out the Raleigh, relieved to find that its tires were not flat. He knew the studio was farther than he had been riding since he'd gotten sick, but he didn't care. It was the quickest way to get there, Connie and Carl having taken the Cadillac and no one was allowed to touch Mom's Chevrolet coupe, which was also missing from the garage anyway.

Besides, once he made it up to Sunset, the grades were fairly level and if he didn't push it, he knew he would be fine.

By the time he got to the studio it was late morning and he was tired but not exhausted. He coasted through the lot, having been granted entrance by the young security guard who had a crush on Connie, and because Hank always promised to give the guard's phone number to her.

By the time he arrived at the studio, it was all over.

He could see it was bad. Mom, Connie and Carl stood in a tight circle near the big barn studio doors. Cedric Sigfried's shaggy white head was disappearing into a Lincoln, along with the director. Connie raised one hand and Mom slapped it down—Hank knew she was flipping Sigfried off. He could hear Connie's voice, loud, riddled with emotion, filling the nearly empty lot with angst.

Carl leaned against the studio wall, his hands in the pockets of his immaculate jacket. He looked down at his shoes, a hank of golden hair masking his eyes.

Standing between them like an umpire, Mom waited—if she was speaking, it was calm and slow. She seemed to be shielding both Carl and Connie, keeping them both safe, especially from each other.

No one had seen Hank where he had stopped several yards away. The Sigfried limo passed by, and he looked in to see Cedric and the director arguing, gesturing. He could leave now, he thought. His family would never know he was here. But as he thought to turn around, Carl glanced up and saw him.

Too late. If he left now, there would be endless questions, recriminations. Disheartened, Hank coasted toward them and stopped a few feet away.

Connie's face was a rigor of torment. Eyes red, cheeks mottled, makeup running in bruised marks and seeming to pool under her eyes. As Hank approached, she stood still, breathing heavily, chest moving up and down.

"I'm sorry, Connie." Carl seemed to be looking for a cigarette, instead found a flask, tilted it to his mouth. He too, looked ragged, stained like an abused work shirt. "What do you want me to say?"

"Nothing. Nothing at all." Connie's voice singed even Hank with contempt.

Mom rummaged through her purse, pulled out a notebook and scrabbled for a pencil.

"Mom, it's in your hair," Carl said, shifting his glance to Hank. He looked liberally shattered.

Her jaw set, Mom gave Carl a piercing look, pulled a pencil from above her ear. "I will talk to Mr. Sigfried. There has to be a way to mend this. You both have a contract with the studio. He can't violate that, in other words, fire you from the studio. But I believe he can remove you from a project for 'improper behavior'. Although the interpretation of that wording changes depending which lawyer is looking at it."

It did not take mind-reading skills to uncover what was going on in everyone's heads. The Cleveland Twins had been fired from the picture; an excuse of budget overrun would be given out; their scenes would be cut, but the real reason was Carl's recent unflattering publicity, even though worse had been tolerated by the studio by more established box office draws.

Carl provided unwitting confirmation about his transgression. "How was I to know she was Sigfried's niece's daughter, or whatever? And I only slept with her. She wanted it. She seduced me!"

"Carl, shut up." Mom made quick notes, wrinkling the paper, her hands shaking. "Connie, don't worry, honey. We can make it work. I'll go to Mr. Sigfried's house this afternoon. He's agreed to talk to me."

Connie fired because of Carl. There was always a first time. It was bound to happen, and Hank knew what would happen now. He saw it on Connie's face, on all their faces. What Carl had worried about a month ago would come to pass. The act was going to break up.

Mom seemed to notice Hank for the first time. Nodding at him, she continued with her notes. Hank said nothing, but he felt sorry for Connie, especially. Not so much Carl, who deserved this kick in the gut. But Connie didn't.

"Let's get you home," Mom said, taking Connie by the arm. Shaking her arm free, Connie turned and stalked down the street between the studios to where the Caddy was parked in the lot behind. Mom followed, and then Carl, and Hank trailed behind, rolling his bicycle.

"I'm not riding in the same car," was all Connie said, but everyone knew what she meant.

"I'll take the Caddy," Hank heard himself say. His bike

would never fit in Mom's little coupe unless he held onto it rolling along the ground outside the window. "Connie can ride with me."

Pulling a cigarette out of the glove compartment, Connie slammed the car lighter in and waited, rolling the cigarette over and over her fingers.

"I'll kill him. I really will kill him this time."

Hank pulled out into the traffic, and, driving slowly, quickly fell behind the coupe as Mom screeched away to dump Carl at home and drive to Sigfried's villa in Beverly Hills. Remembering the last time he was there the night be-fore he got sick, a cold feeling of dislike filled Hank, as if, he knew strangely, that he could blame Sigfried—or thank him maybe—for changing the course of his life. This reminded him of the favor he wanted to ask of Connie, but prudently he waited.

The lighter popped, Connie lit up, and with shaking fingers twirled the radio knobs until something quick and loud with lots of brass tuned in.

"My brother is a cretin. He is a beast. He lives not by his wits, but by his dick." Connie drummed the dashboard to the time of the music, and her words tumbled out in time to the beat. Then she looked at Hank. "Let's go get a drink."

"Con, it's Sunday."

"Don't worry, sweet Hank. I have a plan."

She directed him along quiet suburban Hollywood streets. Soft air breezed through Hank's open window, and the smell of cut grass. She stopped him in front of a garden apartment building, one-story cottages in the shape of a 'U', bordering a fountain of blue tile.

He parked in front and she got out, and when he hesitated, she leaned through the window and smiled. "Come now,

Hank. She's just a friend of mine, a 'starlet' friend. I need a drink, is all, and I know she'll have something."

Well, if this would make Connie happy, and Hank needed her to be happy to agree to his plan, he decided he would go in.

The starlet's apartment was in the front, and the girl who opened the door was very pretty, with close-cropped pixie-cut cinnamon hair, a pointed chin, and a slim, pert body, generous breasts enveloped in a dragon-emblazoned robe.

"Oh Connie, is this your little brother? The other one? Oh, yes, he's cute." Seizing Hank's arm, she pulled him inside, and Connie clunked in after, kicked off her shoes, walked to a wooden table covered with bottles and glasses, and filled three with something brown and bright.

They were like Mutt and Jeff, the friend who told Hank her name was Mary stood a good ten inches shorter than the statuesque Connie. Refusing the offered whiskey or brandy or whatever it was, Hank watched the girls stand before him, clink their glasses and exchange a glance that carried more packets of information than the ordinary telegraph.

He didn't know what ideas they transmitted to each other, but he hoped it didn't have anything to do with him and a possible teasing seduction.

Indeed, Connie was already relaxed, almost giddy, as she poured two more and they clinked glasses again. Watching them from the couch, Hank couldn't help thinking that Connie looked relieved.

"So," Mary said, as she, to Hank's relief, flopped not on the couch next to him, but into a heavy chair near the window, draping her legs over one arm. "What brings the prima donna into my neck of the woods?"

Pouting, running both hands through her hair, a feat of

majesty with cigarette in one and whiskey in the other, Connie launched into Carl's betrayal and her getting fired from
the picture. Tears came again, a rolling cough in her voice,
sighs and sobs. Hank watched impressed, but something
about this performance wasn't quite right.

Mary seemed to suck it all in. Getting to her feet, she
wrapped Connie in her arms. "Poor baby, what a snake! He
deserves to have his balls cut off and served to him for breakfast." She seemed genuinely rattled, concerned to the point of
tears herself. Hank relaxed, feeling as if he too had had a
drink. So Connie had not dragged him here to offer him up
as a main course to the feast of the starlets. She really did
need a drink and a good bitch session.

So after a half-an-hour of shared membership in the We-
Despise-Carlisle-Cleveland club, Hank brought up his plan,
blurted it out, in fact as Mary, having now a little too much to
drink for her small size, sat beside him and petted his hair.

Flopping onto the couch on the other side, Connie's mouth
fell open in astonishment, followed by a grin.

"That girl that Mom threw out of the house? That pretty
Mexican girl? You want to get in touch again?"

The room got very hot, all of a sudden. Hank tried to keep
himself loose, as Connie fussed with his sideburns. *Mom
threw her out of the house?* Why had he forgotten about that?
Desperate to hear more, the last thing he wanted was for
Connie to know that this part of his memory had been
erased.

Connie proceeded to tell Mary all about it. Hank listened,
needing to hear it all. He didn't care about Mary hearing the
story he starred in and didn't know it. She was very drunk
and would never remember any of this anyway.

"She is a beautiful girl," Connie blathered on, while Mary

leaned back her head and tried to keep her eyes open. "Brilliant, too. She was at that fancy school on a scholarship—I guess her father was educated, and they were pretty well off, living, where was it—I don't think you ever told me, Hank."

Connie ran her hand down the side of his face. "Poor Hank. You really did love that girl. It ended so suddenly, huh? I remember seeing her around, and then PFFT! She was gone."

Mary nodded, her eyes closed. "PFFFT!"

Hank smiled at his sister, hoping he looked interested, not flummoxed.

"She looked so cute in that school uniform, with her hair in a ponytail. Must have been hard, the only Mexican girl in that snotty school. I ran into her in the living room once, looking at that trash of Mom's, and as I walked in she whipped out a little tablet and started drawing those stupid little statues on the mantle."

Connie offered her drink to Hank, who shook his head, fascinated about this bit of intelligence. "She said she wanted to be an architect or a designer for the pictures. I actually didn't laugh at her, Hank, you will be glad to know. I could see she was dead serious."

Nodding, Hank pretended to recall this fact about Luz. Memories of the drawing, little doodles on her school folders, nipped at him.

Turning to him, Connie shifted her knee onto the couch. "What were you two up to, young Hank, that got Mother so pissed off. I could only guess, but now it's time to fess up. Then, maybe I will do what you ask."

Someone had turned the heat up, or maybe it was the sun burning through the windows and doors. Connie narrowed her eyes, watching Hank as his face warmed. *He didn't re-*

member. Maybe nothing happened. Why didn't he remember?

"Oh, so my guess was correct. The witness is clearly holding back the truth, your honor." She leaned close, to his ear. "So Miss Chagall is not the first."

Shivers ran through Hank's thighs. He felt as if he had cycled two centuries. But he kept the smile on his face and shrugged. He could act too, when the situation demanded.

Connie slapped her knee and snapped her fingers. "I'll do it, my lad. I will call this girl's Dad, and say I am a high school friend, and I really want to get in touch with her. OK?"

They left Mary snoozing on the couch. Connie crawled into the front seat, leaned her head back as Hank drove them home. The wind curled her hair, licked his forehead, and he could remember cool hands on his forehead and chest and the icy release from fever. Only he was feverish again, he thought, but in a completely new way.

Nineteen

SILENCE MADE HANK uneasy, as he was unable to hear the chorus of voices in the continual background of his life. Mom was at Cedric's pleading for her children, Dad had gone off somewhere. Absent more and more, Dad especially seemed not to like to spend time in the living room under the quietly surprised gaze of his father's urn. Carl was in his room, door closed.

Connie unsteadily and softly went upstairs, after whispering to Hank that she needed a nap and a long soak in the tub, but she would perform his deed first thing in the morning. He felt a little nervous about that, determining that he would make sure she remembered.

Then there was the problem of Susan. Hank sat on the couch, his legs out before him, and gazed at his grandfather. Afternoon air, carrying floral scents, curled in from the patio. Picking up the phone, Hank dialed Susan's number.

Joseph answered. "Ah, the boy wonder." Joseph's voice was slow and drawly, but he sounded lucid. "I think I owe you an apology."

"It's OK. You already apologized."

Joseph continued, "Well, anyway. I'm sorry for being such

an asshole yesterday. I would offer up an excuse, but I don't have one."

"It's OK. Really," was all Hank could think to say.

"Good then. I'm walking more. I'm trying to get off the dope. I want to get back to work like any other good American boy. I miss the ghosts and they miss me."

"You going back to work at the cemetery?" Hank thought this was an ambitious goal, but if it got Joseph out of the house, all the better.

Joseph's voice softened, barely heard above the hiss of the wire. "I'll stay out of your way. She really missed you, while you were gone—Oh hey, this one's for you!"

A clatter, swift talking in the background, then Susan's voice, uncertain, "Hello?"

"I miss you," was all Hank could say.

She was silent for a while. "When will you be back by?"

She had never asked him that before. He always left her bungalow without an invitation to return, as if there was no need for it. Now things were changing course, and he really didn't know.

"Tomorrow?"

She agreed to this. "Tomorrow."

Putting the phone down, Hank looked at his hands, which were shaking. Climbing the stairs to his room, he tried fiercely to remember what had happened. But it was as if he was pushing at a door that refused to open. Lying on his bed, he stared at his desk, trying to see Luz sitting there, laughing at something he said. Connie implied that he and Luz—if that were true, it would definitely be memorable. But had it really happened?

He too must have slept. When he went down stairs, the afternoon had worn away while Connie slept off her brandy.

At some point, Carl must have slipped out, gone down to town to hang out with friends. When Mom came home, she found Hank in the living room, stretched out on the sofa again, trying to read the comics, but finding his mind wandering between two women. Dad was not home yet.

"He won't budge," Mom said, walking straight to the cocktail wagon. "He doesn't want Carl on the set, and so, he says he can't let Connie in there either. He knows he has a three film contract, but we are arguing whether this picture is number one. I think he was impressed by the way I came at him."

Hank pretended to pay attention, but he was really listening for the hitch in her voice, a subtle hesitation, a garbled word. He could hear them mixed in her speech. Sitting down at the other end of the couch near his feet, she patted his bare ankle. "I have to say I was glad you showed up, Hank. Good show of family support. Cedric noticed you."

Great, Hank thought. Would he have to display himself at awards ceremonies and charity events, as well?

"What if the act split up? Wouldn't that be better for everyone?"

Turning her head, Mom stared at him over her reading glasses. Shoving them up on her head, she said, "No, Hank, that would be far worse for everyone. The Cleveland Twins are unique. Brother and sister, and talented at everything: singing, dancing, acting."

She leaned back again, gazed in the direction of the mantle and its bizarre collection of mismatched pieces. "Neither of them have a chance going solo. The competition is tremendous. Pretty blond actors are a dime a dozen."

"But Connie, she has something special, don't you think?"

Mom gave him a look again, curious, wondering. "Maybe.

151

She's good at making connections, getting to know the right people, keeping her M.O. Straight. But splitting up is out of the question."

Having said more than he wanted, Hank remained silent. He knew Mom was protecting Carl. It was hard to imagine what might happen to Carl if the act broke up. He was far more dependent on the whole set-up than Connie.

They sat in silence as the room darkened, and odors of chicken and thyme circulated through the house as Joaquin did his magic in the kitchen. Hank worried not so much what would happen to Carl if the act broke up. He would be fine—he would land on his feet. But the bigger question was, what would Mom do?

That night Hank slept the sleep of the dead, followed around by dreams. In one of them someone sat on his bed with soft breath in his ear, faint smell of lilacs.

"I made the call, you lazy bones," the breath said.

When he opened his eyes, sun brightened the day outside his windows. Getting up, he went down the hall to Connie's room, tapped at the door. Silence. No one was home. Every-one had left him behind.

Twenty

THIS WOULD BE the oddest meeting, the most wrought with potential unpleasantness, that Hank could imagine. The return call had come not from Luz, inquiring after a high school friend she didn't remember, but from Susan. Hank and Luz would meet at Susan's house, at a time of day when Susan would take Joseph to the hospital for a check-up.

He mulled, as he prepared for the meeting, fussing with his clothes, knowing he couldn't be too choosy because he was determined to cycle to Susan's for the first time since he had been ill, about why she was doing this. Was she tired of him and trying to pawn him off on an old girlfriend? Was she a martyr, seeing how in love with Luz he still was, and giving up on him? Was she forcing him to choose between them?

The chosen day was Friday, Luz's day off. He hadn't even spoken to Luz yet. He had chafed all week, snapping at his mother, ignoring calls from friends to go to movies or hang out on Sunset. He rode every day, and his endurance built quickly. Carl was home all day, getting on Hank's and every-one's nerves, drinking too much. Connie was gone all day to who knew where, shopping, visiting girlfriends—if she was hustling auditions, she didn't give a hint. And Hank only gave glancing thoughts to Dad, who was sometimes not even home for dinner.

And Mom. After negotiations with Sigfried, she holed up in her room, and Hank could hear her talking. She had bought a Dictaphone, recording the words she knew she would soon lose. But he had no time for any of it. His only goal was Luz.

Hank set off that day with the certainty that the familiar road, the long coast down to Sepulveda, felt somehow longer. Not because he was still weak—he was stronger than ever— but because it was taking him farther from home than he had ever been. With the house and family out of sight, he melted with the city in an anonymous way, venturing into a wilderness with no roads or even trails, where no human being had ever been; animals understood the landscape, but a blundering man was a blight.

His heart already beating hard from his ride, Hank coasted into Susan's driveway. Cars were parked neatly on the street, children were in school; on the empty street the only other human in sight was a mailman hauling a bag of mail. Arrowing up the drive, he coasted into the yard on the newly greening grass, and saw Luz.

She stood near the kiln, holding a greenware piece. Her hair was down, curled around her face, lapping her shoulders with blue-black. She wore a man's t-shirt—one of Joseph's?—and slacks. Her lips parted as if she were startled, and Hank watched them shift into a smile.

Having already hopped off his bike, Hank stood frozen, heart thundering, his breath trapped in his throat. Putting down the greenware, some animal figurine, Luz brushed her hands on her pants, came toward him, and stuck out her hand.

"Hi, Hank."

Her voice was soft and girl-like, so like, so familiar, that a wave of dizziness washed over Hank, as if they had travelled back in time and were sixteen, standing in his backyard be-side the pool.

The bike was between them. He wanted to shove it out of the way and pick her up, crush her to him, taste her lips again and feel her breasts against his. They were large and prominent. And he remembered the heft of them in his hands when they—

As all this went through his mind, she pulled her hand back, her smile shifted into embarrassment. "You look a lot better."

Hank found he could breathe again. Her demeanor changed into the professional nurse, talking to a patient.

"Yeah, I'm all over that." *You're a complete idiot,* he told himself. He sounded like a conceited asshole.

She touched the handlebars of the Raleigh. "You still ride. Is this the same bike?"

Nodding, he watched her long-fingered hand, skin already creased around the knuckles, hands that were washed and cleansed dozens of times a day.

He said, "I have a Peugeot now, a cross-country racer. I use that for my long training rides."

I sound like a ten-year-old, he thought, wondering why the power of speech and his voice had shrunk and shattered.

She nodded, smiling again. "It's good to ride a bike. Every child needs one."

Hank felt a little stung. Was she implying his cycling was childish? Uncertain, he pushed the bike toward the back porch, leaned it against the wall between the porch and the cellar steps.

"Would you like some coffee? A coke?" Her voice followed him across the yard like a child, touching his leg.

"That's OK, just some water." He started up the steps, into the kitchen, and she was right behind. As he walked to the cupboard to get a glass, he felt his body warm, and wondered what Luz knew about him and Susan.

In Susan's kitchen—surprisingly neat; washed dishes in the drainer, table cleared and wiped and a vase—Metlox, of course—filled with random flowers and dried stems, Hank filled his glass, turned and looked at Luz. She stood near the door, looking uncertain, fingering the edges of her shirt.

Susan's place smelled vaguely of alcohol and musk, and the cinnamon-like smell of her. Hank didn't like being inside, as if he were inside Susan. Luz didn't belong to this place of Susan's, although here she was, and she had been while Hank was ill.

"Miss Chagall has been teaching me about ceramics." Luz lifted her chin, watched him with her coffee eyes. "Do you want to see?" Almost shyly.

Relieved to have a reason to go back outside, Hank nodded. He followed her to the garage studio, watching her walk, briskly but swaying, her butt round and pushing against her flowing shirt.

Coming through the door, the memory of when he had entered and thought he saw Luz at the worktable working on the donkey, came at him with force. It was not Luz, but Susan, and they had fucked right there on the floor. He felt his face grow warm again, hoped Luz did not see.

And she didn't, because she moved to a shelf and picked from an array of animals: a small cat, a leopard maybe, or a jaguar. She brought it to him.

"This, of course, is my best so far." She turned it in her

hand, gave it to him. "I wouldn't dare show you my cata-strophes. They are all appropriately consigned to the trash can."

As she spoke, and he felt the glassy skin of the cat, and looked at its piercing, yellow eyes, Hank felt awash in love. Memories flooded back, talks with Luz, intelligent and prob-ing, funny and sarcastic; he remembered talking to her more than anyone, ever. Luz loved to talk about the world, and Hank could listen to her opinions forever. He wondered again, as he had then, if she had inherited her intelligent ana-lytical powers from her father.

Curling his fingers around the cat, feeling its muscled curves, he remembered another side of Luz, magical, dark, scary, probably inherited from her mother. The way she saw things that Hank never saw, said things that puzzled him. The way she looked at the photograph of his grandparents and proclaimed a truth that he had never seen before.

"Papi never approved of my attempts at sculpting. He didn't like me spending money on clay." Luz ran her hand along the edge of the workbench, where bottles and cans, paints, brushes, a zoo of greenware animals crowded. Hank caught fragrances of oils and mixtures, sharp, like incense.

Hank remembered suddenly that Julio del Mar was dead. Connie had told him, after she made the call to the law office where he used to work as an assistant.

"I'm sorry about your dad."

Grief came and went on Luz's face, she swallowed it away. "He took everything so hard."

Hank thought she wanted to say more, but she sighed, took the cat back from him and laid it on the shelf. Next to it was a smaller figurine, wolf puppy, coyote? But Luz picked up another one, and handed it to Hank.

"For you. That is a gift."

A raven, the figurine easily filled his palm. The raven wore a sombrero and a bandana around its neck.

"Because you fly like a bird, on your bicycle." A smile lifted the corner of her mouth. Hank couldn't stop himself. He reached over, his hand moving without thought—he had nothing to do with it, his body took over, and he touched her hair, ran his finger along the side of her face.

Luz's eyes widened. She seemed to stiffen. Hank pulled his hand away.

He knew his touch had changed. Susan had changed it. Luz felt it, and he thought maybe he had frightened her. He lifted the raven; he and it exchanged beady glances.

"Thanks. He's great."

They made small bits of talk, there in the studio, Hank on the stool for climbing to the high shelves. Luz leaning against the table, told him about school.

"Nursing school is hard. I used to stay at the hospital, in the dorm, most of the time. The other girls are fun. We go out together sometimes, with the interns. It's quite a party."

Jealousy nicked at Hank, but he squelched it. What right did he have? He was the one who cast her out—or rather, his family did.

"How is your mom?" he though to ask, grasping at anything to hear her voice.

Smiling, Luz shrugged, picked at a dried glop of red pooled on the table. "She's good. She misses Papi a lot, but she is busy, taking care of things, the house. She's very involved in the church, too, of course."

Hank knew she lived in a modest neighborhood of middle-class Mexicans, maybe better off than most because her father had a good paying job. Her father had supported her while she attended the fancy private school, bravely, alone.

Then Hank remembered how they met; she and Hank hit it off the first time they met in a reading study circle. They liked the same books, movies. She looked Mexican but she spoke and acted like the other girls, with something more, indescribable.

What had happened between them, and how could he correct this tear in his memory? More recollections tumbled into his head; they loved being together, one time they snuck out to a film. Several times they rode bikes together. Luz had an old rusty Schwinn; Hank remembered tuning it up for her, cleaning and oiling, replacing bearings, tightening the spokes.

When it came time for him to fill in the years between, he found he had little to say. He graduated, he turned down, for now, the idea of college. His parents didn't seem in a hurry for him to leave their nest—if he got accepted to a school, they would support it, but, they seemed to want him at home.

Luz had used the money Julio del Mar left her—a huge sum, it was implied, and she seemed honored and shocked that he had deeded that to her—to go to nursing school. And she put the rest away, saving it, she said. For what she would not say.

Silence hung between them. Hank could not take his eyes off her, and she glanced at him, then away, then back, as if she struggled with how often she should look at him.

Hank considered. He didn't know how long he could stay. He knew he didn't want to be here when Susan and Joseph got home. But he needed connection. He needed to see Luz again. He wanted, in the worst way, to invite her home, but he hesitated. He wanted, in the worst way, for her to invite him to her home. He had never met her mother.

She said, fingering the half-painted rooster she had been working on, "I may give up nursing, go to work at Metlox. Miss Chagall says I have a talent for this. In fact, she really is impressed with some of my glazes." She folded her arms, looked at Hank as if to get his opinion.

He couldn't think what to say. He was absorbed by her beauty, watching her watching him. She took his silence for assent, she figured, because she took down the jaguar again.

"This is special. I made the glaze from the ashes of my father."

A cold hand slid down Hank's back. He found he couldn't look at the jaguar anymore, but he could see, in the corner of his eye, how its head turned to regard him and the yellow eyes sparked with recognition.

When he glanced at Luz, he saw her watching him, her eyes bright, narrowed. *You saw that, too,* her eyes said.

Hastily she replaced the jaguar on the shelf, and as Hank stared at it, he saw that it was just a ceramic figurine, precisely painted and smooth as glass.

Swallowing, he tried to think of something normal to say, some comment on the weather—how warm it was getting.

But all he croaked out was, "Ashes, huh?"

Nodding, Luz pushed a bolt of hair behind her ears. She still wore tiny gold globes in her pierced lobes. "My mother did that. Yes, Catholics don't, but Indians do. She wanted me to have a piece of him, I guess."

Hank slid off his stool, approached, drawn, really, to her side. She smelled like fields of grass and a hint of carbolic.

"How did you learn to do that?" A strange thought travelled through his mind. "Did Susan show you?"

"Actually, no. Actually I taught her." Gazing up at him, Luz's cheeks flushed slightly, and she kept his gaze as she ran her finger back and forth along the stained table top. "My mother uses ashes. She paints with them, mixed in her colors. I just thought, well, why not mix them in the glaze? Susan suggested a slow, low fire; it worked perfectly the first time. We made quite a team."

It was macabre, ghoulish, but Hank couldn't really care about that, standing so close to Luz for the first time in three years. He tried to imagine Susan's face when Luz revealed her special formula. But all he could see was Luz, smell her, watch a silver-blue light travel through the strands of her hair.

Before he could stop himself, he slipped his hand around her back, pushed her to him, and kissed her.

She did not resist this time. And she kissed back, deep and hard, her mouth tasting like cloves and marigolds. He felt the mounds of her breasts against him and grew hard. They didn't hear the car, or the doors slamming, until Hank saw a movement in the doorway, and Susan's face, watching.

Twenty-One

SUSAN VANISHED from the window the moment Hank saw her and pushed apart from Luz, who seemed to know what had happened, because she turned back to the table and reached for the rooster.

Coming into the doorway, Susan's face was clear, expectant, almost self-satisfied. Hank's heart tumbled inside him, an acrobat of conflicts as he watched her, seeking a plan; what should he do, what should he say?

Susan wore a navy hat with two white feathers like dove-wings, her blazing orange hair neatly coiffed in big rolls down her shoulders. In a pert navy suit, a glazed brooch in the lapel, she was someone else, a business woman or a church lady.

The few seconds of voiceless silence siphoned away Hank's breath. He watched Luz as she calmly sat down at the work table and picked up a pencil.

"Oh, Susan, you're back," Luz said, holding her pencil in the air. "How is Joseph?"

"A walking miracle," came his voice from outside, out of sight. "Ready to sit the fuck down."

Grimacing, Susan almost smiled. Her mood was strange,

Hank thought. She didn't look as if she was going to spiral into a jealous rage, or turn and stomp away.

"We're starving," she said finally, gazing at Hank. "Lunch?"

"Sounds great," Luz said, and, as if this were a cue in a play, Luz got up and followed Susan out the door. Hank sat frozen for a moment, completely at sea about what just happened. His only thin veil of protection was that Susan wasn't, at least at the moment, going to make a scene about what she had seen.

That afternoon began a strange and pleasing phase in Hank's life that he couldn't have predicted or completely understood.

The world shifted as spring drew its subtle breath over Southern California. Aside from the usual narcissus and lilacs spreading a dizzying floral haze over everything, bougainvillea and bird-of-paradise colored the landscape with garish bright hues. Luz's glazes took these colors and intensified them. Hank's routine shifted. He came to see Susan on Tuesdays, Luz on Fridays, and the entire trio on weekends. Susan always with one excuse or another, was never there on the Fridays, Luz's day off at the hospital and her studio day at Susan's. Joseph defied the odds and by the end of the week he was walking with two canes. He was persuaded somehow, by his sister, to leave the Fridays to Luz and Hank.

Mostly, Hank just watched Luz work and they talked. There was never a lag in the conversation. Hank spoke more words about the events of his life, and the world, in one afternoon with Luz than he did in an entire year at home. He gathered, after three weeks of this, that Luz knew far more about him than he knew about her.

But Susan accepted him into her bed, lips, and body. In

fact, lovemaking with Susan was more intense, focused, and driven, than he had ever known. Reveling in this, he tried to keep his mind divided in two, not thinking about Luz, who was never there on Tuesdays.

It was a sweet, fine time in Hank's life. But as all sweet times, fine or not, this one too must come to an end.

Hank rode home on a warm Friday night, leaving Susan's house after a barbecue on the patio, attended by the Chagalls and Luz and Hank and an army of brightly glazed animals ringing the bricks—an audience prepared by Luz who laid them out in a dress circle. They had wine, and Hank, not generally one to drink spirits, got a little drunk.

After, remembering, as he rode home how he couldn't keep his eyes off Luz, a sense of guilt tugged at Hank. He had, he knew, practically ignored Susan. He had no idea how she felt about his attention to Luz, especially when he danced with Luz to a crazy song Joseph was singing in a well-trained tenor voice, because he had not looked at Susan the entire evening. Except when he kissed her good-by, chastely on the cheek. Her eyes were in shadow, her mouth inexplicable.

To ease his thoughts, and to delay having to go home to a house of pain, and to increase his mileage, he decided to take the very long way around through Hollywood, do a hill-climb up to Sunset, then home. He would not have attempted such a thing if he had not been a little drunk, but it was Friday night and warm and spring brought people out of their houses and into the streets; odors of grilled beef and music spilled from yards.

Hollywood Boulevard was a forest of neon, a raging river of automobiles and people flowing back and forth between bars and bistros and movie houses. On his bike Hank dodged cars and wove between people on the sidewalks. Eateries poured their fragrances into the street; music of a different type, fervent, brassy, loud, echoed from the clubs.

Coincidence was a given in Hank's life, especially lately. Taking a route he rarely took, on a Friday night, it was inevitable that he would see someone he knew.

It was the flash of silver hair, shifting blue to red in neon glow that caught his eye, on a girl exiting a club. Instantly Hank thought it was Connie, out for a night on the town; the girl looked his way and stared, as if she knew this was Hank, crazy enough to be out on a bicycle at night on Sunset.

But as he slowed, ready to hop off and say hi, he saw that she wasn't Connie at all, but he did recognize the man with her. Kenneth Cleveland reached for the girl, pulled her back to him, and tucked his arm into hers. Her features too sharp, eyes layered thickly with mascara, the girl tucked her head—she was taller than Dad—and kissed his forehead. Her movement jiggled his glasses, and as he righted them he smiled at her in way of most men other that his father. As Hank glided past, staring, Dad and the girl crawled into a waiting taxi.

A honk directly behind Hank startled him, he looked around, a car pushed past, the passenger glaring at him, and when Hank glanced back, the taxi was gone, melding with the flow of traffic into the mild, nervous night.

Hank arrived home just after midnight, having narrowly missed fatality at the wheels of two different drunken drivers on Sunset. Weary from the long ride and the after-effects of alcohol, he coasted into the garage and carelessly rested the Raleigh against the Peugeot.

He didn't want to go inside yet. The night was velvet; the city lay scattered on its hem. Taking the time to get a glass of water in the dark and vacant kitchen, he went back out to the pool.

Waves disturbed the surface, and it was not vacant.

At first he thought Mom was floating on her back, resting on the bed of water, watching the sky. But as he circled the pool's edge to the deep end, he saw that instead she was watching the pool bottom.

Tearing at his shoes, Hank managed to fling one off, but in his panic, gave up and jumped in. Reaching her in seconds that seemed to be ages of precious time, he seized her hair and lifted her face out of the water.

Eyes closed, mouth open, cheeks and lips blue from lack of oxygen. He struggled with her body; it dragged against the water, as if it didn't want to leave its wet comfort. Prudently, thinking clearly as his heart and stomach lurched with horror, he shoved his way to the shallows, realizing it would be far easier to get her out of the pool from there.

His shouts roused Joaquin, who scrambled from the kitchen door, hastily fumbling with his robe. When he got close enough, Joaquin gripped Mom's shoulders and arms, and between the two of them, they hauled her onto the brick.

Lights came on in the houses, the neighbors, and in moments, as Hank shivered and tried to catch the air, any air around him, Joaquin administered respiratory aid in a very professional manner.

Mom's face waxy still, limp and heavy. Naked. Dead.

Hank felt hands on his arms, a towel. Turning, he saw Carl, his face stiff with shock, the faint smell of alcohol enveloping them both. "I called the hospital."

Standing for shivering moments, while all they could hear in the overwhelming silence was Joaquin grunting and the swish and slap of Mom's arms as he raised them and lowered them, and pressed on her back.

Eternity went through Hank's mind in a moment of standstill time, before he heard what he had not expected to ever hear again. Mom coughed, loudly, and again, her voice rasping and pained. Her right arm moved, hand to her face, she brought her knees up and rolled onto her side, retching. A clear puddle of pool water spooled from her mouth and nose.

Hank stood rooted, unbelieving, rolling back the footage in his head. He had just come home in time to save his mother's life. Any delay of even a few minutes, and she would be dead.

Carl kicked a patio table out of the way, knelt, picked Mom up as if she were a child, and carried her toward the French doors. Joaquin, shaking himself out of his shocked relief, ran to open them, and Hank trailed them inside.

Laying her on the sofa, Carl wrapped her in blankets carried in by Joaquin.

"Where is Dad?" Carl sat beside Mom, rubbing her face and hands. They looked, to Hank, the same color as that of the porcelain marquess. "Is he home?"

"I don't think so." Hank pulled his towel close as a shiver raced across his shoulders. "I was just getting home. If I hadn't felt like staying outside, and gone out to the pool—"

Carl rubbed the bags under his eyes, his craggy dimples dark and deep, his lips pale. He was drunk again, Hank knew, had been pretty continually since the break-up. But sober now, and behaving in a quite soldierly and disciplined way in this time of need. Hank was impressed.

Mom breathed, and coughed, and breathed. She didn't open her eyes, she said nothing. The brothers eyed each other, questions unasked, waiting for later.

Twenty-Two

MOM WOULD BE OK, they said. She needed rest. She was in an oxygen tent. She had pneumonia. She will be just fine. Please, go home now.

Hank and Carl sat in the living room as the day raised its paw and swiped at the night. Carl pointed his glass at the marquess. "You see, she didn't fall. That means Mom won't die."

They hadn't turned on any lights, just sat in the pale light from the French doors, where the city sat and the pool waited for its next victim. Now it was morning. Saturday morning.

Nearly asleep, Hank raised his head from the back of the couch, recrossed his ankles on the coffee table. Every time he dozed off, Hank was jumping into the pool again, or falling in, or diving to the bottom to pick up the little marquess from where she lay on the pool floor.

"It's so weird without her here." Carl rubbed his glass across his forehead. It was empty, but he made no move to get up to refill it, Hank was glad to see. Hank wondered if Carl were referring to Mom or to Connie but he didn't ask.

Sitting up, Carl reached over to touch Hank's foot. "Hey, I've been meaning to ask, how come you knew Dad wasn't home?"

They had spoken about everything else: Hank's just making it home in time and his heroism. Carl taking control of the situation, directing the doctor to Mom on the couch, explaining calmly what happened. Even comforting Joaquin, who was visibly shaken, crossing himself, muttering prayers neither of them had ever heard him say before.

Leaning his head on his hand, wishing Carl would fall asleep so he could, Hank told him what he had seen down in Hollywood. The entire incident had flicked through his mind on and off as he tried to puzzle out what happened and why.

"Oh, yeah. He was with her again," Carl said, sighing, waving his glass in the air. "I've known about that for a while. Con told me." He shook his head, rubbed the sides of his mouth as if it tasted bad, and Hank could believe that by now they both did not smell like fresh flowers.

Carl said, "Con knows everything. That's been going on for a month or so. She's his latest. Was she young? Blond?"

Hank nodded. "Young, blond, and at first I thought she was Connie. But she wasn't pretty enough."

"No one is." Carl upended his glass; nothing came out. Sitting up, Hank took it away from him. Shrugging, Carl leaned his head back on the couch, and so did Hank. They were, he thought, bookends.

Carl sighed. "Think about that, young Hank. Dad likes them young and looking like his daughter. Think there's a connection?"

Under ordinary circumstance, unexhausted and clear of mind, Hank would have become annoyed, but now he thought about his dad having the hots for his own daughter.

"I don't think so. Mom was young and blond once. She's still blond, but she's no longer young."

"Yeah, you're probably right." Carl coughed, curled his hands behind his head. Hank stared at him. Carl accepted Hank's opinion? Carl continued. "But it's hard. You of all people know how hard it was, hard it is, with someone as pretty and sexy as Connie around."

Discomfort curled around Hank's chest. This seemed to be, to Hank, Carl's confessional time, and Father Hank was present and listening. He really didn't want to hear it.

"You know, that one time you walked in on us was the only time. And don't think for a minute that anyone got taken advantage of. It was Connie's idea. She was curious, and I sure had the hots for her."

Sitting up, Hank folded his hands in front of him, pulled his feet off the table. His head throbbed and a curious ringing in his ears strengthened, and Carl's voice tuned in and out like a bad radio signal.

"And now, she wants nothing to do with me." Carl's voice faltered, or maybe it was the ringing or was it singing, in Hank's ears. He worried that Carl was going to cry.

After a moment, Carl continued, his voice steady again. "I didn't do anything to that girl, you know. I know no one believes me. We went to the hotel room sure, and I thought we were going to just drink and party and probably end up in the bed together, but she chickened out, cooled off. I was a gentleman. I'm always a gentleman. If the girl doesn't want it ...."

He blathered on, voice fading, winding up high and then slow, like a warped tape or film. Hank needed sleep. He could, any minute, he told himself, get up and leave Carl to his wallow. But he didn't think he had the strength, as if Carl's voice were keeping him pinned to the sofa like a butterfly in a glass specimen case.

The sound of a car pulling up saved him. Carl stopped talking. They waited in the semi-dark to see who it was, the philandering Dad or the all-night-party girl Connie. Connie won out. They could hear the sound of her heels thumping in the vestibule, the clank of her purse being deposited on the hallway table, a sigh, and two more heavy clunks as she kicked off her shoes.

When she came through into the living room, she was perfectly silent, betrayed by a sharp intake of breath when she saw them on the couch.

"What happened?" she snapped, her voice strained and a little hoarse. "You two camping out together like we used to do as kids in the backyard?"

She flopped down in the chair Hank generally occupied, near the open French doors. "Is there any coffee?"

"Joaquin isn't up yet. It's Saturday." Hank couldn't keep the anger out of his voice. He saw, in the dimness, Connie tilt her head.

"You're up. Carl's up. He knows how to make coffee."

To his credit, Carl said nothing. Hank wondered if he had passed out.

"Connie, listen. There was an accident." Hank knew he sounded tired, his voice muted as if he were speaking underwater.

Sitting up, Connie gripped the arms of her chair.

"What?"

Hank explained and Connie got to her feet, paced back and forth in her stockings as he told the story. She wore a blue cocktail dress, tight and form-seeking and rainbow-sleek. Peeling off a pair of short blue gloves she threw them on the couch next to Carl.

"Oh my God, oh my God." Connie's hands were fists at

her sides as she stalked back and forth like a soldier doing turns for punishment.

"She's going to be all right, the doctor said."

"Why? Why would she do it?"

Carl was silent, eyes closed. He made no movement. Shifting forward, Hank thought about getting up, changed his mind. He had asked himself the question over and over. He and Carl had spoken, asked, pondered, tried to come up with reasons.

Did Mom lose her balance and fall? Was she drunk? Or did she do it on purpose? And if so, why? Carl thought it was because of Dad's infidelity. Hank knew a more pure reason, but he said nothing of it. Not yet.

"Is Dad at the hospital?"

Hank didn't answer, and neither did Carl. Connie stopped pacing. "Oh."

Hank's role as the keeper of the family secrets seemed to be compromised. It was evident that he was the only one who didn't know Dad had girlfriends, but he realized he should have known. And he could, at least, pretend he did know.

Reassuring Connie that Mom was recovering and Connie didn't need to go to the hospital, Hank sank back down on the sofa, and thought he heard her tread away, softly, like leaves, to the French doors, to the pool.

And when he woke up several hours later on the couch, Carl was gone, and sitting up, Hank could see Connie curled in one of the lounge chairs beside the pool. Someone had put a blanket over her.

Twenty-Three

SUSAN LEANED against the headboard, hair threading across her shoulders like a skein of wool upset by a cat. She held a glass of water. Hank had just slid off her, pulling from her, cold shock cycling through him.

"I don't know, Hank. She said someone was sick at home. She's taken some days off from the hospital to take care of whoever it is."

He had felt, the last two days while Mom was in the hospital, that his ribcage was made of paper maché, and would break and crack any time if anyone put too much pressure on it. And then there was the difficulty with his hearing, which seemed to be getting worse. But he had heard Susan, and he knew with certainty that he could not stand not to see Luz this Friday.

Susan's attitude confused and frightened him. She didn't seem to care, either way, about his passion for Luz. He knew this couldn't last, that this wasn't normal, that any other woman would throw jealous fits. But neither Susan nor Luz seemed to care about the way they shared Hank, as if they had made a pact.

"But who is it? Her mother?"

Susan dipped her fingers in the water, put them in her mouth. "She didn't say, and I didn't pry."

Sitting up, Hank ran his fingers through his hair. He felt as if he were on a tightrope between two sky-scrapers and couldn't decide, or remember, which way to go. Before Susan, before this winter, he had a plan, of sorts, to live and home and ride his bicycle, maybe sign up for some races. But now, he felt like he had entered a race and no one had told him the route.

"I don't see what you are so worried about. She'll be back next week."

But he didn't believe it. He spent time, before leaving Susan's, in the studio, petting her growing zoo. The raven Luz had given him occupied a place of prominence on his desk, centered in the middle of his blotter, which he never used. It was like, he thought, having Luz's father, Julio De Mar in the room with him.

When Friday came, word was Mom would be coming home from the hospital soon, likely this weekend. When Carl told him what happened, Dad was appropriately devastated; Carl said uncomfortably that Dad started to cry. Dad went to the hospital every day, and was spending every night at home.

Hank felt a deep round hole open up inside him. He almost felt like weeping, but stifled it, kicking himself. Get a grip, man. Pull it together. He wondered if this was what Joseph went through when he was in a battle, bullets trying to kill him, seeing his buddy's heads blown open and pieces of brain ending up in his lap. Hank hadn't heard the end of the story Joseph started. In fact, most of the day when Hank was there, Joseph was asleep, having been, Susan admitted, up all night and out of the house. She did not agree to imagine what he was up to.

That Friday, without Luz, Hank wandered through the house. No one liked to swim since Mom's accident, so he walked around the pool and back inside a few times. No one was home. Carl, after his drunken confession after Mom's accident, seemed to be avoiding Hank. Dad was at the hospital, and Connie—he never knew Connie's schedule any more. But today, as he stalked around, unable to lie down or sit down or even tune the Peugeot, Connie showed up.

Hank encountered her sitting in the kitchen, a glass of Coke in front of her, smoking a cigarette and flipping through Variety. Joaquin was at the market, and Hank, seeing Connie there, almost turned around.

"Wait a minute, Hanky boy." Connie blew smoke, squinted as it travelled across her face. "What are you doing home? I thought you had a standing appointment every Friday afternoon."

Sighing sharply, Hank felt a spike in his irritation. "You are my social secretary then? Keeping track of me?"

Giving him a curious sideways look, Connie raised one eyebrow. She was growing her roots out, the golden straw color showing as the platinum hung onto the strands. She wore a swim suit under a shiny robe, maroon, spotted with white. "Hank, it is my sworn duty to keep track of everything, including my little brother."

"What the fuck do you know about me, anyway?"

Now both eyebrows rose in amazement. Hank wished he had met her with his habitual silence, but it was too late now and he felt a little bad about it. The damage had been done. Putting down her paper and turning in her chair, she appraised him.

"Perhaps it is time, dear son, to speak of your life, and how

I can help you get your freaking act together." She gave him a smile, eyes bright, head turned at an angle as if she was in front of the camera. "For one. I know where you go every Friday afternoon. And I know who you see."

The counter behind Hank, on which he leaned, arms folded, itchy and breathless, went colder. The room was hot actually, the back door open to capture any unwary breeze from the ocean.

"Hank," Connie's voice went sweet, coddling. "It's OK. I think it's really cool, actually, to use the vernacular of my betters. But you know what. Me knowing? I can help you out. Today, especially. So what's the issue?"

"You don't know anything about what I do on Fridays."

"Oh, don't I? Well, for one thing, you get on your bike and you ride down to Venice. I know because I followed you a few weeks ago." Connie picked up her Coke, swirled it, but didn't take a drink. "I think, actually, it was before you got sick. I saw the pretty lady, Miss Chagall, right? She is gorgeous, in a bohemian kind of way."

He should have known. He was supposed to know everything. But he had to grudgingly admire Connie's talent for observation.

As if she read his mind, Connie added. "I am an actress, after all. My entire life is research, observing the human condition. I have studied you a long time, my Hank."

Hank's heart ticked up a beat, and he thought he might take the bait, although he knew he couldn't quite trust her. "So what is this thing you can do for me?"

Shifting to face him, crossing her legs, Connie picked up a pencil and examined it, in a way, Hank thought, very like Mom.

"I know where Luz lives."

This data caused Hank's heart to thunder, and sweat broke out on his palms and under his arms. The thought of going to Luz's house terrified and excited him at the same time, in the same manner when he was setting out on a century ride.

Surprisingly, it did not take Connie very long to change her clothes; Hank thought she had just thrown on a skirt and blouse over her bikini. In sandals, she clacked down the stairs, where he waited, having put on a fresh shirt. He wanted to stop for flowers, but he was damned if he was going to let Connie see him doing anything like that.

Hank drove. His hands kept leaving damp marks on the wheel of the coupe Connie had bought, needing a car, she argued with Dad, because the studio was no longer coming for them, so she could get to restaurants and parties where she was making a lot of new friends and potentially finding new jobs. Sitting next to him, smoking Connie seemed, since the break-up of the act, calmer, more reasonable, less likely to fly into a rage.

"So how is it you know where she lives?" Hank kept his eyes on the road, and thought he sounded off-hand, casual.

Making a smoke ring, or trying too—they both had their windows open—Connie looked out the window at expanses of lawns greening with spring rain, bordered with color. The air was fresh and Easter-like.

"I've known a long time. It was back when she used to come over. You would sneak her into the house."

I did? How come I don't remember any of it? He knew she glanced at him, but he kept his gaze ahead.

She continued, "So one day Carl and I followed her home. We were bored, you know. We'd never seen you with the same girl that often. In fact," she snorted, coughed, and stubbed out her smoke in the ashtray. "We thought you were a fag, because you are so pretty. So we were glad to discover differently."

This was not news to Hank. And at this point he no longer cared. But he was disappointed. More memories of Luz came crowding in, spindling him with nerves because there was so much he had somehow forgotten. Walking Luz to Sunset, get her a cab—which she didn't like, but if she stayed too long, she had to get home quickly so her parents wouldn't be suspicious. They held hands sometimes. She walked with a pleasing sway, and smelled of chocolate and mango. The first time they ever kissed was that last day, in Hank's room. It was the last day, because a wall came up in his mind and he couldn't remember anything else.

He felt himself growing hard, remembering that kiss, and he hoped Connie wouldn't notice anything. But she was turned away, her elbow on the car door, drumming her fingers on the side panel to the music on the radio. During the pauses, they would hear their father's voice exclaiming the virtues of soap or whiskey.

Connie directed him through Hollywood, southeast into downtown, and then full east, to streets lined with *bodegas* and *panaderias*. Brightly colored garish marquees and odors of tortillas. Women with multiple children in tow crowded the sidewalks, carrying brightly colored bags of groceries.

Leaving the packed traffic of battered vehicles, Connie directed Hank into a quiet avenue lined with small oaks, the same rusty cars parked at odd angles, children kicking balls in the middle of the road. The houses were stucco, like Susan's, aproned by tidy gardens. They travelled the street for four long blocks, until Connie, peering out the window to her right, as if seeking the place of memory, told him to stop.

"There. Pull over into that parking place up there."

Hank did so, and Connie turned toward him. "Back there, the yellow one."

The yellow one was a small bungalow tucked between similar others, one brown, one white. But the yellow one, Hank could see, could be none other than Luz's and her mother's, because it was the most beautiful house on the block.

There was no lawn, but a garden of riotous color; the steps rose to an arch of pale pink roses, leafing out, blooming earlier here than anywhere else. Blue trim around the windows and a blue door. Brilliantly striped curtains, one of them fluttering through the opening. It was hotter here than in Westwood, farther from the sea's cooling breath.

Children called and screamed—there was a school down the block. The air smelled fresh and floral. Connie was looking at him.

"Well, aren't you going in?"

Hank couldn't move. He was afraid of what it might do to Luz to see him on her porch, invading her sanctuary. She had never invited him here, as if she were ashamed, but he didn't see what she had to be ashamed of. The neighborhood was nice, delightful, in fact, warmer and more alive than Susan's edgy Venice street.

"Go on. You wanted to see her today. Today is your day. Go on!" Connie's voice was soft, urging. She had hidden her perpetual sardonic smirk under a sisterly smile. She was a very good actress, he thought, opening the car door.

Connie's snicked open just after. "I'm coming too. Moral support and all that."

"No. I don't need any of that." Hank was on the sidewalk. He needed to do this alone. He needed to cut himself away from her.

Shrugging, Connie nodded. "I'll just wait on the sidewalk. Luz's mother might feel better seeing your older sister is with you."

Giving her a rolled-eye look, Hank turned away and started up the steps. His heart thundered, pounded, but he kept going.

At the top of the steps a little garden opened up on either side of the walk. A child's tricycle sat near the steps. Hank climbed onto the porch, looked back to see Connie standing on the sidewalk, holding her pocketbook in front of her. She had even put on gloves. She gazed at him through green sunglasses and nodded.

Turning back to the door, Hank lifted his hand to knock, and it opened.

He stared into a dark, cool room. No one stood in the doorway, not Luz or her mother, whom Hank had never met. A dizzying wave went through him—*the magic of Luz, a door opening by itself.*

Then he heard a sniffle, a cough, and it came from somewhere lower, and as he looked down he saw a small child, about three maybe, clinging to the doorknob.

He was a pretty boy with black curly hair, eyes the color of licorice and framed by lashes miles long. His cheeks were flushed red and he gazed up at Hank, eyes round with curiosity.

Footsteps behind the boy, the sharp quick voice of Luz. "Diego! What are you doing out of bed?"

She swept into view, hair pulled back from her head, wearing a cotton shift and an apron. Her eyes were for the boy, and she swept him up, then started, almost tripped, when she saw Hank in the doorway.

Twenty-Four

"*O DIOS MIO.*" Her eyes widened; she gripped the little boy, staring at Hank. He couldn't read her face, he faltered, wanted to run. But Connie was coming up the steps behind him.

Then a smile, uncertain, but real, brought up the corners of Luz's mouth. Hearing Connie she frowned, peered out through the open door to see who it was.

"Oh, Hank. Is that your sister? Won't you both come in?"

"Thanks, Miss del Mar." Connie swept past Hank as Luz pulled the door open wider. "I could sure use a glass of water. Hot isn't it?" Her voice faded as she disappeared into the house.

Hank stood frozen, seeking any clue from Luz. The little boy, Diego, gazed at him, fingers in his mouth. Shaking her head, she smiled again, and without a word, tilted her head toward the room, inviting him in.

The room was dark, cool, one window open for a breeze. A braid rug, heavy wooden furniture; bright colors flowed over the walls, with paintings of bright, magical beings, flying and playing musical instruments. An array of photos on a white-painted table, and Hank recognized Julio del Mar, sitting stiffly beside his wife.

So I did meet him. Where, and when?

And there she stood in the kitchen doorway, fragrance of oranges and spices circling around her, a small woman; had to be Luz's mother Rosa.

She was tiny, a little round in the middle, nose prominent, eyes narrow and piercing, lips parted in surprise. She wore a simple cotton dress, much like Luz's, and a woven apron. But her hair was the surprise, made Hank stop and stare. Her hair was perfectly white, strung in two braids, one draping her shoulder, the other disappearing down her back. Her face looked young, eyebrows thick and black. Wiping her hands, she waited, looking at her daughter for the introductions.

Luz made them, and Hank stumbled forward, holding out his hand. A silence followed, as Mrs. del Mar looked him up and down. He quailed, waiting, keeping his hand before her, ready. Even Connie, standing beside the sofa under a painting of a white bird in a sapphire sky, kept her mouth shut.

Mrs. del Mar stared up at him, closed her mouth, sighed. Then, Hank watched a keen admiration shift the muscles of her face, and the barest wisp of a smile. She took his hand and shook.

"*Esse chico, cara mia*." She said. "Please, sit down. I will bring a tea."

"Oh, Mrs. del Mar, please don't go to any trouble." Connie leaned forward, gave Rosa a brilliant smile.

"*No, no problema, señorita*. No trouble at all." Her English, unlike Luz's, was heavily accented, but clean and good.

Sitting down, Connie crossed her legs. Hank stayed near the kitchen doorway; behind him was a dining table littered with medical books, papers, a typewriter. A half-drunk cup of coffee.

"What a beautiful little boy," Connie said slowly, a breath of awe in her voice. Hank turned to look at his sister. Her face was rapt almost, as she gazed at Diego. Hank had never seen her look that way before, at least not in a very long time.

"How old?"

"Diego is almost three." Luz's smile was strained, but Hank thought that it was because she was talking to a well-known entertainer sitting in her living room. "My little brother. A late one, you know, just before my father passed away."

Connie nodded in a jerky way, and murmured condolences. But she wouldn't take her eyes off the boy, who gazed back at her, solemn, unmoving, his head against Luz's shoulder.

Luz glanced at Hank, who gripped the table behind him. "He's been sick. I was so worried, you know, with polio going around. I stayed home to take care of him. He's getting better, but he's not out of the woods yet." Muttering something in Spanish to the boy, who did seem tired, she excused herself and left the room, vanishing through a doorway.

Connie sat still as stone, her gloved hands folded in her lap. Hank's chest opened, relaxed, as if his heart had liquefied and pooled in his stomach. Here he stood in her house, met her mother, and her mother, Rosa, seemed to approve of him.

Hank could hear Luz singing to Diego in a back bedroom. He could hear Rosa moving in the kitchen amid the clink of plates and silverware, the rising whistle of the teakettle. He could, he though, just stay here. Never, ever go home.

"Let's get out of here." Connie rose, skirted the coffee table, grabbed Hank's arm. He pulled against her and she looked at him, her eyes rimmed with tears, her face flushed with fear. "Please, Hank, I'm losing it. Please, get me out of here."

"But let me at least tell them we are going—"

"No. No!" She ran to the door, opened it. Hank waited, torn, the sounds of the women in the house, the coolness.

"*Hank!*"

Following Connie down the steps, Hank stopped on the sidewalk, looked up at the house. The windows remained vacant; no one came out onto the porch.

Hands shaking, Connie had a cigarette going by the time he got into the car. But he didn't start the motor. He turned to look at her.

"OK, I'm a shit. But I couldn't. Hank, I couldn't." She pressed her hands to her eyes, the cigarette burning between two fingers.

"What? They invited us in." Heat filled him and he pounded the back of the seat. Connie dropped her hands and stared at him.

"I wanted to stay."

Her eyes narrowed. "Then stay. I can drive myself home." Pushing open the door, she scrambled to get out of the car. Hank understood the mood she was in, although he didn't know what had triggered it.

"Forget it. You'll get yourself killed."

Connie sat, two feet on the curb. Pulling them in, she sat stiffly, picking bits of tobacco off her lips. Hank started the motor, anger flooding him, intense and sharp.

"What the fuck is the matter with you?"

Lifting her chin, Connie stared at the visor, pulled it down, flipped it back up. But before she could speak, Luz appeared in the window beside her.

"You're not leaving?" Luz was looking across Connie at Hank, pure fear on her face, almost desperate.

Hank stared at her, wanted to flow through the car somehow and appear at her side, hold her, brush her with kisses. But he couldn't, as Connie inhaled sharply, impatiently between them.

"Connie's not feeling well. I've got to get her home. Tell your mom I'm sorry."

"Oh." It was clear Luz didn't believe him. She didn't even look at Connie, but kept her gaze on Hank for a moment, and they looked at each other across a great gulf. Then Luz stepped back, and Hank drove away.

He was going to drop Connie off, then go back. Connie seemed to calm down by the time they arrived at home. They hadn't spoken a word since they left Luz's house until they were in the driveway at home.

"That little boy," Connie said, brushing ash off her skirt. "He was sure cute, wasn't he?"

"If you thought he was so cute why did you drag me out of there?

Connie looked at him, apologized. "I just had a sort of panic attack I guess. You know me. It happens sometimes. Don't be mad."

But Hank was mad; he pushed open the car door and left her, walked through the kitchen, said nothing to Joaquin, who stood at the open door Frigidaire.

Joaquin said, not looking up. "You think I have nothing better to do than answer the telephone all day?"

"Why? Who called?" Hank felt like a spear had been caught under his ribs. He stood, wondering whether to eat or puke.

"You all fly around like a flock of frightened pigeons when *Señora* Cleveland isn't here." Joaquin slammed the Frigidaire door; held a bunch of carrots by their green feathery tops as he would a chicken he was going to gut.

He muttered something in Spanish that Hank couldn't quite make out. Then, in English, "She talks and you fall under the spell of her words. She's *la bruja,* the old priestess. She makes people forget what they should know, the way she talks."

Hank stood near the table, as Joaquin picked up his big chef's knife and began to sever the carrots. Little bits flew up like orange confetti. Hank didn't remember seeing Joaquin this annoyed before.

A flush covering his cheeks, Joaquin gestured with his blade. "You need to stop listening all the time and remember and do what you are supposed to do."

"What are you talking about?" Hank's heart clawed at his ribs. For a moment, he thought he was going to fall over.

Joaquin stopped chopping. Hank thought maybe an explanation was coming, but instead Joaquin fished a big onion out of the basket and executed it with a huge swipe of the blade.

"Go read your messages. I have to get the dinner."

They were piled beside the phone and there were several. Sorting out the ones for Connie and Carl, Hank found his: one from the hospital, saying his mother had asked for him specifically to come see her before she came home tomorrow. The other from Joseph Chagall, asking for a call back. *Urgent.*

As Hank stared at the messages written in Joaquin's neat script, the writing getting quicker and careless as the phone kept ringing, Connie walked past, looked at him, shoes in hand, then started up the stairs. He turned his back, his hand on the phone.

Carl appeared in the archway to the living room, drink in hand. He looked tragically and romantically dissipated, and his eyes followed his sister as she climbed upward.

Hank said, "You've been here all this time? How come you didn't answer the phone? Joaquin is like a mad bull in there."

Carl shrugged. "I guess I fell asleep."

Turning his back on him, Hank dialed Susan's number, if for nothing else, to distract him from his moments seeing Luz. Joseph answered after the first ring. His voice was quick, blurry. He needed to see Hank, he said. He needed Hank to help him with something for Susan, something that he wanted to do for her.

Hank made a half-hearted promise to show up, but Joseph insisted that it be tonight, late—he wanted Hank to pick him up down the block, not at their house, but at the corner. Close to midnight.

Hank started to turn Joseph down, but then thought, what the hell. Hank knew he wouldn't be able to sleep much tonight anyway.

That done, Hank faced Carl. "You need to snap out of it," he snapped, disgusted. "Come with me to the hospital."

Family, Hank thought, as Carl obediently poured the rest of his drink down the bathroom sink, ran a comb through his hair and gargled.

Mom had a private room in the private wing. Dad was there, sitting in her suite. He had been reading to her, and she sat up in bed, against pillows, in a quilted bed jacket. Her hair neatly wrapped in a ribbon, her dark grey-streaked roots showing, Mom looked thinner than ever, but her cheeks held a good color. Flowing past plaid curtains, sun came in through the window. Flowers in varying states of freshness and decay filled vases on the tables and window sill. The room smelled antiseptic and clean; the nurse, far less lovely than Luz, stuck her head in the door and nodded approvingly.

Mom gave Hank and Carl both hugs, something she rarely did any more. Her arms were strong, but very thin. Dad rose from his chair. He wore his reading glasses and a tan polo shirt and slacks; he laid the book down on the bed.

"I'll leave you to it, then," he said in his velvet voice. "Carl, come with me for a second. The nurses want your auto-graph."

Dad closed the door behind himself and Carl after sending a knowing gaze at Mom, and Hank wondered whose idea this visit really was. Mom patted her bed and Hank sat. Si-lence, edged with birdsong and faint voices, movements and bangs and rolling carts of the busy hospital corridor, settled between them.

Waiting, Hank looked at the flowers and cards, and smelled the bitter odor of antiseptics. Mom just looked at him, blue eyes wide and excited. An unpleasant thought in-truded in Hank's mind, wound around like a monkey tail. To confirm it, he watched as Mom reached behind her pillow and brought out a small pad. She picked a pencil from be-hind her ear. Hank had not even noticed how odd it was for a patient to have a pencil behind her ear, but he was so used to seeing Mom that way, he hadn't questioned it.

He stopped her hand, encircled her wrist. "You can't talk at all now?"

Her lips thinned, and she gave her head a short shake. Her eyebrows formed a V of worry. She began scribbling on the pad.

"I don't want the others to know."

"Mom, they have to know. You are coming home tomor-row."

"I need your help. You can talk for me."

190

Putting down the pad, Hank stared at her. He hated to talk. He listened, he didn't speak. People spoke for him, read his mind, said what he was thinking.

And Mom knew what he was thinking. She started scribbling again, a long paragraph, taking minutes and minutes.

"We can do it. You can ask me yes or no questions. You can answer the phone for me. We can play back the Dictaphone. I have recorded hours of words."

Hank sighed and she grabbed his wrist, squeezed, her fingernails digging in. "You have to do this," she mouthed, and he read her lips clearly.

He felt the air go out of the room. He felt his life closing in, as if he were in a box, no—a coffin in the ground, with only a straw to breathe through.

"OK, yes or no questions."

She nodded furiously.

"Did you fall into the pool by accident?"

Her mouth slammed shut and she stared at him, the familiar Mom-calculating-wheels-turning-behind-her-eyes look. Then, to his astonishment, she shook her head.

He blinked, then pressed on. "Were you going to kill yourself?"

Again, she shook her head, and confusion filled him, but he continued on.

"You went into the water on purpose?"

A nod.

"You didn't go in thinking you would drown yourself?"

A shake.

"But when you got into the water, you thought you would do it?"

Hesitation, and then a slow nod, a shrug.

"Did you think of it because you were losing your voice?"

A shrug: *"I don't know."*

Hank could understand that. But he wanted to keep Mom in her corner.

"Did you think of it because Dad is unfaithful?"

She gave him an exasperated look, eyes narrow, lips pulled in. Shook her head rapidly.

"You've known about all his girlfriends?"

A nod, a shrug. *"Yes I've known and I don't care."*

This he could not understand. "How could you not care?"

He had broken the rule about a yes or no question, and she picked up her pad. *"It runs in the family. I am beyond caring."*

Hank looked at her. "Grandfather Joel?"

Mom's pencil stayed poised over the pad, as if she were composing something else to add. Hank stared out the window at a row of trees brushed by wind.

Finally she scribbled a short note. *"Get out of here. Come back in a half hour. This will take a while."*

Twenty-Five

EIGHT-THIRTY in a sweet velvet night, and Hank was parked across the street from Susan's house. He was here early because as soon as he dropped Carl off at home, he drove straight back to Luz's house. Luz was not at home, Rosa told him, holding the little boy who still seemed fever-ish and fussy. Luz's house looked warm and cozy inside, candles burning on a blue-painted sideboard on the wall behind Mrs. del Mar. She invited him to come in, but it could be a few hours before Luz got home.

Carl's mood improved greatly after his session with the nurses. They all knew who he was, remembered him from several of his small roles in pictures with Connie. None of them knew or cared about the recent bad publicity. They didn't believe Carl's accuser, either. He spoke about it all the way home, said he was going to make some changes. One of them was television. He was going to see if he could get onto one of the variety shows as a singing act.

Since Mom's 'accident' Dad had spent every day at the hospital with her, made arrangements for a live-in nurse for Mom when she got home, organized Mom's room to perfec-tion, setting up the bed and arranging things. Hank had some odd prayerful notion that the live-in nurse might be Luz, but he knew that would be highly unlikely. It was as if Dad cherished something he had nearly lost, as if he were trying to paste the broken marquis back together.

Mom's note, three pages of it, was folded into Hank's trouser pocket. When she handed it to him, her eyes held a kind of desperate light, needy and yearning. These were not Bess Cleveland's eyes, but the eyes of a wary spirit, *la bruja*, like Joaquin said. Looking frail and weak, but any moment could gut you with a razor talon.

Leaning back into the seat, Hank closed his eyes, remembered Mrs. del Mar in the doorway, looking at Hank in a piercing way, not at all unfriendly.

"You need to listen," she said finally, as Hank was turning to go, having refused her offer to wait for Luz. "There is a voice in your head that is saying the truth."

Hank's ears still rang, buzzed, and he only noticed it when he thought about it. He had heard enough truths for one day, he thought.

"Thank you, Mrs. del Mar. I'll try to listen."

She nodded, but he didn't think she believed him.

On the way to Susan's he stopped for a quick dinner at a diner on Wilshire. The smells of the evening's cooking at the del Mar's ignited a firestorm of hunger, and he devoured one-and-a-half hamburgers, French fries, and a vanilla shake.

He didn't care that Joseph might be miffed at him for showing up way before midnight, but he had to see Luz. Even though her mother had not said where she was, he knew she was here. If secrecy was a must, he would think of something.

A light was on in the studio. A string of Christmas lights ran from the back-porch to the clothesline. Another string adorned the clothesline itself, wound around its pole. An audience of figurines encircled it, as if it were a May Pole. Was it May already?

Crickets pulsed in the grasses. Someone was grilling. Hank crept to the studio window and peeked in.

Two gooseneck lamps illuminated the work bench. Susan and Luz sat before it, heads together, shifting dry ingredients in a wooden bowl. Beyond, he could see their faces reflected in the window, a pair of sirens concocting a potion to lure their personal Odysseus in and keep him captive. Susan's scarf was red, Luz's blue. They both wore khaki work shirts and shorts. Luz's ankles were wrapped around the legs of her stool. She was barefoot. Susan wore tennis shoes without socks.

Glancing up, Luz saw Hank's face reflected in the window before her. But she gave no indication to Susan, just smiled quickly, then turned her attention to Susan, who was saying something about the glaze mixture.

Watching for a while, Hank left them to lie down on one of the lounge chairs to stare at the sky and think about what Rose del Mar might have meant.

What other truth would there be to learn? One he was afraid to ask about. He had his chance, back there in the hospital. He could have asked Mom about the day she threw Luz out of the house and why he couldn't remember that. But he chickened out.

Fingering Mom's pages in his pocket, he wondered if the truth might be there in her written words.

But he must have fallen asleep; a shred of a dream left him with the idea that Susan on one side and Luz on the other had each kissed his cheek. When he came fully aware he was alone on the patio still, flanked by a ceramic donkey on one side of the lounge and a poodle on the other, each perched on little tables that had not been there when he lay down.

Checking his watch, he found he had slept for over two hours. It was nearly midnight. His stomach lurched at the thought of helping Joseph in whatever insane idea he had, but he wanted to follow through, lurch off on some crazy journey with crazy Joseph.

Getting up, he found Luz by herself in the studio, model-ing a human figurine. Going in, he stood close to her.

"You saw me, in the window," he said. He couldn't stop himself from touching a curl of hair covering her ear.

"I saw you asleep on the patio, too." She didn't look up from her work, making a neat cut along what was looking to be the long skirt the figurine was wearing.

"I'm sorry about leaving you like that, earlier." Hank sat on the stool next to her. "I wanted to stay. I went back there, tonight, but your mother told me you were out."

"And you knew where I'd be."

Her voice was teasing, soft. Hank watched her eyelashes move as her eyes followed her hands.

"Diego looked like he was feeling a little better."

Luz nodded, smiling. "I am so relieved."

Sliding onto the stool next to Luz, Hank inhaled the musty odor of wet clay. "I let Joseph talk me into some kind of caper tonight. He says it's a surprise for Susan."

Putting down her knife, Luz looked at him; a wrinkle crossed her forehead. "What kind of caper?"

Hank shrugged. "Beats me. But I thought I'd better tag along to keep him out of trouble.

Luz nodded. "You know he's very unstable."

She could have meant this two ways: Joseph's mind or his ankles. Probably both.

Picking up the knife, she incised another fold in the skirt, "He had a terrible experience in the war. I used to sit with him, and he tried to tell me about it, but always got to the same part in the story and stopped, and it was as if his memory had been erased."

Hank found himself fingering a shard of greenware. The same thing in regards to Luz had happened to him. This had nothing to do with seeing the horrors of war. But how in the world had he forgotten her name for so long or even the memory of her coming to the house? As he looked at the piece in his hand, he saw that it was a small human leg. A memory nudged him, and before it ran away laughing, he saw Luz's face, hair tangled, eyes closed, moving from side to side.

Connie told him Mom had thrown Luz out of the house. Moving closer to her, Hank folded his arms to hide his shaking hands.

"Do you remember when my mother—"

Luz gave him a sideways glance. "I don't like to remember that. It was humiliating."

The room went cold, as if he were standing in a refrigerator. What had happened? What had he done? What had Mom done?

Luz looked at him now, scrutinizing, as if judging. He looked away as she touched his upper arm. Just as he was certain she was going to say something, they both heard a clunking sound at the studio door.

A four-legged stick-creature against the porch light behind him, hunched on his two canes, Joseph stood just outside the studio. Hank wondered how long he had been out there. And he wondered where Susan was. Joseph had, just now, knocked one of his canes against the wall.

"I know she's beautiful," he said, "But you and I have a date, buddy."

Sighing, Hank nodded and gave a smile to Luz, who still looked disturbed. She put down her knife. "I'm going with you."

She brushed past Hank and ran into the house. Hank's heart tumbled around, confused, while Joseph shrugged.

"You can't say no to a nurse."

Twenty-Six

THE SANTA MONICA CEMETERY gates stood open, just as Joseph said they would be, but he directed Hank to park the Caddy on the street. All the way, sliding along quiet streets through Venice and into Santa Monica they said little, Luz in the passenger seat beside Hank, Joseph in the back seat filling the car with cigarette smoke.

A breeze built up, crawled its way up the hillsides, cooled Hank's skin as he got out of the car. Around them, wind stirred palms and pepper trees and sycamores; a paved lane wound up a short rise; mausoleums dotted the hillside, white against the black fabric of the grass.

Hank and Luz glanced at one another as Joseph slid out of the back seat. This was the cemetery where Joseph worked. Perhaps they were coming for something he left here.

They followed Joseph along a winding lane to the corner of a barn-like building, a storage shop discreetly hidden under trailing vines of bougainvillea and jasmine. Except for the breath of the wind in the trees, the cemetery surrounded them in eerie quiet. Joseph led them through an unlocked door into a place of tools and machines, all for the careful interment of the dead and the comfort of the living. Grass clippers, two power lawn mowers, shovels, picks, hoes, rolls of green cloth, folded canopies, folding chairs and in the center of it all, a small tractor.

"C'mon," Joseph said as he picked a key from a wall of keys. "I need you to open the doors for me."

"Joseph, what's up?" Worry gnawed at Hank. Joseph might have worked here, but that didn't give him the right to break into the workshop in the middle of the night.

Joseph hoisted himself onto the tractor seat, saying, "I told you. This is for Susan. She's put up with me all my damn life and I am going to repay her big time."

With that the tractor coughed and spit and began to growl and move forward, barely in time for Luz and Hank to get the garage doors open. Joseph drove through the parking lot, and down the winding drive, Luz and Hank running behind him.

The sound of the tractor echoed across the level graveyard and into the surrounding neighborhood. Hank prayed no one would be curious enough about the sound of a motor grumbling through the cemetery to call the police. Like a red-haired pasha on his royal elephant, Joseph bounced on the seat, driving with purpose, at the old machine's highest speed.

By the time Hank caught up with Joseph he had somehow climbed down off the tractor in front of a starkly white mausoleum. Flanking the door were twin figures, holding identical ewers from which flowed marble rivers. These conjoined over the entry archway into Latin words that Hank did not understand. Behind him Luz stood, catching her breath.

"Hank, help me up here." Joseph was on the top step, a pry bar in his hand.

Why would this door be locked, Hank wondered, if the gate to the cemetery was open? Would the families have keys to let them in? Would they have a secret password, like "sesame", to open the doors?

"I don't think we should break in here." Hank took the pry bar from Joseph, who offered it to him. Luz stood warily at the base of the steps, looking around as if on guard.

"Yes, we should. Go on, Hank my lad, you're stronger than me."

Hank shook his head, and Joseph pushed his shoulder.

He said, "If you don't help me, and soon, we *will* get arrested with the night watchman drives through. Which will be in about 30 minutes."

Cursing under his breath, Hank understood how he had been manipulated. He hesitated only a moment, while Joseph tried to grab the pry bar from him.

"All right, hang on." Hank pushed the bar between the iron doors, and with one quick jerk, the doors sprang open much more easily than he expected, and the force threw him backward. Joseph caught his arm.

"C'mon." He disappeared inside.

An old smell, must and mold, floated out of the black interior. That and a hit of flowers, like an old garden deep in heavy soil. Hank walked in, and saw a flashlight bobbing ahead, dimly reflecting off of vertical ranks of bronze plaques engraved with the names of the dead.

Joseph had stopped before one of the plaques along the left-hand wall, two rows from the bottom. The pry in his hand, he produced from somewhere a hammer, and began pounding on the marble facade, hammer blows ringing.

"Jesus, Joseph, what are you doing?" Hank didn't want to get any closer as bits of rock sprayed onto the floor. Passing him was Luz, moving up behind Joseph, but saying nothing. She scanned the plaques as if reading the names; some of them she even touched.

Joseph didn't answer him, but continued to pound. If any watchman was anywhere close, they would definitely be heard.

"Hank, help me with this."

Hank moved to help, getting down on his knees as Joseph gave one last heave with the hammer. The marble separated from the wall in one piece, and clattered to the floor. It was far heavier than either of them could handle, and Hank pulled Joseph back as the rock fell.

Dust flew up around them, glittering a million minute fire-flies around the flashlight beam. By now, Luz was several feet away, reaching up to touch another plaque. As the stone fell, she started.

Coughing, Joseph reached into the crypt and pulled out a metal container shaped like a genie lamp. "Hi, Dad," he whispered, and a cold finger traveled up Hank's spine.

Seizing Joseph's jacket Hank pulled him to his feet. Luz approached, and between the two of them they herded Joseph out of the crypt, leaving behind hammer, pry and fin-gerprints.

Below in the funeral home lot they saw lights moving. The night watchman had arrived, and would be making his rounds, checking the doors to the mausoleums. But as soon as he saw the open shop doors, he would know something was amiss.

"We can't go that way," Joseph whispered. He indicated the rise behind them. And they stumbled up the grassy hill past headstones and angels and biers glowing murky white against the blackness. They were as quiet as they could be, their breathing ragged. None of them looked back, but they couldn't hear any footsteps behind.

As they reached the top, Hank thought they were home free. An expanse of hillside spread before them, spotted with heavy shadows of thickets of trees for shelter. They wouldn't be caught, he thought.

He coughed as dust filled his throat.

They froze and looked down the hill behind them. The watchman's light swung around in their direction. Luz clapped her hand over her mouth as if to stifle nervous laughter.

Hank didn't care if he or even Joseph got caught, but he worried about Luz. To his relief Joseph grabbed his arm.

"We need to split up. Luz, you circle around to the street, get the car. Go around the block and pick us up on the north side."

Luz shook her head, eyes wide and glinting in the darkness.

"Take this." Joseph thrust the urn at her, and she cradled it in her arms. "Get him out of here safe."

Hank leaned in, kissed her. She gazed at him a minute, then took off running through the forest of gravestones.

Joseph directed Hank as they hobbled toward the north end of the cemetery. He expertly led them to a gap in the fence, one he could, evidently find with his eyes closed, because here darkness seeped into every seam. Crossing the street, they turned up an alley, and at the end, like the coach of Dracula, the black Caddy appeared, and they vanished into the night along with the ashes of the dead.

Part III

DIEGO

Twenty-Seven

THE BROWN EYES in the skull's sockets watched Hank. The bony face was level with his as he lay on the sofa. He could have been looking into the remains of Grandfather Joel, until he remembered where he really was.

Sun filtered through the curtain behind him. A yellow-painted room, a bright rug and a human skull, staring at him inches from his face.

Odors of strong coffee, tortillas. He was not at home, smelling Joaquin's cooking. He was at Luz's house, and the staring, serious skull observing him was a mask, and behind it a little boy. If this was a dream, why bother to wake up?

Diego had wrapped himself in a blanket that someone, probably Luz, had draped over Hank and had fallen to the floor. Covering his eyes, Hank pretended to be in terror, and the little boy giggled.

Voices murmured from the kitchen. Sitting up, Hank stretched, wondering how long he had slept, remembering that today mom was coming home.

Luz appeared in the doorway wearing the same clothes she'd worn the night before, her hair loose. Kneeling beside him, Luz looked at him carefully, almost assessing.

"What a crazy night." Hank sat up. "So Joseph thinks that having his father's ashes will help him deal with whatever happened to him over in Italy?"

Sitting on the couch beside him, Luz leaned back. Hank wondered if she had slept at all. "That's what he thinks. Maybe it will work."

"I don't know if I want to hear the rest of that story."

"Me neither." She looked at him; he wanted to kiss her.

I will never ever leave here. "You were pretty cool out there, under fire. You saved the ashes."

Sitting up, Luz pulled her hair into a pony tail and let it go. Diego climbed into her lap.

"My little skeleton boy," she murmured to him.

Hank's next words burst out, as if pulled from his mouth by Diego's pudgy hands. "Luz, my mother needs a nurse. Would you be my mother's nurse?"

He saw her stiffen. She stopped stroking Diego's head.

Hank sat up. "I mean, she's coming home from the hospital today." He told her everything, Mom's neurological problem, her 'accident' in the pool. Luz listened, but she said nothing, sat as stiffly as a bird trying to evade a predator.

"Please, Luz. You could do it. You would be great." He knew she would do it. She would have to do it. He knew, deep down, she was the perfect choice. No battle-axe or Charles Atlas, but his beautiful Luz.

Luz got up from the couch. She walked into the kitchen without looking back.

Following, Hank was drawn as if by a rope strung from his heart to hers. Through the kitchen windows he saw Rosa del Mar hanging laundry. Her back to Hank Luz picked up a sponge and started worrying a pot with it.

"Luz, listen. It would be the perfect revenge."

Hank could not remember, his head burned trying to remember why he didn't hate his mother for throwing Luz out of the house. He must try to remember that Luz would despise Bess Cleveland with all her heart.

"She would have to rely on you. She couldn't say no. She already said she needs me to be her voice, but what if it was you I brought to her?"

Luz scrubbed, her elbow working up and down. Standing behind her, Hank watched her shoulder muscle bulging. How strong she was. She could lift up the world.

Now he should confess. Now he should tell her he couldn't remember. Now he should ask her what really happened.

"Then we could be together," he said. "I could see you every day."

She still didn't reply. She dipped the pan in the soapy water, started in again. Diego came in carrying a metal truck, ran it across the linoleum, making truck noises.

"Please." Hank touched her hair. *I love you.*

This he remembered. How much he loved her. How could he have forgotten about her?

Luz turned to face him. Her cheeks were red and her eyes angry.

"How can you ask me that? How can you, Hank?"

Dropping the pan in the water, ignoring the splash of water onto the floor, she left the kitchen, walked into the front room and through the front door. Hank trailed her, appalled at how much he had upset her.

Going down the steps she started along the sidewalk, Hank a few feet behind. The morning promised heat. Magnolias lining the street were starting to bloom.

They reached the corner, and Luz turned, walking rapidly.

Hank couldn't believe how fast she could walk. He trotted up, fell in step next to her.

"Luz, I need you to help me with this. Mother needs to see that I love you. That I want to be only with you."

Stopping in the driveway of a tidy bungalow, Luz inhaled sharply. "If you want to be with only me, how come you let her do that to me?" Her fists closed, knuckles white.

Hank could think of nothing to say. He stood, near her. At least she was speaking to him.

"That's what I thought." She started walking and Hank followed. At the next corner she turned right again.

"I was stupid, an idiot. A moron." Hank knew he was all these things. The thought that he let his mother abuse Luz stabbed him like a knife. *Why can't I remember?*

Luz stopped and looked at him. The fury in her face impressed him.

"Is that all you have to say? You disappeared. You made no attempt to contact me. It was as if you completely forgot me, what, an upstart Latina, no better than the maid to have a fling with. Never good enough or white enough to be in the company of one of the great Clevelands."

Tears rimmed her eyes. "My father should never have sent me to that school. He wanted us to be better, he wanted me to be better than what he could do in this country. He was an attorney in Mexico, did you know that? And all he could do here was work as a file clerk for a bunch of *pendejos* who treated him like shit."

Pressing her cheeks she turned her face away. "And all I did was break his heart." Her hands muffled her words, but Hank could hear the strain in her voice. He touched her shoulder, but she shrugged him away, faced him.

Her chin raised, she said. "I can't believe you asked me

that. Your mother is nothing to me. The best thing that ever happened to her is losing her voice."

Hank followed her back to the house. On the porch, where Diego watched through the screen door, Luz stopped him.

"You better go. Your mother needs you."

The door slammed behind her. Hank saw her pick up Diego and take him away, down the dark hallway to where the bedrooms must be.

He found a pack of Connie's cigarettes in the glove compartment, lit one, tasted the smoke. Luz's house didn't look as bright; he could see from across the street where he parked the car, cracks in the stucco and broken tiles on the roof. And inside the charred remains of what had been his heart.

By the time he got home after looping around Beverley Hills, driving into the canyons and back out again until the gas gauge read nearly zero, Mom was definitely home. Since Hank had the Caddy, Dad had used Mom's coupe, top town, to ferry her and her jungle of flowers home from the hospital. Many of them remained in the back seat, wilting in the sun. Pulling in behind the roadster, Hank reached in as he passed and broke off a blue bachelor button.

His mouth tasted sour and the house looked dull and dark. Dread nagged at him from the horrifying thought that he might never see Luz again. But if there was one other person than himself he could blame for that, it would be Bess Cleveland.

From Mom's bedroom upstairs Dad's voice boomed with laughter. Joaquin came down, a smile on his face. Seeing Hank standing at the bottom, he tried to scowl.

"Now you show up. Your mother's asking where you are, young Hank." He jerked his thumb over his shoulder. "Get up there. She is hungry, thank God."

211

Joaquin lowered his voice. "She is skinnier than a praying mantis. I will cook her such a meal!"

At least someone is happy she's home, Hank thought as he climbed the stairs. Stopping outside the room, he lit another cigarette, opened the door.

Mom sat on the side of the bed. Dad was crossing the room, carrying the Dictaphone. Carl turned away from the window, where he stood looking bored. No sign of Connie.

"'Bout time you showed up." Carl shifted his gaze toward Mom, indicating that Hank should watch out.

"Where have you been, young man. Why couldn't you be here to welcome your mother home?" Dad placed the Dicta-phone on a table beside the bed that had been brought up from downstairs, its surface already stacked with pads, a dozen sharpened pencils in a glass, pot of coffee, water pitch-er, spare reading glasses, and a stuffed Teddy bear.

Mom looked small, thinner than she had even in the hos-pital, dwarfed by mountains of linens in the bed and stack of writing pads on the table beside her. She had wrapped a spotted green turban around her head and wore a matching robe. Indicating Hank should come to give her a hug, she wore a sloppy, rather pathetic grin.

The sight of this hardened Hank's heart even more. When Mom saw him approach with his cigarette, her eyes nar-rowed slightly.

Good. Let her ask for a smoke. She won't get one from me.

He dutifully let her hug him. Dad brought over a saucer. "No cigarettes in the sick room," he said. Hank took a long draw and stubbed it out.

"Where's the nurse you're supposed to have?" Hank sat on Mom's dressing table chair, a brass confection with a fuzzy pink seat.

"There won't be one." Carl leaned against the window frame. From here at least, he looked sober.

"I will take care of your mother until she is able to get around on her own." Dad fussed with the items on the table, moving things around. A big chair had also been brought up and stood on the other side of the table from the bed, books and magazines piled next to it, a standing lamp behind.

So much for my Luz scheme, Hank thought, leaning back, one elbow on the dressing table, knocking over a bottle of perfume.

Mom watched Hank. He thought he saw doubt in her eyes, but more likely it was scrutiny, calculation, a method of discovery.

Sitting in the big chair, Dad loosened his tie. "So where were you last night? Your mother was distressed that you weren't here when she got home. Carl tells me you were out all night."

Shrugging, Hank said nothing. He watched Mom and she watched him back.

"Hey Hank, get this." Carl took off his jacket. The room grew hotter and hotter, Hank noticed, and it wasn't from the heat of all the lies sealed up with them.

"That girl, the one who accused me, changed her story. What a kick, huh? Mom says she'll talk to Cedric about Connie and me being rehired."

"That's interesting." Hank kept his gaze on mom. "She'll *talk* to him, huh?"

Dad shifted in his chair. "Of course, as soon as she gets her voice back."

"I don't give a shit, actually." Carl ran a hand through his hair. "I don't think I want to work with Connie anymore."

They all turned to look at him. Carl smiled crookedly,

pleased to be, Hank thought, the center of attention once again.

"I've been talking to people on my own. If Connie can suck up, so can I, so to speak. I have an audition for a TV show."

Dad snorted. Mother glared at Carl, as one might stare down a tiger. Hank wondered at this change in Carl. What had made him suddenly grow balls of his own? It had to be more than the adoration of a bevy of star-struck nurses.

"Congratulations, Carl," Hank said, just as Connie came through the door.

"The prodigal daughter returns. Hank and Connie both missing in action." Carl sat on the window seat, crossed his legs, turned to look outside again.

Connie breathed heavily, as if she had just run up the stairs. Hank was curious about the look of her; sundress clean, ironed, sandals in her hand, hair a curly soufflé. But there was something paler about her, as if she were a ghost of herself. Her smile strained, movements jerky as she scraped up all the available energy in the room.

"So glad you're home, Mommy." She fluttered to Mom, sat next to her, swept her arms around her. "I was so worried."

Worried enough, Hank thought, to stay out of sight of everyone for as long as possible. No one asked where she had been, however. Hank noticed that.

While Connie rubbed Mom's hands, an action, Hank could see, that Mom didn't like, he said, "So Carl was telling us he has an audition. Television show, he says."

Connie whirled around, too quickly, Hank thought. *Snake-like.*

"Oh really? Television?" She said the word as if Carl said he landed a gig in Hell. "What will you use for your audition? A soap jingle?"

Standing up, Carl stretched. He walked around Mom's bed to stand a few feet from Hank.

"No. A love ballad. I'm learning to croon."

Now it was Connie's turn to snort. Her eyes were too bright, too wide. She had smeared makeup across her face carelessly. "You, a crooner? What, you going to be the next Mel Torme?"

"A prettier version, certainly." Carl smoothed back his hair.

"Well, good luck. Better hope the sponsors don't find out you're a rapist."

"Constance, that's enough." Dad stood up. Hank could see Mom's fingers digging into Connie's skin.

Carl looked at her, one eyebrow raised. "Oh, maybe you didn't hear. Your little friend recanted. She said there was no rape. The papers reported she made a mistake."

A slow recognition slid over Hank. He watched Connie's face, to see if his intuition was right.

Pulling away from Mom, Connie got up, walked across the room, opened Mom's cigarette holder, found it empty, slammed it back onto the dresser.

"She's an idiot. Someone got to her, that's all."

Carl said, "Oh, and who would that be? Mom maybe? She walked into that girl's apartment and threatened her?"

Connie paced around the room, ended up beside Hank. "Who knows? Who cares?"

"I do." Carl approached her, his face full of a level of contempt Hank had never seen before. "I do because you and your starlet friend, yeah, she's Cedric's niece or something, and yeah, I met her in the hotel bar and she was very friendly. But you cooked all that up with her to get the rotten publicity you needed to break up the act."

It all made perfect sense to Hank. In fact, he started to laugh, and Connie glared at him. "Mary. Mary the starlet—'is this your other brother?' Of course. You didn't take me to her place to drown your sorrows, it was to celebrate. It's perfect, Con. You are a master."

Mom stood up. She stared at her three children as if she had never seen them before. Walking toward them, she came up to Connie and lifted her hand.

Getting to his feet, Hank seized Mom's wrist before she could strike Connie. Carl stood frozen. Connie stepped back, chin raised.

"Mother, you know it was time. I need to be on my own. You would keep us handcuffed together like slaves in a chain gang the rest of our lives. I can't do that. Carl can't do that." Her voice was raw, grating.

Face red, eyes murderous, Mom stood trembling. She rested a hand on the dressing table after Hank let her go.

Dad appeared, took Mom's arm. "Come along, sweetheart. You need to lie down."

Taking her back to the bed, Dad folded Mom under the covers as if she were a doll he was saying goodnight to. She lay, staring at the ceiling. The utter silence in the room was eerie and strange.

Then Connie began to hum. She did a twirl, executed a quick tap-step.

Scowling at her, Carl moved, grabbed her arm. "Cut that shit out!"

She scratched his cheek. He lifted an arm and Hank re-capitulated his intervention, grabbing Carl's wrist.

"You fucking ruined my life, you bitch."

"I did you a favor, Carly. You will have to cut the apron strings, just like I did. And it's tough out there, flying on your own." Connie smiled. All this time she had been here, she had not looked at Hank at all.

Dad came over, pushed Carl away from Connie, pointed at the door. "You all get out of here if you can't behave like human beings. Your mother is sick!"

Connie ruffled her hair, picked up her sandals from where she had dropped them. "I'll be back later, Mommy, to tuck you in."

Dad did not look amused. Standing a few feet away, Hank wondered if Connie was high on something. Carl fingered the scratches on his jaw. One of them looked pretty deep.

Hank felt himself retreat, seeing them as if Mom and Dad and Connie and Carl, all characters in a play and he was observing, trying to figure out what was going on.

And finally, the closed closet of Hank's memory. What had Mom done to Luz and why he couldn't remember?

He remembered dropping Joseph off at home, helped him into the house with his genie-lamp of father-ashes. He thought of Susan, brown eyes and lines of freckles.

Grabbing Carl's arm, Hank pulled him along, out of the room, past Dad and Connie's astonished faces.

"C'mon," he said. "I'm getting us both out of here."

Twenty-Eight

AFTER STASHING the Peugeot in the Caddy trunk, Hank backed out of the Cleveland driveway, Carl in the seat beside him, offering him a drink from his flask. Hank declined, but he did accept a cigarette, knowing that once at Susan's he wouldn't be able to smoke.

He told Carl he had met the infamous 'Mary', which was her real name. She was a distant relative of Cedric Sigfried and had been Connie's comrade-in-arms for years. Hank was relieved to know that Carl was not the notorious womanizer he led people to believe.

"I've maybe gotten all the way only five or six times." Carl opened the window; air flowed through his hair. Hank drove in his usual sedate manner and Carl made no remark about it. Hank realized the only people who liberally complained about his driving were the women of the family.

Carl glanced at the urn between them. "Why, exactly, did you want to bring Grandpa Joel's ashes for the ride?"

Hank stared straight ahead. Carl had not asked why Hank propelled him down the stairs and into the living room, swiped both the urn and the marquess off the mantle and led him to the car. Carl got in the passenger seat, cooperating, probably, because his brother's behavior was so unlike him, and waited while Hank rolled the Peugeot out of the garage.

"Hank said, "You'll find out soon enough."

"What a carnival freak our sister is." Carl waved his hand out the window as the car moved along Wilshire. Late Saturday afternoon, glorious and sunny, made traffic to the beach cities heavy.

Nodding, Hank couldn't agree more. But he didn't give a rip about it. He had a way to remember now. Susan could help him. If he could remember, he could go back to Luz to ask her to forgive him. The thought of living without Luz made him feel as if he had a hole in his body so big everyone could see through him to the other side.

When they reached the street of Venice bungalows, Carl glanced at Hank curiously as he drove up Susan's driveway. Hank had hoped, stupidly, foolishly, to see Luz's battered ja-lopy that was always breaking down parked on the street near the house, but it was not there and he knew it wouldn't be.

Getting out of the car, Carl stood, nodding, looking around.

"Look familiar? You and Connie sussed out this place a long time ago, didn't you?" Hank spoke to Carl over the Caddy's roof, Grandfather Joel and the marquess in his arms.

Shrugging, Carl gave him a half-sheepish smile. "We had to know where our little brother was getting some. It was written all over you that you were seeing a girl."

Carl prudently said nothing judgmental about any of it, because at that moment Susan appeared, coming from her studio. Her cheeks were flushed. Hank could smell the heat of the kiln and his skin prickled. Was she already firing pottery painted with her father's ash?

Walking up to Hank, ignoring Carl, Susan kissed Hank fully, several seconds, on the lips. In spite of all that had gone on before, Hank felt himself stir at the touch of her mouth.

Resting his chin on his hands, Carl looked at them over the Caddy roof. Susan glanced at him. "You're the brother? Carlisle?"

Carl nodded jerkily, all the while smiling.

"Pleased to meet you." Taking Hank's arm, Susan led him up the driveway and into the back yard.

The kiln was indeed going. Joseph lay in the chaise lounge, asleep under a plaid blanket, the same place Hank and Luz had left him this morning. Setting sunlight filled the space, touching everything with brilliance, as if the entire scene was a ceramic tableau flaked with gold. Joseph's hair, the ring of figures under the laundry pole, the kiln, all appointed with precious metal.

Hank had worried Susan would be angry he had helped Joseph run off in the middle of the night to rob the cemetery of their father, but she seemed the happiest he had seen her, ever.

She led Hank into the studio. The genie lamp stood on the workbench; brushes and knives cluttered it as if Susan had just finished and put a figure in the fire. A coffee can held more ashes, Susan showed him. She could make numerous items from them.

But for this, she said, she did a bowl. A very special bowl.

"Wow," Carl said from the doorway. "These are really nice." He was looking at the array of figurines on the shelves. Hank could see that some of them were different in style, heavier, sturdier, beings of the earth. These would be Luz's, he thought, while Susan's were fluttery and light, of the air.

Hank set Grandfather Joel and the marquess on the workbench.

Picking up the marquess, Susan said, "Ah, the Messien." She turned it over, saw the mark. "I was right. What a pity the pair is broken."

Another broken pair. One partner wishing the other were gone, and when it was gone, wishing for it back.

Putting down the marquess, Susan looked at Hank, then at the urn. "You want a favor?"

He nodded. She gave him a half-smile, then pried the lid off the urn. Carl made an uncertain noise behind them, but didn't move from his place at the doorway.

With a spoon, she dug into the ashes. The stuff was whiter than Hank expected, not like charcoal or cigarette ash at all, but the ash the color of bone.

"Your grandfather that died?"

Staring at the little cone of ash on the spoon, Hank nodded again.

"And what would you like, something practical, like a vase, or a platter?" Susan took an empty coffee can and spooned the ash into it. "Or a figure. A farmer, a sage, a dwarf from 'Snow White'?"

Hank thought, still struck dumb by the sight of incinerated bone moving from the urn to Susan's can. Then it hit him.

"A bicycle racer."

Giving him a sideways glance, Susan nodded. "A bicycle racer, bike and all? Complicated. Will take me a while."

She got busy, taking a box of talc and jars of crushed colors and began mixing. Each color would have a modicum of Grandfather Joel mixed in. She arranged these, then with wire cut a slab of clay from the big block, wrapped in damp cloth, on the work bench.

Turning, Hank grabbed Carl's arm and took him onto the

patio.

"Sit," he said, went inside and found two beers in the refrigerator.

"What is she doing, Hank? With the ashes?" Carl took a low swallow of beer. They sat in two splintery wooden chairs beside of the still sleeping Joseph.

"She's going to help me remember." Hank leaned back, knowing he would have no results until the next morning. And he wasn't going anywhere until the figure was complete. That was why he brought the bike, in case Carl wanted to take off somewhere. But Carl showed no sign of leaving.

"Beautiful," Carl whispered, taking another drink. Hank wondered if he meant the beer, lovely spring evening, or Susan. Probably all three.

"Carl, what do you remember about that girl I was friends with in high school? Her name was Luz del Mar."

Carl tapped the lip of his beer bottle on his nose. "That Latina girl? Very cute. I could hear you guys talking for hours in your room."

Hank's heart skipped up a notch. "Do you remember Mom's reaction? I mean, what did she think of the whole thing?"

Sitting up, Carl rested his hands on his knees. "What do you mean? Why are you asking me?"

"I just wanted a new perspective. I sort of got in touch with her again."

Carl nodded. "You got Connie to help you. I wondered what she was up to."

"She took me to Luz's house. But, she had one of her moods, and we had to leave." Hank didn't want to talk about Connie. "It's just that, I don't remember that much about Luz. But now, that I've seen her again, I wonder how I could have forgotten."

"You are in love, young Hank. I can see that." Carl leaned back again. "Memory is a tricky thing. We only remember what we want to, really."

Hank didn't agree with that. He wanted to remember everything about his time with Luz when they were sixteen.

The sun left the scene, the scent of the nearby ocean intensified, along with a breeze cycling through the top of the palm in Susan's front yard. Carl left to get groceries to shuffle something together for dinner, Joseph continued to sleep, unmoving. Hank sat in the chair, drank another beer, and stared through the open studio door at Susan as she worked.

Carl was just returning with hamburgers and buns when Susan emerged from the studio at the sound of a ringing alarm.

Sitting up, Joseph threw off his blanket, swung his legs over the side of the chaise lounge. He looked wide awake, not groggy at all, nodded at Hank, gazed curiously at Carl as he set two bags of groceries on the patio table between the ceramic piggy jar and the donkey.

Susan was opening the door to the kiln.

Getting to his feet, Joseph hobbled toward the kiln, Hank following. Wearing gauntleted oven gloves, Susan pulled the rack free.

In the center was a medium-sized bowl, the interior the bluest dark-sky blue Hank had ever seen. A pale pink rim framed a spray of stars, two moons, a ringed planet, all reflected in a black sea.

They all stood around it, staring. Susan pushed it toward Joseph, whose face was rapt. Then she took it inside the studio, where it would continue to cool slowly.

Hank looked at Joseph, trying to see any recognition there.

As if reading his look, Joseph shrugged.

"There's just one thing missing."

"What is that?"

"Nurse del Mar."

Hank gazed at Joseph, dumbfounded. What did she have to do with all this? What did Joseph mean? He followed Joseph back to the patio where they sank back into their chairs. Picking up the groceries, Carl shrugged and went into the house.

"Why Luz? Why her?"

Joseph had closed his eyes, opened them again. "She's in charge of the memories, dear Hank. She stirs the ashes, finds the threads." He cocked his head, as if reading Hank's confusion on his face. "She was the one who showed Susan how to mix ashes into the glazes, you remember?"

Joseph picked up a small figure from the table. It was a man in a business suit. Then another, a chef; and a baker, and a doctor. "All these. Guys I went to war with. I have a stash of their ashes. I woke up in the hospital in Italy with all these little bags tucked in my kit, with names written on them with indelible ink. 'Flannel Suit', 'Chef', 'Donut-boy', and 'Quack'. I don't remember their real names any more, but 'Donut-boy' was the crazy lieutenant I told you about." He rotated the baker-figurine in his hands. "I know they died. I know I was the only one to get out of there. But that is all I know. Luz, she was very interested in my stash. She helped me talk about them, the only person who asked me about them. Not one of those self-satisfied, over-rated Army shrinks asked me about them."

Sitting back in his chair, Hank felt all the hope drain out of him. Luz was the key to the memory, the only key that would open this particular lock.

"Is she coming over?"

"Beats me." Joseph picked up Hank's half-drunk beer, swallowed the remainder. "I thought you had brought her."

Carl grilled, showing no sign of wanting to ditch these odd companions for the headier attractions of Hollywood. Joseph plugged in the Christmas lights and put a record on the record player. Hank took a plate in to Susan, set it on the empty stool beside her.

Luz's stool.

The racer was taking shape. She had squared him so he looked as if he and the entire bicycle were at top speed; she cleverly embedded the wheels into a ceramic stand. Now she was painting on the slip, and this she would carve and etch with her distinctive flowing details.

She paid no attention to him, so he left, wondering who would summon Luz. But he soon had his answer. Joseph was checking his watch as he and Carl shared a bottle of good whiskey.

"She should be here by now," Joseph said. There had been, apparently, a prior arrangement that Luz return in the evening for the ceremony with the bowl. Hank said nothing, just sank into his chair and took the bottle from Carl. He didn't want to suggest that it might be his fault Luz wasn't coming at all.

But he was wrong, and happy to be wrong. A few minutes later she appeared around the corner of the house, coming up the driveway.

She wore slacks and a light jacket; her hair was tucked in a cap. She carried a shopping bag over her shoulder. When she saw Hank, she gave no indication that his being there made any difference to her whatsoever.

Hank and Carl got to their feet. Joseph also tried to rise,

but Luz went straight to him and laid a hand on his shoulder. "No bother. I see you are ready. Hello, Hank." Luz put her bag on the table.

"Hello, Luz. This is my brother, Carl."

Luz shook Carl's hand. Carl's lips parted and for once he seemed incapable of speech. As Luz turned away, making for the studio, Carl caught Hank's eye and waved his hand under his own chin as if he had just been scorched.

Luz said from the studio door, "Joseph, I'm sorry I'm late. The car wouldn't start and I had to take the street car and walk from there."

Hank cursed himself. He could have gone to pick her up, if he had known she was intending to come even though there was a high probability that he would be here and she might not want to talk to him at all.

Joseph struggled to his feet and Hank gripped his hand to help him. Joseph's skin was cold, clammy. He really believes he'll get that memory back tonight. Hank was half-believing, because he believed in Luz. But it was crazy to think firing of human ash into a glaze could resurrect lost memories.

The three men stood in the doorway. Luz's back was to them as she and Susan murmured over the quality of the mixtures. A moment of silence, then she left Susan, pushed past the men, and went to her shopping bag.

Crickets filled the silence. Laughter came from somewhere down the block from one of the houses on the canal. A fragrance, flowery, heavy, floated across Hank's nostrils. But a moment later he saw that Luz had lit a wad of herbs and laid it in a lopsided soup bowl that had an ill-experience in the kiln.

"Will someone bring me the bowl?"

Joseph reached for it, but stumbled. He still wasn't steady

on his recently healed ankles. Carl shook his head, and it fell to Hank to take the dark sky moon bowl of Chagall to Luz.

She took it from him, her finger brushing his. She did not look at him.

Squatting beside the low patio table, she tipped ash from the burned herbs into the bowl. Looking over her shoulder at Joseph, she motioned him to sit beside her.

He lowered himself to the ground. She waved smoke from the herbs over him, urged him to inhale the odors from the bowl. She had laid multi-colored beans and kernels of corn in the bowl, along with dark powder.

Picking it up, she placed it on the still-glowing grill.

The bowl would crack, break, and be destroyed by the heat. But it sat there as the ingredients inside scorched and burned and filled the yard with obnoxious smells. Hank hoped none of the neighbors would feel compelled to call the fire department.

Then Luz picked up the bowl with her bare hands.

Carl and Hank yelled *"Don't!"* at the same time, but she smiled and shrugged at them. She carried the bowl back to Joseph, who lay on his back on the grass, staring at the stars as if he had never seen stars before.

"Dip your fingers in the ash," she instructed. "Smear it on your face. Taste it. It is the taste of memory. No locked doors can withstand this. It goes to all places. It finds every shred and brings it back to you."

Her voice was soft, sing-song, and slightly accented. Joseph obeyed, striping both cheeks and his forehead with black as he lay on the grass.

Luz sat next to him, leaned forward. Hank and Carl sank onto the chaise lounge, side-by-side. Maybe he was drunk, maybe they both were drunk, but Hank could feel magic on his skin, taste it on his tongue. He glanced at his brother, whose face was open and staring like a child.

Even the crickets had fallen silent. It was as if they were suspended in a glass globe enveloped by space and stars. The earth fallen away.

Joseph closed his eyes. The outlines of his face were sharp as if trimmed with moonlight. His breath accelerated. Luz watched him, eyebrows close together, seeing everything. Hank wondered if she could see his memory, watch it like a movie on a screen.

With a grunt Joseph sat up. He stared ahead, almost gasp-ing to catch his breath. Seizing a cushion Luz propped it against the chair-legs and Joseph leaned into it, closed his eyes, opened them in astonishment.

The Christmas lights gave dim illumination to his face, the strange whiteness vanished as Joseph began to speak, recite the text as if from memory, which it was.

"It was black night, no moon. He made me drive with the lights off. I was sure we were going to die right then and there, in the truck; it could fly right over the edge of the cliff. Those hills, sharp and steep, all of rocks and olive trees. Mountain goats were always falling off those rocks, much less people in machines.

"But he was crazy, Donut-boy. He carried hair from Ger-man soldiers wound in a string around his neck. He says he shot an American lieutenant once, killed him dead in a fire fight." Joseph licked his lips. Carl handed him a beer from which he took a long swallow. Hank leaned forward, elbows on knees, hands so tightly clasped his thumbs began to cramp.

"But we got there, alive and well, and scared enough to mess our pants. This castle, a ruin of a castle, actually, but a good hideout, hard to get to. I said, why don't we just phone in and ask for artillery, but no one had brought a field phone. This Sargent, he loved pointing out the futility of my ideas. The others just laughed.

Joseph looked them all in the face, his eyes wide as if he had just woken up from a twenty year sleep. "I determined then that I was going to live. These guys might get iced trying to storm a medieval castle full of starving, insane Krauts, but I wasn't about to join them. Castles were built not to be taken. They had slots for arrows and battlements for dropping stones and boiling oil. But I didn't say this to Donut-boy. He could not be reasoned with when his mind was made up.

"So we start up there, Donut-boy in the lead, Chef and Baker and Flannel Suit fanning out behind, and me, myself, and I taking up the rear. I had a rifle, but I was a lousy shot— barely passed gunnery school. That's why I was a driver."

He ran his hand through his hair, fingered his beard. A movement in the corner of Hank's eye told him Susan had come out of the studio to listen.

"Some of them had hand grenades. The idea was to creep up close enough and lob grenades inside there. Inside of what? The wall we were approaching was four stories of solid rock. If they were in there, and we threw the grenades over this low place beside it, they would know we were there and shoot us dead. They had a machine gun up in there.

"But that was Donut-boy's plan, right? I hung back. Let them get killed. I was only the driver."

Hank understood how Joseph felt, but he also wondered if Joseph could really stand by and let his fellow soldiers die.

"So, they go up, I'm halfway down the slope, watching that castle. And sure enough, Chef lobs a grenade in the low place, followed by Baker. Donut-boy gave a whoop as the things exploded.

"Then silence for a long time. Probably only a few minutes, but a few minutes can be a really long time. Then I see it. I think my angle, being lower down, was better, so I could see it and the others couldn't. There was a little movement on the low wall. I could see it in the light from something burning inside there.

"A head and a rifle and as the Kraut got ready to aim I got off a shot and goddam what do you know, I got him."

A worried look fell over Joseph's face. "Only, it wasn't a him. We get up there—there's no return fire or noise, Donut-boy clapping me on the back and Flannel Suit shaking my hand, and we see who it was looked over the wall."

Joseph looked at Luz, shaking his head. "It was an old woman. All alone up there but with a gaggle-load of weapons and stuff to make bombs. The old woman I saw, or thought I saw, when I jumped off the streetcar."

Luz reached out a hand, touched his arm, but said nothing. It was hardly anyone's fault, Hank thought. Joseph was saving their lives. That old Italian lady was going to shoot them.

"We figured she thought we were Germans, maybe. But why would those assholes leave their mother to guard that place up there, all by herself? Fiends, heartless fiends." Joseph kept shaking his head. "But that's not it. That's not what I didn't want to remember, even though the memory stopped there, on the road up the mountain.

"So we feel pretty shitty about that, and we leave, go back, to make up some sort of report or story. The guys don't blame me. They saw the rifle she had aimed at us. But we all felt pretty bad. I wanted to get the hell out of there. We go back to the truck.

"I'm driving as fast as I can, with no lights and in pitch

black on a road on a sheer cliff. Donut-boy is on my ass, call-ing me evil and saying we should have gone back to get some of her hair. Boy, when he said that I couldn't help my-self. I elbowed him in the nose.

"Then everything went sideways. We were falling, off the road. I had driven us fucking off the road when I elbowed Donut-boy. I was screaming, we all were screaming. Then the screaming faded, got farther away. I heard a boom, big and loud."

Joseph drew his knees up, held them with his hands. He continued to stare at Luz. "I was thrown out, I guess. When I woke up, there was a little light. The sun was coming up. I sit up, testing myself, no bones broken, except for my head maybe and who cares about that? I wonder where the guys are. Did they leave me here? Was this all some kind of joke?

"I can't yell. There might be Krauts anywhere. I remember driving off the road, and I get up onto my knees. I'm dizzy as hell. And then I see it.

"Down in the ravine, maybe fifty yards down, the truck. It's charred to a crisp, black and still smoking. I can still smell the smoke, even now." He fell silent for a moment, remem-bering. Hank thought about what the smell must have been like.

"I go down there. I was an idiot, going down there. I should have gotten straight out of there. Of course, they're all dead. Burned."

He was silent a long while. The crickets started up again, a car raced past on the street in front of the house. When Joseph started speaking again, Hank jumped.

"I just stayed with them. I told myself, I couldn't get out of that ravine anyway. If the Krauts got me, they got me. To while away the time I made little pouches out of bits of canvas—some of it might be from their clothes, or from the truck itself. We all had this kit, you know, with a needle and thread. Came in handy. Writing the names on each pouch was hard, though. I didn't have a pen, but I shaped each pouch a little differently, so I could keep track of whose ashes were whose. A wide one for Chef, a skinny one for Flannel Suit, like that. Donut-boy I really scored. I found a shred of his shirt with part of his name on it."

Leaning back on the cushion Joseph closed his eyes. End of story, Hank thought. Nothing more to tell other than about hospitals and psychiatrists and broken ankles.

Susan knelt beside Joseph, put her arms around him, lowering her head so that the tips of her hair touched his lap. Hank wanted to reach out, touch her, touch Luz, who stayed seated, quiet. He needed to ask her to do the same for him but he didn't know how.

Carl got up, brought out another bottle and some glasses. Even Luz had a sip. She got to her feet, stretched, began to wipe out the bowl with a cloth from her bag.

Setting his empty glass down beside Carl, Hank went into the studio.

The Cyclist was done. Even the sinews of his thighs and calves were visible; head down, goggled, he spun the course, wheels turning, going round and round. Jars of glazes were mixed and ready for application.

After a while, Joseph hobbled wearily on his canes and left them, telling Susan he didn't need any help. As he said this, he glanced at Hank as if letting him know he was giving Susan the permission to finish the Cyclist.

Susan, unlike Hank, seemed energized and went back into the studio to finish. Now she would apply Grandfather Joel's ashes. Outside, Carl picked up the car keys while Luz packed up her bag.

"Don't go," Hank managed, reaching for her hand.

Her eyes glinted in the Christmas light glow. She looked away from him, as if she hoped to see an answer in the darkened geography of Susan's back yard.

"I see you're not addressing me, Hanklet. I'm going home." Carl took Luz's hand, kissed it. "A pleasure to meet you, Beauty. Take good care of our Hank here."

Picking up the half-drunk whiskey bottle, Carl looked at it, up-turned it to let it drain onto the lawn.

"Lucky grass," he said, and left them alone. Hank heard Carl taking the Peugeot out of the trunk. He hoped the racer wouldn't be too banged up.

The light from the studio made a silver square on the lawn. A chill edged the night, and Luz pulled her jacket around her, and to Hank's immense relief, settled down onto one of the patio chairs.

He lowered himself to the chaise, rubbed his knees. "How did you do that? Can you really do magic?"

Luz shrugged. "An old family secret. My mother can do magic. She taught me a few things."

"That was quite a story."

"Yes it was." She fell silent, and they both remembered.

What a crazy thing war is. No wonder Joseph came home a mess. Hank thought, looking at the tiny figurines of Joseph's fellow soldiers. He didn't want to touch them.

"I found his stash of ashes when I was going through his things," Luz said, seeing him looking. "I asked him one day about them, but he couldn't tell me anything. Then I asked him if I could have his permission to take a bit of ash from each to make a glaze.

"At least he could tell me about the men, and I decided to

try to make each one." She picked up Donut-boy, the insane lieutenant baker. "My figures are cruder than Susan's, but by the time I got to Donut-boy, I was getting pretty good."

Hank thought the figures were fantastic. "These are really good, Luz."

They sat in silence for a while. Hank watched Luz pick up each man, turn him over in her fingers like Hera deciding the fate of mortals. He could do no more than watch her, when he wanted to fold her into himself, feel and taste her skin and lips again.

Should I bring it up again, apologize about asking Luz to be Mom's nurse? Around them the soft night penetrated Hank's bones; the Christmas-light string colored Luz's cheek with a sheen almost like gold.

Then he remembered Mom's letter. Pulling if from his trouser pocket, Hank looked at the folded yellow legal foolscap marked with Mom's heavy square script.

"What is that?" Luz asked.

"A letter from my mother. She wrote it while she was in the hospital."

Hank watched Luz sit a little straighter, stiffen. Don't leave. Please stay.

Sighing, Luz looked at Donut Boy lying in her open palms. "Read it to me."

The Christmas lights provided a red-moon glow. His heart thundering under his ribs, Hank began.

> *My mother once told me that memory is like soap. Heavy and solid, but as it is used, it grows smaller. It transforms into lather and bubbles, and drains away with the water.*
>
> *You children never met my mother and I thank*

God every day that you never did. Virginia Ronert was a hard woman, bitter, angry. Later in this missive, con-fession, whatever it is, you will learn why. But there was one thing about her, that I, her only daughter, inherited, and that was her voice.

I never took up singing. It seemed stupid and frivolous, maybe it was because my mother sang like Christel Goltz, that famous German opera soprano. Weddings, funerals, and church. She made the rounds. I suppose Connie and Carl got their voices from her.

I just remember one day, sitting in church, listening to my mother sing. I was maybe nine years old. It was winter in Oklahoma, gray and cold, not even the sweetness of snow to block the bleakness. But I re-member as I sat there, listening, bored, the sun came out.

The church walls changed, somehow, to blue or turquoise; the people sitting in the pews took on color, black and brown and gray transformed to gold and scar-let and green. It was my mother's voice that did that. She could change things, just by singing. I wanted to learn how.

I couldn't sing like her but I could talk. People told me I sounded like a damn lawyer. I could argue the corn cobs off the stalk. I argued with crows and cows. I always made my point and I always won.

I'm not going to bore you with the story, again, of how I got myself into law school, talked my way in, really. That's not why I'm writing this. Oh, maybe it is, as a way of explaining what I did, not the why of it, but the 'what' of it.

I met your father, Kenneth Cleveland, that

summer before I left for college. My mother, for all her faults, was determined that I would go to college and be schooled like she never was. You've heard the story. Your dad was riding a bicycle out from Waynoka, right near the cemetery. I was driving my mother's old Ford into town for groceries, with her in the passenger seat telling me to slow down or speed up or hold the wheel a certain way. We saw the car ahead clip him and over he went into the ditch.

Now comes a part of the story you didn't know, Hank, and this is only for you. I had never met or heard of Kenneth Cleveland. Oh, I knew about the Cleveland farm, a big, prosperous place north along the river. But my mother knew who he was, this young man lying in the ditch with a broken arm. She never said anything, but I could tell she knew him and she didn't like him.

So, when we started up, your father and I, we kept it secret. Oklahoma Law School opened in 1923 in Norman, Oklahoma and I was one of the first students. Norman was as far from my mother as I could get in those days. Your father came with me and worked in a grocery store. And we got married there, in secret.

But you know all this, or at least, this is nothing I kept secret from any of you. But there is something.

Looking up, Hank caught Luz staring straight ahead, a deep vertical line on her forehead, as if behind that wall of bone and skin she was shuffling memories faster than an adding machine. Getting off his chair, he slid to the grass, to be closer.

My mother found out. She came on a visit to surprise me—strange because Mother hated traveling. And of course your father was there and it was all too plain to her that we were married.

Mother flew into a rage. I had never seen her so angry before, and she had a temper. She kept asking if Joel Cleveland, Ken's father, knew we were together. The look of her face, beet red, will always live in my mind.

Luz's hand slid onto Hank's shoulder. He froze, didn't turn to look up at her, because if he did, she might disappear. His heart turning over in uncomfortable leaps, Hank kept reading.

Mother kept shrieking about an annulment. Ken kept demanding to know why. Your father, a quiet, reliable man, really learned the power of his voice that day, because Mother had to give up. She couldn't out-shout him.

And when Mother answered, her voice cracking with hoarseness, 'ask your father!', a terrible thought slid into my mind.

On Hank's shoulder, Luz's hand tightened. "She knew," she breathed.

Luz's voice made Hank falter; he lost his place, found it again.

And so, yes, we learned the truth, but it was never from Mother or Joel Cleveland. It was from your grandmother's best friend, Rosie Gantry, who is still alive, I believe. We traveled back to Waynoka but we didn't tell my mother or Ken's father we were in town.

Lines were crossed out, blackened with swipes of the pen so that Hank couldn't read them, as if Mom had tried to begin this paragraph and kept revising.

> *I learned that Joel Cleveland was my father. Mother made up a story about my father dying in a grain silo. I've told you children that same story, all these years. Joel Cleveland, a well-off farmer, married to your grandmother Annette, who died in the influenza epidemic was both Ken's and my father. Now I knew why Mrs. Cleveland, who headed all the church and school committees, hated my mother and me.*

"She knew," Luz said again. "That picture of your grandmother, and your grandfather. I saw that in her face. A broken heart, and deep, deep anger."

Everything in Hank's body, stomach, heart, sank toward the cool grass underneath him. Mom and Dad were half-brother and sister. But they stayed married, raised children, made a life for themselves as far away from Waynoka, Oklahoma as they could get.

There was more, in the letter, about Grandpa Joel, and how he had known all along. Ken told him about the girl, Bess Ronert, whom he loved. And Grandpa Joel did nothing about it. He just let it happen.

A strand of Luz's hair brushed Hank's cheek. She was leaning over him, staring at the letter, or at the ground. The scent of cinnamon encircled Hank. His heart thundering, Hank reached for her, to press her closer so he could kiss her. He felt her moving, soft, pliant, coming closer.

Susan emerged from the studio with the Cyclist. Luz pulled away. They watched Susan load it into the re-heated kiln.

Getting up, Luz picked up her handbag. "A cyclist, huh? I should get going. It's late."

Near the kiln, Susan said from the shadows, "The Red Car is closed by now. Let me drive you home."

Hank watched Luz shake her head. He stayed on the grass, as if all the power of his legs had been sucked into the earth.

Susan was insistent; she seemed to want to get Luz away —had she heard the content of the letter, from inside the studio where she was working?

Hank was helpless to make her stay with him. He had no right to ask. Luz probably hated that he and his brother were even here to see this private little ceremony. And now she knew the shameful fact of his parents.

Following them to the driveway, Hank said to Luz as she got into Susan's car, "I'll come by tomorrow."

"Don't Hank. We're busy." Luz looked at him over the car roof, the way Carl had looked at him.

"I will. I'll sit outside on the sidewalk until you talk to me again."

Shaking her head, Luz disappeared inside the car. Susan didn't wait, reversed out of the driveway in a hurry. Hank stood alone in her yard with only crickets for company.

Curling up on the chaise under the blanket, he stayed awake, and when the alarm went off, dutifully turned off the kiln. Resisting the urge to open it and see the cyclist because he knew the risk of damage, he got back onto the chaise lounge, found a few swallows of whiskey in a bottle under the table.

Mom and Dad, brother and sister, growing up in the same town and never knowing. Deciding to stay together even when they did know. And Hank thought of Carl and Connie, and what they admitted to doing that afternoon all those years ago when Hank walked in on them. Barriers that he always thought rigid and tall, like prison walls, were crumbling to dust.

Why did Mom throw Luz out of the house? Dad and Mrs. del Mar? Hank couldn't picture it. Dad might have his little dalliances with young blond actresses but Rosa del Mar?

He had been lying there maybe thirty minutes when he heard Susan's phone ring. Who would call this time of night? Joseph did not seem up to answering it, or maybe he was too drunk or tired, but it rang and rang. Stopped. Started again.

Cursing, Hank got to his feet, and trailing the blanket behind him, crossed the kitchen, found the phone on the table against the dining room wall and picked it up.

"Hank, is that you? Where is Joseph?"

"Asleep. *Luz?*"

"Yes, yes, it's me. You have to help us."

A shock traveled through him; his blanket fell to the floor. He was fully awake. "What happened?"

"Diego. We can't find him. He must have wandered off." Her frantic voice cycled higher, was cut off. He imagined her clapping her hand on a sob.

He put the phone down. He could hear her calling his name. When Hank got to the driveway he rolled up his cuffs, swung his leg over the Peugeot and pumped into the street, through the brisk night, heading for East LA and Luz.

Twenty-Nine

HE WHIZZED THROUGH intersections, cadence rapid, dodging the occasional car. Even now, at 2 in the morning, people were out driving around.

All Hank could think about was getting to Luz's house. She had called *him,* of all people, to help her find Diego. He wished for the speed of experimental jet planes, fold time and be there in seconds, not hours.

Thirty-five miles to Luz's house in East L.A.. If he could maintain a speed of twenty-five miles per hour, he would get there in less than two hours. It seemed an impossibly long time, and he slowed, considering. There had to be another way. He had no car. By the time he rode home and took Mom's car, no time would be saved. Pounding the handlebars in helpless frustration, Hank blew through an intersection and ran straight into a crossing car.

Hitting the brakes, Hank slid sideways, saving the front wheel from warping, but slamming into the rear passenger door. Before he could get his balance, he bounced off the ground.

Hank heard the car's brakes squeal and saw it lurch to a stop. Scrambling to his feet he lifted the bike to check the wheels and gear. Pain stabbed his left elbow, the same one he had fallen on weeks ago, and he nearly dropped the Peugeot.

A woman stood near her driver door, clinging to the handle.

"Oh, thank god you're all right. Can I take you anywhere? Does your bike work? I didn't see you, honestly. I didn't see you."

She rambled on from her place near the door. Hank couldn't answer. His heart thundered in his ears; he knew she was offering him a ride and was concerned and all that, but it didn't matter. Thoughts flashed through his mind, bits of film on a screen, distracting bits.

He thought he shook his head. He maybe even said 'No thanks I'm fine'. The next thing he knew he was on the bike, riding. It was working fine, even though a biting pain paralyzed his left elbow. The bike was working fine. And he knew where to go.

These were not the memories he was seeking, but they were there, firm and splendid in his mind, in Technicolor with sound and music. His legs, shivering with adrenalin, moved him swiftly through the night; the tongue of ocean breeze licked his skin and fingered his hair as he went.

He knew he was halfway to Sepulveda on Washington when he hit the car. Now he headed west, back toward the beach and Mission Way.

The thing with the baby. He remembered that now, and the puzzles snapped neatly into place. The thing with the baby.

It was about the same time, he thought, spring heating into summer, school about to let out.

Now, in sharp focus, as if it were yesterday, he remembered. Connie had been sick and now he knew why. She didn't go to rehearsals and stayed in her room and would only talk to Mom. Hank didn't care so much about that, but Carl was very upset by the whole thing. Sitting in the kitchen with Joaquin, eating a pile of scrambled eggs, thinking about going for a long ride, Hank was astonished to see Connie enter the kitchen, snag a Coke from the fridge and leave again with only a smile and a wave.

Dressed to perfection in a white suit with red polka-dot collar and cuffs, tight skirt and white heels, she looked stunning. She was nineteen then, the Cleveland Twins getting lots of auditions and just starting to land small roles in musicals.

Hank had only seen her once or twice the last five days leaving her room to go to the bathroom, hair mussed and crushed, in an old bathrobe and barefoot, pale and looking terrible. Mother said it was the flu, and the boys should stay away from her.

But now Hank knew what was really wrong with Connie back then and what was wrong with her now. He coasted along Mission Way under marching ranks of palms. To his left, the Pacific gurgled and crashed under the safety of darkness, invisible but ceaselessly present.

That sunny spring day three years ago, Hank just rolled into the driveway after a sixty-mile ride, feeling drained and pleasant, gnawing pain gone for a little while, drained along with his muscles and brain. Emerging from the garage, he came in through the kitchen and a wall of voices and weeping met him.

In the front room, as Hank stood in the doorway, curious, he noticed first the incongruity of two policemen standing near the mantel. They were large, strong men, holding their caps. One was older than the other—the young one looked completely overwhelmed at the sight of Connie pacing back and forth on the other side of the sofa from them, crying, shaking her head. Mother spoke rapidly with the older cop, who was looking at her with a cold expression. Carl and Dad did not appear to be home.

"You see she is distraught," Mom was saying, her voice calm, almost delicate. "She has had a recent trauma and is not coping well. She didn't know what she was doing. I will take full responsibility for this. Anything that needs to be done, I will do."

The policeman kept his eyes on Connie as she walked back and forth. She still wore the pretty suit, but now it looked wrinkled, and there was a grass stain up one side of her skirt. Hank's mind wandered over the possibilities and the ones that came into his mind made him smile.

Mother's back was to him and she hadn't seen him yet. Connie was evidently not seeing anything, just walking back and forth, straightening her jacket, squeezing her hands.

"Mrs. Cleveland, the Los Angeles Police Department will let you know if there will be any charges filed. The family is pretty upset about it. Luckily there was no physical harm done." The cop put on his cap, and the younger one copied him.

"This won't happen again," Mother was saying, turning toward the door. Hank drew back, dipped down the hallway and into the dining room, out of eyesight but not earshot.

"She will be properly looked after. Please assure the family that I have everything in order and that if there is anything I can do for them, it will be done."

The older cop paused as Mom opened the front door. "Mrs. Cleveland, this is a serious matter, you understand. The family may not understand that your daughter is, er, disturbed. You shouldn't contact them under any circumstances, unless they ask to speak with you."

"Of course, officer. Absolutely no contact. Thank you for bringing her home, and not to the jail. I do thank you for that."

Now Hank wondered if Mom had bribed the cops to keep the incident secret. It certainly died away, not a whisper in the papers. The family of the stolen baby must have been well compensated.

Hank remembered everything as he approached downtown Santa Monica in the cool darkness. Mom had closed the door behind the policemen, gone into the living room, took Connie by the arm, and led her upstairs.

All the while, Mother's voice moved like a river, talking, talking, low and constant in Connie's ear as they went. Hank followed, trying to catch what was being said. Mom had no idea, he thought, that he was there. And Connie, evidently, would never remember.

"You need to rest, sleep, forget about everything. You are hurt and tired...." Mother's voice faded as she closed Connie's bedroom door behind her. Hank pressed his ear against the space between the door and the door jamb.

Connie. "Oh Mommy, I'm so sorry. I never meant to hurt anyone. I just wanted to hold her. She could have been mine, right? That sweet, golden baby. She was sitting up in the buggy, looking straight at me. I knew she was mine—what was she doing in that stranger's buggy?" Connie's voice rambled up and down the scale, and all the while Mother's voice encircled the room in clouds of words, obscuring everything.

Hank remembered trying to catch Connie's voice in Mom's flood of words sweeping memory away. Like he was swimming in the water of voices, trying to save Connie. He thought he knew by now what had happened; Connie's short illness followed by this crazy, desperate act. He heard the word 'abortion', not from Mom, but from Connie, over and over. She wanted the baby. She wanted to marry the father. He had offered to marry her.

He remembered now wondering if Carl was the father. But he was wrong about that, had been. Besides, he had the feeling now, as he coasted onto the sidewalk in front of the Lady Windermere Hotel, that he was about to meet the father of the child Connie never had.

Leaving the Peugeot in deep shadow near the private garage behind the hotel, Hank found the back entrance, always unlocked for certain people coming to the hotel who did not want to be noticed. It led through a dark, vacant kitchen to the service elevator.

Mother's voice, the very voice she now had lost forever, low and soft, always a buzzing his ears, background, controlling everything. Hank knew that Bess Cleveland had something to do with his not remembering Connie kidnapping a baby. He wondered what Connie remembered; did Connie understand why she had done what she had now done?

As he rode the elevator to the eighth floor everything slowed. His body was asleep, he felt, but his mind sharp and alive, an electric thing.

The hallway was silent, smelling of floral spray and cigarettes, framed in dark wood and the swirling pattern in the carpet in muted blues and browns. He tried to imagine the colors of the Cyclist fused with Grandfather Joel's ashes.

As he closed on the room, the same one he borrowed months ago to meet Susan, Hank stopped, his body, for the moment, refusing to function as he understood the next epiphany. Where Diego was had nothing to do with the accident or the pain in his elbow. This memory leaked from his mind in Mom's flow of words, from the smell of the ashes as they baked.

He knocked on the door of 818. There came a sound like breathing, a soft rustling, footsteps; the door opened.

Connie gazed at him, her face drawn and blank, as if she were addressing the postman or milkman. Then her eyebrows moved, her eyes sharpened.

Behind her, inside the room, a groan, then, "What the—"

Pushing through the door, Hank nudged Connie aside. She didn't resist, moved like a zombie. In her pale silk robe she looked ghostly pale, washed out, a bright spot trained on her, erasing any contrast. Except for her eyes, dark, blue, stunned.

"Where is he?" Hank choked out the words, looking away from her. A murky light from the window, curtains open to capture ocean breeze, lit the room. He recognized the smell of the place where he was to meet Susan, a new rug or crisp sheets. Through the broad opening into the next room, he saw the bed, a rumpled range of covers and in it a man.

Sam from the Pottery—'I help out in the studio prop shop'—rising on one elbow.

Standing beside the door, Connie motioned stiffly toward a settee near the window. As Hank moved toward it, Connie watched him, jerked forward, and knelt protectively over Diego.

The little boy was asleep, nestled under a blanket. Hank could see his hair and nose and eyes, lashes against flawless baby skin. Asleep, not afraid or hungry or crying. Something tight under Hank's ribs un-knotted itself.

"Connie, give it up. I need to take him home to his Mom." Lowering his voice, not wanting to wake the boy, without rancor, Hank thought, without blame, but she heard something in his tone, impatience maybe, a wish not to be here or to listen to her side of things.

"How did you find us?"

"It wasn't hard putting two and six together." Hank knelt beside her, grabbed her chin, pulled her to face him. How to tell her it was like magic, Indian magic?

"Your friend Mary responds well to monetary bribes." An easy lie, a quick lie. He surpassed himself in that one.

An embarrassed smiled crossed Connie's face, apologetic, almost. "A true mercenary, our friend Mary."

"She's not my friend." Hank sat at the settee's edge, looking at the sleeping child, wanting to pick him up, but afraid somehow, to risk waking him.

"Connie," he said gently. "What was going through your mind?"

"She's in no state to talk about that." Sam's cool voice came from the bed. Getting up, he stood over Hank, big man in a sleeveless t-shirt and boxers, hands on hips. He smelled of over-ripe bananas. He could probably pick Hank up and throw him out the window without a getting out of breath.

Taking his sister's hand as she drew her fingers across Diego's forehead, Hank said, "Why, Connie? Why did you do it?" His fingers brushed the warm child-skin, and a thrill went through him.

"I couldn't help it. He might have been mine." A big tear traced her cheek, slid down her chin, hovered.

"I know what's going on. I know why you took him. I just don't understand it."

She looked at him, blank, wondering stare gone as suddenly as it had come, and he saw her jaw set hard, lower lip jutting out.

"You are such a damn idiot, Henry Cleveland. A clueless drifting balloon brain. You are around all the time but you see nothing."

Hank stared at her, the sound of her voice cutting him—if this was acting, it was academy material.

"Oh don't stare at me as if I just sprouted antennae." She whispered harshly, still, he thought, able to keep her voice low as they sat next to the child.

"Connie." Sam had no such compunction. Diego gave out a small whimper. "You don't have to tell him anything."

"Oh shut up, Sam." Leaning over Diego, Connie gave out a soft *shhhhh.* "He could have been mine, but instead, he's yours."

Hank glanced up at Sam, whose features were lost in shadow.

Sam shrugged. "I don't know what you're talking about," he managed this time to keep his voice low. "That kid was given away, you said. You said you found him with that Mexican nurse."

Connie stared at Diego, shook her head, pointing her chin at the child, her hair straying back and forth like the pendulum of a clock.

"I found him, but he's not mine, he's yours."

Hank felt rather than saw Sam make an impatient gesture and retreat to sit on the foot of the bed. Hank touched Connie's arm. Her skin was cold.

"Connie, he's Luz's little brother. He doesn't belong to any of us."

She threw him the same fierce look; he could see her jaw pulsing in the lamplight.

"You are not only deaf, you are blind. Look at him Hank. I knew it the moment I first laid eyes on him, when we visited

Luz and her mother."

Obeying his sister, confusion blowing through him, Hank looked at the sleeping boy. His eyes, large under thin lids, lashes long and cheeks like pomegranates. And lips, full, and moving in and out as if in a dream of eating.

Somehow, the room had been cleared of all the air, and when Hank opened his mouth to take a breath and speak, he couldn't, because he couldn't draw any anything at all into his lungs.

Mom's voice, talking, talking. Loud, fast in his ears. Hank was sixteen again, Mom at the mantle at home, marquis behind her, face set and red around the edges, blotched with white. Mother gazed coldly at Luz as Hank tried like an idiot, inadequate and stumbling, to introduce her. Luz smiling, wary, ready to be polite and say *Hello Mrs. Cleveland.*

Mom threw Luz out of the house. Was that when it happened? His room, photos, kisses, alone in silence?

Connie was watching him. She saw the recognition cross his face. He couldn't look at her. Instead found himself standing up. *Why hadn't Luz told him?* Why had she disappeared and then when found again pretended Diego was her little brother?

Why had she not let him know he had a son?

He took everything so hard, Luz had said about her father. Did she blame herself for Julio del Mar's death? The disgrace his only daughter brought to the family? And where was the father, Mr. del Mar would demand, Hank thought. And he could see Luz, proud, silent, never revealing.

But Mom knew. Hank realized suddenly, a punch to the stomach. Mom knew.

Thirty

"MAYBE THIS is what it would take, to get you to see what was right before your eyes. St. Henry, the keeper of the family secrets. You didn't even know the biggest secret of your entire life." Connie raised a hand as if to slap him into wakening, but Hank grabbed her wrist.

The girl Mom threw out of the house. "What happened? When Mom threw Luz out. What happened?"

Giving him a quizzical look, Connie tried to get her wrist free. "You're hurting me. Don't you remember anything?"

"No, I don't." His hand turned to steel around her wrist. He tightened, wanting to break it. "I don't, just like you forgot you had an abortion and she made you forget. Just like she made me forget."

Whimpering, Connie tried to twist away from him.

A shadow moved between them. Blinding pain shot up Hank's left arm as Sam seized it and jerked him backward. He sank to the floor, nausea flooding his throat. He could hear Sam's voice, angry, quick.

"What is he saying? You never had that kid? Our kid? You lied to me? You got rid of it?"

Connie sobbed, and as Hank's vision cleared, he saw her

crouched on the floor next to him, her hands on her face. Fury got him to his feet. His arm was going numb with pain, but anger that Sam might have hit his sister cleared his pain-fogged brain.

But he was wrong. Sam knelt down, pulled Connie up by her shoulders, and held her, big arms around her back. Hank could see her shoulder blades through the thin robe, and he too felt very, very sorry for her.

Stumbling for the phone, Hank muddled for Luz's number, and dialed. Mrs. del Mar answered on the first ring, her voice quick and worried. When Hank told her he had found Diego and he was safe, she started to cry. She managed to blurt that Susan and Luz were in the car, scouring the neighborhood.

"Gracias a Dios," Rosa del Mar repeated over and over. Hank got her to write down the apartment phone number, but he would be leaving here in fifteen minutes to bring Diego home.

Hanging up, he turned to Connie and Sam, sitting together on the other side of the bed. At least, Hank thought, Sam was turning out to be a decent sort of guy. It was obvious he was in love with Connie, and had been for several years, apparently. Hank wondered if Mother had broken that relationship as well, considering that Sam was not good enough for her girl.

A relationship of any kind, especially mother and child, would get in the way of The Cleveland Twins' career.

"Con," he said as gently as he could. "We need to get Diego packed up and ready to go home."

Sitting next to Sam, Connie looked at Hank over Sam's big hunched back. She wiped her nose. "What's wrong with your arm?"

"Nothing a good cast won't fix. C'mon, Connie. Get cracking."

There wasn't much to organize. Connie had thrown a handful of clothes and toys, including the metal truck, into a suitcase when she sneaked through Diego's open window. As Connie dressed, not bothering to screen herself as she slipped into her dress. Hank looked out the window, but Sam watched admiringly, the story came out. The little boy didn't even wake up as she picked him up and carried him to Sam waiting in her car.

Hank wanted badly to carry Diego out to the car, but his elbow was swollen and bruised to the point of immobility, so he had to allow Sam to do the honors. Just as he was about to close the door behind Sam, Connie and the still sleeping Diego, the phone rang.

Rosa del Mar's Spanish mixed in with English, was able to tell them that Luz and Susan had called from Susan's house, where they had gone to pick Hank up, if he was still there. They would wait there for Diego, since it was closer.

Hank's heart spiraled up at this news. Luz in Venice Beach, so close, waiting for Hank and Diego. Thanking Mrs. del Mar, he fumbled the phone onto its cradle, chased down the hallway after Connie and Sam, to tell them about the new plan.

Sam drove, Connie in the roadster front seat holding Diego, and Hank in the jump seat, clinging to the Peugeot over his lap with his good arm. Night held on, streetlights dim, palms like sentinels stretching their necks to see over the horizon of the black sea. Hank's heart stayed close in his throat. He swallowed several times to get it back down, afraid it would break free and float away.

As soon as the roadster bounced into Susan's driveway

and stopped behind her car, Luz appeared, running around the corner of the house to the car. She wore her same slacks and jacket, hair flapping like bird wings. Seeing Diego asleep in Connie's lap, her eyes bloomed with tears; she circled the car and opened the passenger door and Connie allowed Luz to scoop her boy into her arms.

Diego woke up. His soft, "Mama?" when he saw Luz holding him sent a spear through Hank's heart.

She carried him toward the backyard, crushing him against her. Sam and Connie didn't move. Straining, Hank was able to lift the Peugeot with his good arm and set it down on the driveway, where it quickly fell over with a clatter. But he didn't care. He crawled out of the jump seat and followed Luz.

She was sitting on a patio chair, rocking back and forth, hugging Diego. A shadow near the kiln was Susan, but Hank couldn't talk to her. Pulling a chair over Hank sat as close to Luz as he could get.

Looking at him over Diego's head as he began to fuss and squirm, Luz bit her lip.

Hank touched her hand, then Diego's. "I know, Luz. I know." The words escaped him in tight bursts.

She closed her eyes, opened them, and then let Diego down. "He's awake now," she said, straightening his pajamas.

Diego looked at Hank, who, heart pumping, put his hands over his face, peeked out at Diego through his fingers. My son, my son.

Diego examined this performance for a moment, then turned away, more interested in the array of figurines on the patio table, well within his reach.

"Oh, oh." Luz captured his hand as he reached for the

nearest one, which happened to be Donut-boy.

Something else caught Hank's eye. A larger figure stood in the midst of the smaller ones, the Cyclist in his blue and white uniform, on a bicycle the same color green as the Peugeot, head down, racing through the crowd. Hank's breath stopped in his throat.

In the dimness, Hank couldn't read Susan's face. He wondered what she knew, if Luz had told her, or if she had just figured everything out on her own. He had forgotten that she might care about that. He didn't really know how she was feeling.

He had forgotten completely, for the moment, about Connie and Sam. Getting up, he went to the driveway, but the car was gone. Only the Peugeot, lying on its side, occupied the concrete.

His left arm felt heavy, as if it weighed three times as much as the other one. If he didn't move it, the pain was a controllable but distracting ache. He knew he should see a doctor about it, but there was something more important he had to do first.

Luz had risen and picked up the cyclist. She held it in her hand, looked it over, and as Hank approached everything shifted as a swift dawn approached.

Light filled the space; a backdrop of wide-fronded shrubs, leaves bowed with moisture. The shriek of a monkey or a bird, the smell of sweet rot and ungoverned growth of green, living things. A woman stood there, wrapped in brilliant striped garments, ribbons wound through hair the color of polished black marble. She raised the knife in one hand, the golden fruit in the other. Next to her stood a small child, looking up at the fruit.

Hank found himself looking at the woman's feet. They

were brown and lovely, bridled in leather sandals. Then he saw, on a stone table in miniature, another woman, this one in drifting yellow gauze, hair the color of Arizona sandstone. A slim and graceful statuette.

They all watched the woman, even the white monkey in the tree, as she lowered her arm and with a swift stroke, cut the golden fruit in half.

Glitter fell from it, along with the stench of burning. The halves fell, one at the feet of the child, who knelt to scoop it up, the other onto the table beside the gauzy figurine.

The memory flicked into Hank's mind, bourn by the glitter. Luz lying on her stomach on Hank's bed, saddle shoes in the air, drape of plaid school uniform skirt pleasantly, to Hank's admiring eye, outlining her curves. Pointing at the photo of Grandmother Annette and Grandfather Joel, made her pronouncement about them. He came across the room from his desk chair and sat beside her, skin cold as he listened to her tell the history of his family, even down to the detail of his parents' strange relationship.

This part he scorned, laughing, but she was perfectly serious.

"They were deeply in love, inseparable. That was why, when they found out later that they had the same father, they stayed married anyway." Shifted to one side, Luz lay her head on her hand. Hank couldn't take his eyes off her breasts and the line of her hips.

She saw him looking, and a half-smile came and went on her face. Shifting closer, getting up on one hand, she kissed him.

Hank remembered his astonishment. He would never have pressed any advantage with Luz, as much as he craved her. He reminded himself that he loved talking to her as much as looking at her, as he leaned closer, moved a length of hair from before her face, looked at her cheeks flushing with embarrassment.

There were three times, he remembered, in his room; three precious afternoons. She was tasty and smooth, responsive to his fumblings. The skin on her breasts was golden, nipples brown and hard, the smell of her and the taste of her hair, both above and below in the special, sacred place. He once asked her to just lay on his bed nude, so he could look at all her beauty.

A stabbing pain shot through him. How could he have forgotten that?

And that was the day that after, when they went downstairs, Mom was waiting for them.

She did not reply to Luz's "Hello, Mrs. Cleveland. It's nice to meet you."

The room grew icy. Hank couldn't move, he remembered now. It was as if Mom glued his feet to the floor, and he was turned into a statue, leaving Luz alone and vulnerable.

"Well, isn't this interesting," Mom said to Hank, as if Luz was not even there. "Been studying hard, have you? Getting ready for final exams? Spending a lot of time indoors hitting the books?"

Hank could say nothing. His tongue wouldn't move, his jaw wired shut.

Mom moved toward him. Hank remembered Luz looking from him to his mother, as if waiting for him to say something to stop Mom's advance.

"Henry Cleveland scholar. Do you have a tutor? Someone to show you how it's done? Someone who has great experience and is eager to share it with a poor little rich boy?"

Hank tried to move. He heard Luz's sharp intake of breath,

but he could say nothing in her defense. Mother's voice slammed into him like a cold sheet of rain.

"Sometimes these lessons are painful," Mother said. She was close to him now, odors of smoke and carnations, her brilliant hair sealed in place, lips bright with red, in her impeccable gray suit and orchid corsage. "You may think you know what you are doing, then reality brings you up short. The reality of class, my boy. A plain and brutal lesson. Not a class in a school, but a class of people. A class of people who don't belong here. They have their own ways, their own places to live. Their own schools. Sometimes one or two of them try to switch classes, to become what they are not. But it never works. Especially when they use looks and allure and sex to get there."

Hank's face burst with heat. How could he have let his mother say these things in Luz's hearing?

"No, young Hank. You are studying the wrong thing, in the wrong place. Some things it is best not to know about. Some people are best ignored, forgotten. Unseeable, invisible, in their place." Mom touched his cheek. He tried to move back, but he couldn't. Her voice went into a drone, low, seeking, probing everywhere in the folds of his brain.

Then she stopped. Mother turned away from him, faced Luz. He heard Mother say names, bad names to Luz, his dear, dear Luz. He saw Luz run from the room, heard the door bang open. He should go, walk her to the street car, make sure she got home, but he couldn't move. Already the memory leaked from him, levels lowering as it seeped away.

When Mother came back, she started in again.

His back was cold. Hank opened his eyes and saw stars. Distant, blinking. Something soft under his head. His elbow, up on a pillow, throbbed, wrapped with something really cold.

"Hank, *caro mio.*" Luz's voice. Luz's hand on his cheek.

Hank looked at her, hair behind one ear, eyes bright in the dim light. He said, "You came back. I'm so sorry Luz. I should never have let her say those things."

"It's OK now. I see it now. I didn't realize what she is."

Sitting up, Hank realized he was not at home, lying on the sofa, but in Susan's backyard on his back on the grass. Moving his elbow sent a shock-load of pain up his arm.

Luz sat on the grass next to him, leaning on the chaise lounge, Diego cuddling next to her, eating a banana. Susan was no where to be seen.

"You fainted. We couldn't get you up, so we just let you lay here until you came around. I think your elbow is fractured."

Hank couldn't take his eyes off her. "I should never have let her get away with it. I was an idiot. She made me forget you. With her words. She talked and talked and ate up my memory with her words."

Nodding, Luz brushed his cheek again. "She knows a magic, too. But it's not the same as mine."

Hank had to agree, remembering the vision of the woman slicing into the fruit. But he didn't tell Luz about that, or the previous one he had when he walked into the studio those long weeks ago. That magic for now would stay safely sealed inside his brain.

They were silent for a while, sitting among the crickets. The Cyclist stood on the patio table, Grandfather Joel's secret wish, one he made on Hank. Around them, dark retreated in increments that could not be seen until they had gone. Dawn was coming. The air was cold, the grass damp, but neither of them wanted to move.

"You need to get to a doctor, Hank." Susan appeared, wearing her robe, her face pale and scored with weariness. "Luz, you could borrow my car, get him to a doctor and get Diego home."

Hank struggled to his feet. His head felt like a balloon was expanding inside it, but he kept his balance. Susan looked so beautiful, her hair trailing down one side of her face, green eyes looking around her garden as she sighed.

Hank went to her, stood below her at the bottom step. "Thank you. I need to thank you."

He worried, what did she think? He was leaving her for Luz. How long had she known this would happen?

Susan gave him a crooked smile. "My young lover, your girlfriend is my pupil. I have no doubt I will be seeing more of you than ever before."

Feeling his face grow warm, Hank looked at her bare feet, white and longer than Luz's.

"How is Joseph doing?"

She shrugged, shook her head. "Asleep. I think he's catching up on years of lost sleep."

Good, Hank thought. Good.

He and Luz woke up the same doctor who had tended Hank through his meningitis. Shaking his head, the doctor said the only way to set the bone was through surgery. Hank disliked that idea, but by now he would have cut off his arm if it would help the pain go away.

The doctor drove him straight to the hospital and the deed was done. Luz left him in the doctor's capable hands, taking Diego home to his worried grandma. They touched hands through the doctor's car window, the spark of her touch stayed with Hank all through the anesthesia and even when he woke up to find Carl sitting at his bedside.

Thirty-One

JOAQUIN'S EYEBROWS rose several inches when he saw Luz and Hank walk into the kitchen together. Then a smirk grew on his lips.

"The beautiful *señorita* has returned *a la casa.* Or should I say, *dos señoritas?*" With his spatula Joaquin indicated the guest house. "Will there be more for dinner?"

Hank held Luz's hand tight in his. Yes, the beautiful girl has returned to the house, three years after being thrown out. No one was going to throw her out again.

His head turning side to side, Joaquin stabbed his spatula under a tortilla. "Only one arm to hold her with. *Que lastima.*"

"One's enough, *no importarle a uno.*"

Diego moved against Luz's leg, tugging to get away from her firm hand, as if he wanted to run straight to Joaquin. Joaquin's dark gaze took in the little boy.

He nodded, smiling. "*Hola, companero.* Are you hungry?"

Leaving Diego with a slice of warm tortilla and in Joaquin's capable hands, Hank took Luz into the dark and quiet living room. Hank wasn't worried that Dad would ever find out about the origin of the Cyclist, which Hank placed on the other side of the urn from the marquess. The marquess was back on the mantel shelf, along with Grandfather Joel's urn, even though half of his ashes were gone. It wasn't likely that Dad would look inside or even pick the thing up.

They had already quietly moved Joseph and Susan into the guesthouse, after retrieving scorched-smelling and somewhat damp clothing and belongings for them. They also packed up a box of the figurines that had survived the fire, including the blackened hulks of the soldiers, all of which besides Donut-boy had survived Joseph's bonfire intact.

Luz spent a period of time on the phone in the hallway with Joseph's and Mother's doctors, writing things down. She had a list of necessities and a prescription for Joseph for the all-night drug store down in Hollywood. Carl obediently went to get it filled.

They waited in the dining room before slices of flank steak and a platter of asparagus. But no one was hungry except Diego. The telephone rang, and rang, and Joaquin refused to answer it, so Hank trudged back into the hallway.

"Hank?" Connie's voice, breathless, rushed. "Is the little boy OK?"

"Where the hell have you been?"

Silence, the hiss of the line. For a moment, Hank worried she had hung up.

"I'm with Sam. Not at the hotel. At his mother's house in San Pedro."

"You know that Tarzan hunk broke my arm?"

"He's real sorry about that. But he thought you were going to hurt me."

Hank almost laughed. "Right. He weighs ten times what I do and he's worried I'm going to hurt you."

Another silence, and Hank's anger drained away. "Are

you OK?"

"What is the studio saying? Are they looking for me, miss-ing in action?" Her voice was small, almost child-like.

"Sorry, Con, I have no idea. I've been kinda busy." Luz watched Hank from the kitchen doorway. He couldn't quite make out her expression. "Con, you need to come home."

Another silence, but not as long. Connie's voice came through strong and sure.

"No. Not yet. I can't face her. Not yet."

Then he heard the click, and knew she was gone. But something about her voice untied one of the many knots his family was so good at twisting around him. An important truth that he shared with Connie, and Carl. They were in this together and had one enemy that united them, like Joseph in the Italian hills. And that enemy was Mom.

Hank went back to Luz and hugged her with his one good arm.

Movement, voices in the kitchen. Carl had returned with an armload of drugs and supplies. And Hank heard Joseph exclaim, "We have the same name, *hombre*!!"

Joaquin stood with his arms folded over his taut belly, a knife in his hand. One eyebrow raised, nostrils flared. Uh, oh, Hank thought. Joseph has met his match.

Joseph was the only one who ate, and talked. Susan sat si-lently, and Carl pulled his chair in next to her, chin on one el-bow, smiling at her in a ludicrous way, Hank thought.

She's here, in my house. The woman who had pulled him away from here, into a world he knew was there but was an-other country behind that border of class and work Mom spoke so strongly about. It was OK in Mom's book that a half-brother and sister could fall in love and marry and have children, but it was not OK to cross that gulf of class.

Susan watched him. She had washed her face and combed back her hair, pulled it under a scarf. There was the slightest smirk on her mouth, but her eyes didn't match it. Then her gaze moved just beyond him, and her smirk deepened.

Turning, Hank saw Luz behind him, in her nurse's uniform, white shoes, hose, cap and all, hair bundled at the base of her neck. Her cheeks flushed when she saw him looking, and she straightened her wristwatch.

"I'm ready to face the lioness in her den."

As he led her upstairs Hank's heart thundered and it was as if the entire house was beating itself on the chest like a great ape. They went along the corridor past Connie's room, then Hank's on the left, which Luz glanced at with a little smile; then Carl's room and then Mom's big suite. The door was closed. Standing outside the door, Hank could hear Dad reading aloud.

Knocking, Hank opened the door without waiting to be asked. He pushed it wide, like a servant, for Luz, who walked into the room with a confident stride. Only Hank saw her hands shake as she smoothed her uniform for her entrance.

Coming in behind her, Hank closed the door. As Dad got to his feet the magazine he was reading slid to the floor. Taking off his glasses, he stared speechless at the two of them.

"Hank. You're home. How's the arm? Is everything OK? And who is this?" he came around the table and looked at Luz, who nodded politely but walked past him toward her patient.

In a chair across the bed from them, Mom was encased in pillows, reading glasses on her nose, feet up on the bed. When she saw Luz her eyes widened; Hank saw her nostrils visibly flare.

"Hello, Mrs. Cleveland. So nice to meet you." Luz circled the bed, held her hand out for Mom to shake.

Mother's feet thumped to the floor. She struggled to rise and when Luz reached to help, she flung away from her and came around the bed, glasses and pad in hand, pencil in her hair, and marched up to Hank.

"Your nurse, Mom. Meet Miss del Mar. Carl said you and Dad were getting on each other's nerves and so he hired her for you." Hank kept his tone innocent, and Mom's face bloomed red. She glared at Dad, who shrugged.

"I think it's a great idea, Bess. She can do a lot for you that I can't, you know." Picking up his magazine, Dad sighed, smiled.

"Well, I'll let you all get to know each other. Hank, it's great that you're home. You have no idea. Just stay off that bicycle for a while, huh?"

Dad wasted no time now that he was set free of the duty he'd volunteered for in the first place.

Standing on the rug in her bare feet, Mom began to scribble on her pad. Luz approached and yanked it out of her hand.

"Oh, I think not, Mrs. Cleveland. Too much excitement for one day. It's evident that you need a bath."

Luz picked at Mom's hair, which looked like a pile of sprayed gauze. "That's the problem with relying on relatives, especially husbands, to assist you. They just don't encourage people enough to get well."

Looking around, Luz saw the bathroom door standing open. "Oh, how convenient. Your own bathroom. Well, I'll get the water running. Hank, you make sure your mother doesn't write anything down while I'm getting it ready."

Mom shook with fury. Hank started to worry that she

would have a stroke or even explode. Taking her by the shoulders, he sat her down in Dad's chair. She reached for one of the pads but he shoved them away, then took the pencil out of her hand. She looked like she wanted to stab him with it.

"You remember Miss del Mar, don't you, Mom? She is an excellent nurse, you know, first in her class at the nursing school. Only the best for my mother." He patted her on the knee and she slapped his hand away.

Hank continued, "Miss del Mar remembers you. I had a time convincing her to help us, but I couldn't think of anyone better. Right, Mom? Someone whose experience is far greater than yours or mine?"

He listened to the water running, saw Luz moving back and forth in the bathroom with towels and soap. "I remember now too, Mom. Funny, the things I forgot about. Important things. Maybe one of the most important things of my life. Oh, wait, Luz brought you something."

He went to Luz's nurses' bag, lifted out a bundle wrapped in newspaper. "A gift for you. From one sorceress to another." He glanced at Mom as he unwrapped the paper. Mom's face paled with fear. He set the gift on the table at the foot of the bed, removing the vase of dead flowers there.

Mom sighed impatiently, stared at what Luz had made for her. A large figure, more than 14 inches, of a Mexican Indian woman in in scarlet, yellow and indigo garments, black hair caped on her shoulders, skirts caught in a mountain wind. She carried a baby in a basket; she swung the child in her arms, and looked as if she were singing to it.

Oh god, hideous, Mother mouthed.

"No, beautiful," Hank said. Picking it up, he brought it to her. "Touch it. Like silk. Smell it. Like smoke."

Have you lost your mind? Mother turned her head away, reached for the phone.

"Who are you going to call? God? The Devil?"

Mother's lips thinned and she tried to slap him. He got out of the way just as her fingers grazed his lower lip. She was pretty fast. He would have to watch that.

You call that doctor right now. I don't want her.

Hank shook his head. "Can't do that. Carl hired her. It's nothing to do with me."

Mother's look told him she knew it all had to do with him.

Luz appeared, ready to take Mom into the bath. Hank decided it was time to leave, and he shut the door behind him. If there was a struggle, at least there was no screaming or name calling.

While Luz was helping Mom with a bath, Hank ate some of the cold dinner with Susan, Carl, Dad, and Diego on Joseph's lap, which seemed to Hank odd but strangely comforting.

Dad heard the story of the fire and made no complaint about putting the Chagalls up for a few months. After all, hadn't Susan nursed Hank when he was so ill? He kept glancing at Diego, as if trying to understand whose little boy this was and why he was here. It was as if he had not put two and six together and as if he never even knew Diego existed. Mom never told him, apparently.

Joaquin loaded a tray with food for Mom and Luz. From inside Mom's room came soft murmurings. Getting the door open, Hank angled through carrying the tray, expecting chaos and blood, but got nothing of the sort.

Only the lamp behind the reading chair, and another shaded one on the dressing table were lit. A hint of herb and flora sifted through the air. A gold light seemed to fall on everything. The Indian woman stood under the lamp on the dressing table, lit from above, or within, Hank thought.

Luz sat on the bed. Hidden by the table piled with magazines and books and the Dictaphone, Mother came into view as Hank brought the tray closer and set it down in a spot cleared by Luz.

Mother leaned back on her pillows. Her eyes were closed, hair curled around her shoulders, luminous and soft; a pink scarf pulled it from her face. She wore a dove-gray bed jacket. Luz had fished a not-so-dead carnation from the bouquet Hank had thrown away and pinned it to the collar. A mirror, along with tubes of lipstick, make-up, eyeliner, lay on Mom's lap.

Luz sat on the bed, leaning against one of the end-posts. She had loosened the buttons around her neck and taken off her shoes and cap. She held a book on her lap.

Hank stood beside Luz, leaned down, kissed her, sliding his hand along her breast. She dug her fingers into his hair.

As he straightened, he looked at Mom. She had been watching them, eyes curious but indicated nothing else. Then she looked away toward the foot of the bed and smiled.

On the end table stood the little marquess. Luz must have fetched it from the living room while the others were eating. Next to it she had propped the framed portrait of Grandmother Annette and Grandfather Joel.

Luz read aloud from *Alice in Wonderland,* while Hank moved Dad's chair closer. A few minutes later Hank heard the door open. Luz turned her head to look, and the book slowly slid into her lap.

Carl, Diego in his arms, circled the bed and stood before Mom's chair. A bolt screwed itself into Hank's guts, then unscrewed itself just as quickly. *This is right.*

Mom's eyes were closed. When Luz stopped reading, she opened them again. Her lips parted, one eye brow drew down. Hank saw her reach up to her ear, as if searching for the pencil.

"Hey, Mom. Meet your grandson Diego."

As Luz rose to stop him, Carl placed Diego in Mom's lap.

Hank found himself on his feet, *she'll kill him. She'll throw him out the window.*

He gave Carl a sharp shove as he raced around the bed, and started to push past Luz, but strangely, she seized his arm.

"Parar, caro mio."

Mom steadied Diego in her hands as he sat sideways, one leg hanging down, and squirmed a little. The deep lines, like cracks in glaze, on Mom's face smoothed away; her gaze covered the boy, taking in every inch.

Then Hank saw something he had never seen before. Maybe he never saw it before because Mom talked them out of existence. But now she was mute, and so they came, tears that bled down her cheeks.

Squirming from Mom's arms, Diego slipped to the floor, and, standing on tiptoe, began to examine the magazines and books and pens on the table next to Mom.

And Hank thought about how his son didn't speak, either. He hadn't heard a word from the boy since he had known him and selfishly, he had never asked Luz about it. Was it a concern, a three-year-old who didn't speak?

Luz moved then; picking up *Alice in Wonderland* she knelt on the floor next to Diego and began to show him the draw- ings inside.

Mom's eyes closed again, her face blank. He couldn't see her thoughts about anything any more. Hank wouldn't hear her thoughts about anything any more.

"Oh, and I almost forgot. Connie wanted Luz to have this." Carl pulled an envelope from his pocket. Taking it, Luz frowned, opened it, read it, handed it to Hank.

Connie had paid for a new car for Luz, saying it was really for Diego, who needed to be driven around in style.

"Don't you dare say you can't accept it. Let Connie do this for you. It's the least she could do," Hank said, handing the envelope with title and keys back to her.

When Hank glanced back at Mom, she was staring at him as if she had seen him for the first time. Sitting up, she fumbled in piles on the table, and pulled out several narrow boxes of tapes, examined each one, and after tossing three of them onto the bed, thrust one at Hank, then tapped the Dictaphone.

"I think she wants you to play it, Hank," Luz said from her place on the floor, where she looked a little stunned.

Mom waved them away and pointed toward the door. *Not here. Take it to your room. Carl can stay with me a while.*

Carl can stay with me. That meant she wanted them both to hear it. Hank took the Dictaphone in his good arm, Luz carried the tape, and they went to his room.

> *Once I threw my son's girlfriend out of the house. Henry was too young to understand what I did for him. What I do for him, for them all. I have to watch every move, catch every single error. I am the anesthetist, one slip of my hand on the gauge, the push of a cc too much or too little, and it all falls apart.*
>
> *She was a beautiful girl. A smart girl. I could see her intelligence in her eyes. An intelligence I don't understand. She could overpower me, if I give her any*

kind of entry into my house and family. So now she is gone. My son is furious with me, but I can talk him down, out and around to anything. I have done it before with Constance. I can do it again with Henry.

But I don't think this will last. I think my time is at an end, soon. I am tasked with holding the pairs together, but my own partnership with the devil is come to pay. For whatever reason, I have been blessed with money, looks, talent, a beautiful family. I am married to my half-brother, but we cannot see ourselves with anyone else.

My father knew all along, but did nothing to stop it. What could he do? For me stopping it would mean death, which is what it would take. Maybe he knew that. It killed Kenneth's mother, though. Annette died in furious anger after our wedding. Joel knew she despised him, she wished, prayed that she could outlive him, but it wasn't to be.

I made a grave mistake that day I shoved that girl out the door, I think. But I will continue on the path I chose. I am doing my part to keep order in chaos. But things will happen. I used to look at my mother's marquis and marquess, that she gave to my father and he in turn gave to his wife. They are very valuable, she said. Just make sure they don't become a broken pair.

About the author

The author of numerous short stories and novels, Jill Zeller lives near Seattle, Washington, with her patient and adoring husband, one self-centered tuxedo cat and the princess of the family: an English Mastiff named Bernadette Delilah.

Her works explore the boundaries of reality. Some may call it fantasy, but there are rarely swords and never elves. More to the point, she prefers to write as if myth, imagination and hallucination were as real as the chair she is sitting on as she writes this. Maybe it is because she was raised as a Christian Scientist.

Jill Zeller also writes under the pseudonym Hunter Morrison. You can find more of her works at:

http://bookviewcafe.com/bookstore/bvc-author/jill-zeller/
http://jzmorrisonpress.com/

About Book View Café

Book View Café Publishing Cooperative (BVC) is an author-owned co-operative of over fifty professional writers, publishing in a variety of genres including fantasy, romance, mystery, and science fiction.

In 2008, BVC launched a website, bookviewcafe.com, initially offering free fiction and gradually moving to selling ebooks of members' backlist titles, then original titles. BVC's ebooks are DRM-free and are distributed around the world. BVC returns 95% of the profit on each book directly to the author. The cooperative has gained a reputation for producing high-quality ebooks, and is now moving into print editions.

BVC authors include *New York Times* and *USA Today* best-sellers; Nebula, Hugo, Lambda, and Philip K. Dick Award winners; World Fantasy and Rita Award nominees; and winners and nominees of many other publishing awards.